Lead
Me On

Dear Reader,

Welcome back to the mountains of Colorado!

For this story, we have to take a little drive over the pass to Tumble Creek's sister city of Aspen, Colorado. I hope you don't mind, but Jane Morgan lives and works here and dedicates her whole life to running the Jennings Architecture office with an iron fist. Jane is the very picture of perfection...but appearances can be deceiving.

I got the idea for this book while I was people-watching. This probably won't surprise you, but I tend to make up little stories in my head about people I see when I'm out and about. Some folks seem to fit neatly into slots, but the people who don't...these are the stories I have fun with. The punk-rock teenager at the grocery store who helps his elderly grandfather slowly down each aisle every Sunday. The conservatively dressed librarian with the tattoo that peeks above the edge of her crisp collar. Or the perfectly composed office manager who's hiding a scandalous past behind her cool facade...

Of course you can't judge a book by its cover, and none of us are exactly who we seem to be on the outside. But some people use their appearances to hide important truths, and my fascination with people's secret lives is what compelled me to write Jane's story. I hope you find her as interesting as I do!

Happy reading!

Victoria Dahl

Lead Me On

VICTORIA DAHL

HQN™

ISBN-13: 978-1-61523-858-3

LEAD ME ON

This edition published by arrangement with Harlequin Books S.A.

® and TM are trademarks of the publisher. Trademarks indicated with ® are registered in the United States Patent and Trademark Office, the Canadian Trade Marks Office and in other countries.

Printed in U.S.A.

This book is for Grandma Winnie.

I love you and miss you.

Also by

VICTORIA DAHL

Talk Me Down
Start Me Up

Don't miss *The Wicked West* by Victoria Dahl writing as
Holly Summers, available wherever eBooks are sold.

And look out for *Crazy for Love*

Lead
Me On

There are so many supportive people in my life that
I couldn't possibly thank them all. My family sacrificed
a lot of time and hot meals for this book, so I can honestly
say it wouldn't have happened without their love.
Thank you, gentlemen.

And thank you to my agent, Amy, and my editor, Tara,
for making the entire Tumble Creek series possible.
I hope you enjoyed your time in the mountains.

I've always said that the romance writing community is the
warmest group in the world, and it's true. Jennifer Echols
is there for me every day, encouraging me when
I need it, and rapping my knuckles when I need that, too.
Courtney Milan did her best to help steer me in the right
direction with the legal details of this book, and hopefully
my alignment wasn't off. And people like Kelly Krysten
offer encouragement with sheer kindness. Thank you!

My biggest thank-you goes to my readers. Thank you so
much for wholeheartedly embracing the Tumble Creek
series. Your notes and kind words mean the world to me.

CHAPTER ONE

JANE MORGAN STARED at the man seated across the table from her. The lunch crowd at the trendiest restaurant in Aspen was a pretty quiet group. There was nothing to distract her from Greg Nunn.

She watched him chew his food, his jaw moving as anyone else's jaw would move when they ate. He wasn't sloppy. He didn't dribble crumbs down his chin or flash an occasional view of partially chewed pasta. He ate the way any reasonable man would. So why in the world did she feel vaguely nauseated as Greg swallowed and wiped his mouth?

"Is your steak all right?" he asked. "It looks a little rare."

"No, it's fine," Jane insisted, and made herself cut off another piece and raise it to her lips.

"I told you to get the prawns."

Jane chewed and told herself not to growl. In fact, he'd mentioned that grilled prawns were low fat, as if Jane needed to lose weight. That was a new development. Maybe he was feeling the strain between them, too.

Greg turned his attention back to his own food, and she stared in horror as he slipped another bite of salmon into his mouth and began to grind away. Surely his teeth worked a bit more vigorously than necessary? Lowering her gaze, she swallowed hard to get her piece of steak down.

They'd been dating for four months now, though they'd been sleeping together only a few weeks. Aspen wasn't exactly a huge dating pool, so Jane tried to step cautiously into those waters. Now she wished she'd held off a little longer.

Before they'd slept together, Greg had been the perfect boyfriend. Smart, attentive and mildly funny… he'd even struck the perfect balance between patience and desperation during the long wait to get into her bed. But now that he *was* in her bed, he was becoming more proprietary every day. Sleeping over every other night. Insisting she attend every dinner and cocktail party hosted by his attention-loving boss. And now he thought he had some input into her lunch selection. Jane felt the walls were closing in around her.

Ridiculous, of course. She wanted a future with a smart, ambitious, successful man, and Greg was on the fast route toward becoming the lead assistant district attorney. But even his promising career couldn't make her forget the fact that he made love like a rabbit.

Jane frowned at the small sound Greg made when he took a sip of water. How could a man of such keen intelligence even begin to imagine that women liked it fast and frantic and shallow?

She'd tried to let it go. She really had. A man couldn't be judged on the depth of his thrusts alone. He was handsome, educated and only a bit vain. He loved his job and he was good at it. He'd be a good father if they ever got that serious. Greg Nunn was exactly the kind of boyfriend Jane needed. Any other woman would be holding on to him with two clenched fists. A couple of months ago Jane had been holding tight herself.

But every time she'd seen him this week, all she'd been able to think about was the absentminded way he clicked his fingernails together when he was thinking. Or his habit of humming when he drove. Not humming actual songs, just hmmmm-ing in a tuneless sigh. And now the way he chewed.

The idea that he might put that mouth on her tonight when they went to his place for dinner… The idea that they might have *sex…*

Jane shuddered and set down her fork. "Greg, I'm afraid this isn't working out," she said without any preamble.

He picked through the grilled vegetables on his plate, pushing aside the peppers. "Hmm?"

"I'm breaking up with you."

A pepper slid off the plate and onto the table. *"What?"*

"I'm sorry. I know I shouldn't be so abrupt. I just don't think this is going anywhere."

"But…" His eyebrows snapped together. "We're going to Fort Collins this weekend so you can meet my parents!"

She smoothed a nervous hand down her practical gray skirt. "Yes, I know. This is really awful of me. You're a wonderful man—"

"Oh, great."

"—but I just don't think there's much chemistry between us."

"Seriously?" He looked genuinely shocked.

Jane pushed her glasses up nervously. "Well, there are sparks, of course," she fudged. "But you aren't in love with me."

"Jane, we agreed from the start that we would take this slowly. I'm concentrating on my career and you didn't want to rush into a physical relationship." Greg leaned forward, his eyes taking on the bright expression of a lawyer sinking his teeth into an argument. "Waiting was fine with me, but I thought we both expected that we'd take it slowly emotionally, too."

"Of course, but—"

"There's plenty of sexual chemistry between us, and we're perfectly suited in temperament. We've got the same goals in life, the same aspirations. And I respect you. I think you're being a little hasty here."

She *was* being hasty. But regardless of her practical nature—or maybe because of it—she could see she had no future with a man if she couldn't bear to have sex with him just three weeks into their physical relationship. Still, there was no way she could say that to Greg, especially since the sex seemed to be just fine on his end.

"I'm sorry. It's not you, it's…" Oh, God, was she really about to say this? Yes, she was. "Me," she finished feebly.

Greg looked as disgusted with her as she felt with herself. "I can't believe this." His fork clattered against his plate. "Unbelievable. What am I supposed to tell my parents? 'I'm a wonderful guy, but Jane decided to break it off right before the weekend she was going to meet my family'?"

"Maybe you could tell them I got sick."

"I'm not going to try to *hide* the fact that you've dumped me, Jane. It's not that much of a goddamn blow."

His voice was getting louder. She'd wounded his pride. Greg hated losing cases, and apparently he hated losing the girl, as well. She recognized the hot fury in his eyes, because he looked the same after a bad day in court. Actually, he'd gotten that look the time she'd canceled a date to help her boss with a project. Maybe she should've paid less attention to his bedroom skills and more attention to his character.

Jane glanced nervously around. Only a few sets of eyes were on them. "I'm sorry. I was just trying to help. Maybe I'd better go."

"Maybe you'd better," he snapped. "And don't call me up when you get lonely in a couple of weeks. That new legal assistant's been eyeing me for weeks. You can bet I'll be talking to her tomorrow."

He'd meant to hurt her, obviously, but all Jane felt was relief. And a fleeting hope that the new legal assistant preferred friction over thrust. "I'm sorry," she said one more time as she grabbed her purse and stood. "I thought it would be better to end things before I met your parents. Do you want me to pay my half of the bill?"

"For Christ's sake, just get the hell out!" Greg snatched up his water and took a gulp, not meeting her eyes at all.

Had he been in love with her? She didn't think so. He looked more furious than hurt. But it didn't matter. She couldn't stay with a man she wasn't attracted to. "Goodbye."

She waited for an answer, but none came, so Jane

turned and walked toward the door. Her feet wanted to run, but she wouldn't let them. She thought she heard a muttered curse behind her—something like "frigid bitch"—but she didn't acknowledge it. She'd been called a lot worse than that in her life. And if that was what he'd said, then good riddance.

Jane stepped out onto the street and took a deep breath. Free. Invisible ropes of tension were falling away as if she'd cut herself free with a knife. This was becoming a pattern with her. Cringing at the thought, she started her walk back to work. It was only half a mile, and she felt totally energized.

A few more hours in the office and then the whole evening stretched out before her like a promise. No sex with Greg. No discussion of opera or foreign films or constitutional law or any of those other things that helped to shape her public persona. After work, Jane was going to go home, take a bath and watch something vile on pay-per-view. Maybe a horror movie. All that and she could still get to bed early and be bright eyed for work tomorrow.

Wow. She was free.

She tried to tamp down the relief that swelled inside her. She'd be twenty-nine on Sunday. The last year of her twenties. In 368 days she'd be thirty. She wanted to marry someday, wanted the chance to have children if she decided to. And if she wanted to marry the right kind of guy, she had to stop dumping boyfriends for superficial reasons.

A woman didn't *need* hot sex to live a good life. Just as she didn't *need* a man with muscles. A rough guy in jeans and boots. A man who would wind his calloused hand into her hair and tell her exactly what he was going to—

"Crud." Jane shook her head to scramble those thoughts. She wasn't that girl anymore, and she never would be again. That girl had been a nightmare of low self-esteem and even lower expectations.

Jane Morgan was a respectable woman and she'd marry a respectable man. She had a few more years to find one, surely, but wouldn't it take that long just to meet someone and truly know him? She was going to have to get over her boredom with safe men, fast.

Despite her stern internal lecture, Jane couldn't stop her grin as she headed toward her office, but once she walked through the door she put on her serious face and got back to work. A half hour later her world was back to normal. The perfect quiet job in the perfect quiet office…until her cell phone rang and she glanced down to see the screen flashing "Mom."

"Oh, no," Jane groaned, taking a deep breath before she dared to answer it.

"Honey," her mom said immediately, "please tell me you've heard from your brother."

Alarm spiked in her blood. "Jessie? Why, is something going on?"

"He didn't come home last night."

Jane's heart stopped, though not out of panic. No, her heart stopped out of sheer disbelief. "That's why you're calling?"

"He left at six last night, and he didn't come home and he hasn't called, and I don't know what to do!"

"Mom…" She made herself take a deep breath and count to ten. "You're being ridiculous."

"I just… Oh, honey, I'm sure your little brother is in trouble."

"Oh, that's probably true," Jane answered. "I just have no idea what that has to do with me. Jessie's twenty-one years old, Mom. An adult, just like me."

"Well…" Her mother sighed. "He never had the advantages you did, baby."

Jane squeezed the phone tighter and glared at a spot of late-afternoon sunlight hitting Mr. Jennings's door. Advantages. The woman was living in a dream world.

"He's not as smart as you."

A deep breath helped bring Jane's blood pressure down. "I've told you not to call me at work unless it's an emergency. This isn't personal time for me."

"It is an emergency!"

"No, it is not. A grown man can't be considered missing after eighteen hours. Especially not a grown man who likes to drink and hook up with skanky barflies."

"Now, that's just mean!"

"Mom, I'm sorry, I have to go. Is there anything else?"

"Well, I don't think so… Wait! Are you coming over for your birthday?"

Jane cringed. Before breaking up with Greg, she'd had the perfect excuse to miss a birthday party with her family. But now… Jane found herself wishing her mom had forgotten her only daughter's birthday, but no such luck. Her mother had been a pretty shabby parent, but not because she lacked kindness or generosity. Just the opposite, in fact. But Jane hadn't needed a girlfriend when she was growing up. She'd needed a mother.

"Sorry, Mom. I'm busy."

"Oh, are you doing something with that new boyfriend?"

"Mmm-hmm. Yeah."

"You could bring him with, you know."

Jane tried to picture Greg in her mother's house, but the idea defied the laws of nature. He'd never have made it past the burned-out car in the front yard.

"Your dad finally hauled off the Corvair," her mom added hopefully.

Well, then. No burned-out car in the yard, so that just left…everything else. Her family, the shop, the house and the other cast-off vehicles scattered around. Perfect. Maybe her mom had added that chicken coop she'd always wanted.

"No, thanks, Mom. I'll call you, though."

"Oh. Okay. All right."

Ignoring the obvious disappointment in her voice, Jane hung up and stared at the phone as the screen faded to black. What did it say about her that she'd rather be alone on her birthday than spend time with her family? What kind of person was she?

The familiar guilt sank its claws into her heart and squeezed.

As an adult, Jane could see the mistakes her mother had made through a clearer lens. There had been no malice in her mom's decisions, just immaturity and desperation. The life she'd subjected Jane to—the poverty and prison visits and constant moves—had been the only life her mother had ever known. And without the early intervention of her stepfather, Jane would've sunk straight into that life, too.

So she wasn't truly angry with her mom anymore. She was just…uncomfortable.

Her family—her mom and stepfather and brother—knew who Jane really was. They knew the kind of girl she'd been, and they saw right through her false transformation into a conservative businesswoman.

The problem wasn't so much her family. The problem was that Jane Morgan was a fraud. And she didn't like being reminded of it.

Better to keep the two halves of her life separated by a wide expanse. That way, no one got hurt, especially Jane.

WILLIAM CHASE CRANKED UP the stereo as he roared down the mountain. The wide-open windows let in the crisp spring air and quite a bit of dust from the road. Chase didn't care. After a blast like that, nothing could ruin his mood.

Fifteen hundred pounds of dynamite chewing up granite as if it were papier-mâché. Sweet mother. Without a doubt, Chase had the best job in the world.

He tapped his hands against the steering wheel and grinned. Blasting days were his favorites. They didn't come often enough, though. It took a lot of planning to execute, plus an unbelievable amount of paperwork. And hell, most excavations didn't require even one single stick of dynamite, just a backhoe and a bulldozer. But when a new hotel was going up on Aspen Mountain, the foundation had to go somewhere, and that somewhere was straight into the bedrock.

Though he'd started Extreme Excavations only six years before, Chase had already made a name for himself as the go-to guy for tough jobs. Not just the big stuff, but the intricate work, as well. Chase could blow out a wall of rock fifty feet wide and leave the hundred-year-old barn that stood two feet away without even the slightest creak of boards.

He was good, and he knew it, and that made the work even better.

Smiling, he turned onto Main Street and passed his favorite coffee shop without a glance. No need for caffeine today. He was high on life. And explosions.

When he pulled into the parking lot of Jennings Architecture, he didn't get out right away. Instead, he let his head fall back against the headrest and waited for his favorite song to end. When the bass-heavy music faded away, the drip of water from hundreds of roofs became the dominant sound. Winter was officially over, and months of grueling work stretched out before him.

Scoring a job with Quinn Jennings was a big coup. Quinn was one of the most sought after architects in town, and though Chase normally worked on commercial projects, he'd jumped wholeheartedly at the chance to work with Quinn on a few residential builds.

Chase cut the engine and headed into the small office building. As soon as he crossed the threshold, he was stopped in his tracks by a large desk guarded by a woman whose posture radiated cool judgment.

A pair of big brown eyes studied him through black-framed glasses. "Good afternoon," the woman said. Her eyes flickered to his chest and then back up. Chase felt a jolt of interest, but the disapproval in her gaze made him wonder why he felt like smiling.

"Hi, I'm Chase," he said, giving in to the smile.

She didn't respond, except to raise an eyebrow. Even her fingers stayed poised over the keyboard, as if she were only waiting for him to move along so she could get back to work.

"I'm with Extreme Excavations," he clarified.

"I see. A pleasure to meet you, Mr. Chase."

"It's just Chase." Another arch of her eyebrow. Chase cleared his throat and tried to shake off the urge to squirm. "Quinn Jennings asked me to stop by to pick up some preliminary plans. I told him I'd be here today."

The woman finally lifted her hands from the keyboard and folded them primly on the desk. "Mr. Jennings is on the phone right now. If you'd care to have a seat, he should only be a few moments."

"Thanks."

"I'm Jane. In the future it may be best to speak with me about project materials. Mr. Jennings has a tendency to overlook those kinds of details when he's working."

"Um…okay. Nice to meet you, Jane."

"Can I get you something? Coffee or water?"

"No, thank you. I'll just…"

Her head tilted toward the grouping of chairs to his right, as if Chase were a child in need of coaxing. Chase nodded and sat down without another word, relieved that this woman wasn't his secretary. He'd live in terror of ever being late to work.

Then again, she was kind of pretty.

Chase's brow fell into a frown, as startled by the thought as he had been by the little zing of interest he'd felt under her gaze. He glanced up to watch her type something on the computer. Her stylish little glasses slipped down her nose and she nudged them up again.

Was she pretty?

Well, despite the fact that she seemed to be made of ice, her full lips looked very soft. And her brown eyes were gorgeous in spite of her reserved expression. The rest of Jane was difficult to decipher. Her black suit jacket was tailored to reveal nothing of her figure, and her shiny brown hair was pulled back into a tight knot. The only jewelry she wore was a pair of small pearl earrings.

In every way she looked like a conservative professional woman who didn't believe in letting loose.

Fingers typing away, she glanced toward Chase, and he averted his eyes to the nameplate on her desk. Jane Morgan.

Something about that rigid exterior made his fingers itch.

He dared another peek and happened to catch Jane licking her lips. The tip of her tongue looked very pink against her mouth. If she wore lipstick, it was the very plainest of colors, but there was nothing plain about that little flash of her tongue.

Chase shifted in his seat and drew her eye back to him. This time she glanced away. A flush crept into her cheeks, and his pulse sped in response. He probably wouldn't even have noticed such a faint hint of color in another woman's cheeks, but it seemed like a significant response for her. She was aware of him, and he narrowed his eyes and let his gaze slide down to her elegant neck.

Her skin looked soft as all hell, and he couldn't help but wonder how a lady like this would respond to being nibbled. But why the hell was he thinking about nibbling a complete stranger?

Before his frown could fully form, he realized what it was. The blast. He was always pumped up after a good explosion. Pumped up and horny as hell. Prissy Jane probably wouldn't react well to that at all.

His cell rang, cutting off the chuckle rising in his throat.

She looked surprised when he murmured, "Pardon me," and stepped out the door. Surprised because he was polite? Because of the tattoo, maybe? Chase was smiling when he answered the phone, though his insurance agent's talk of rising liability rates sobered him up pretty quickly.

Chase paced back and forth across the doorway for a few minutes, arguing his case, but it was no use. The agent swore it was an across-the-board increase and nothing to do with Extreme Excavation's records. "Our goddamn safety record is spotless," he insisted one last time, glancing through the glass to be sure the secretary hadn't overheard him and covered her ears.

Her eyes were on him. She was watching, but she wasn't scowling. Jane the secretary was staring at his chest.

Chase froze and watched her as his agent babbled in his ear. When her gaze finally rose to his, she blinked rapidly before snapping her eyes back to the computer screen.

Well.

He turned his back on her and wrapped things up with his agent, then glanced quickly over his shoulder to try to catch her again. No such luck. The woman was fully focused on her work.

When he tucked the phone back into his pocket,

Chase realized that there was a smear of gray dust across the front of his dark blue T-shirt. Maybe that's what she'd been looking at. "Shit," he muttered, strangely disappointed that she hadn't been indulging in a fantasy of getting dirty with a blue-collar worker.

Shrugging, he headed back inside just as Quinn Jennings emerged from his office.

"Hey, Chase," the architect said, hand outstretched.

Chase shook his hand and took the folder Quinn offered. "Thanks, man."

"Sorry I forgot to leave it with Jane. Next time you'd better call her."

"That's just what she said." Chase dared a look at her, but Jane ignored the conversation.

"Well, apparently I'm trainable after all," Quinn said with a laugh. "Keep it as long as you need."

"Shouldn't be more than a few days."

A hand popped into his view and snatched the file from his fingers. "I'll take that," Jane said. "I'll need to make a copy before it leaves this office."

"Um…understood," Chase answered the back of her head. She was already at the copier.

While Quinn excused himself to head out to a site, Chase checked out Jane's ass, but her straight gray skirt didn't offer much of a view. She was tall, and either curvy or a little chubby, but Chase was a man, and a little softness on a woman didn't scare him at all.

"Here you are, Mr. Chase."

He blinked and took the file. "It's just Chase," he repeated, though he was beginning to suspect she was quite clear on the matter and simply didn't approve.

"Have a good day," she said in answer.

Unwilling to be so obviously dismissed, Chase opened the file and flipped through a few of the papers. "Your boss is good at what he does."

"He is."

He looked over a couple more drawings of the mountain home, then cut his eyes toward Jane. She didn't notice. She was too busy staring at him again. This time it was his arm that had caught her attention, either his biceps or the ink stretched across it. Somehow he suspected it was the black bands of his tattoo.

His heart thumped in excitement. Maybe Miss Prim and Professional wanted to take a little walk on the wild side. Luckily, Chase was in just the mood to accommodate her curiosity.

"Jane?" he said softly, startling her enough that she jumped.

A blush warmed her cheeks as she turned back to the computer. "Is there something more I can help you with?" Despite her pink face, her voice was perfectly cool.

"Yes, actually." He closed the file and approached her desk. "How about dinner tonight?"

Although she froze, Jane didn't look up. "What about dinner tonight?"

Ah, of course. This woman would require something a bit more formal. Fine. He'd play along. "Jane Morgan, would you do me the honor of accompanying me to dinner tonight?" Hell, he even gave her a little bow to top it off.

Jane was unmoved. Literally. Her fingers hovered above the keyboard again. "What?"

"Would you like to go to dinner?"

Her hands finally dropped, banging against the keyboard. "No, I would not."

Chase wasn't exactly surprised, but he felt oddly heavy with disappointment, all the same. "Are you sure?"

She licked her lips again and tossed a brief look his way. "Thank you, but I'm sure."

Damn, her lips were downright sultry now, flushed pink and glistening with moisture. Chase cocked his head. Yeah, her lips were sexy as hell. "Well, if you're sure," he said, stalling.

"I am." Jane took a deep breath, put her shoulders back and began to type.

"Right," he muttered. "Have a good day, then." And there was nothing Chase could do but leave.

THE OFFICE DOOR eased closed with a little hiss. Jane kept typing gibberish. She waited, counting to twenty, before she slid her hands off the keyboard and dared a glance at the glass door. The man's truck was turning out of the lot. She was alone.

Letting out a deep breath, Jane slumped in her chair. "Oh, crud."

What had just *happened?*

Despite the scene over lunch with Greg and her mother's phone call, Jane's day had been proceeding at its normal professional pace. A rush of calls after lunch from contractors driving back to work sites. The quiet buzz of a well-run workplace for a few more hours. That disastrous lunch hour had hardly put a hitch in her stride.

And then *he'd* walked in.

The sight of him filling the doorway had shocked the life out of her. He wasn't big in a body-builder kind of way, but he was tall. Probably six foot three or four, with a wide, solid frame that took up more space in a room than it should. His brown hair was short, nearly a buzz cut, but so thick it looked soft to the touch.

Jane shivered at the thought.

Three solid hours of freedom and she was already thinking about an inappropriate man. She shouldn't have broken it off with Greg. Greg was educated, ambitious and mannered. He wasn't big and tattooed. He didn't drive a dented, dusty truck. He didn't work for an hourly wage at a dead-end job and wear steel-toed boots and dirty T-shirts that clung to his muscles while he labored.

Her skin tingled and Jane muttered, "Oh, crud" again. This Chase guy was exactly the type of man she didn't need in her life. The kind of man who made her skin tingle, not to mention other less visible parts of her. No, he was not the kind of man she needed, but he was the kind she wanted. Raw and primal and *big*.

"I will not be my mother," she insisted to the computer screen. "I will *not* be my mother." The computer stared her down. "Screw you," she snapped, then glanced around guiltily. She did not use undignified language.

And she did not date men whose biceps were ringed with thick bands of stark black ink like some sort of brutal, ancient warrior.

Jane rolled her shoulders and stretched her neck. "I won't be my mother," she murmured one last time.

"And I won't be that girl again." Then she erased the mess she'd made of her Excel spreadsheet and forcibly turned her mind back to work.

CHAPTER TWO

JANE'S MUSCLES WERE liquid with exhaustion as she stepped out of her car the next morning. She'd been too anxious and distracted to follow through with her plan the night before. Instead of heading home for a movie, she'd called up her trainer and spent an hour working the heavy bag at his private gym. Then she'd eaten a whole pizza, watched TV until midnight and overslept.

Jane unlocked the office door and rushed inside to drop into her chair. Fifteen minutes late. She was spiraling.

One night on her own and Jane Morgan was sinking low, her facade crumbling like mountains of melting snow in the parking lot.

It didn't matter that she took care to dress professionally and maintained a manner more prickly than a librarian. It didn't matter that she refused to show even a hint of friendliness to the dirty contractors and groping developers and sexist engineers, or that she made very, very sure to date only *appropriate* men.... She hadn't changed at all.

Jane was still attracted to the same kind of guy she'd dated in high school: tattooed, rough and ready to ride.

"Crap," she groaned. She'd had a very sexual dream about Chase the night before. And just that dream had gotten her off in a way that Greg hadn't even approached.

Though, she reasoned to herself, he didn't seem *exactly* like the kind of guy she'd once run around with. And he wasn't exactly the type of man her mother had favored for years.

Despite the fact that his jeans had been creased with age and dingy with ancient dirt stains, he'd smelled of laundry detergent. His hair was cut short and neat, belying the dark curves of a tattoo that curled straight up the back of his neck and disappeared into his hairline. And most important, he couldn't possibly be an ex-con. Extreme Excavations specialized in blasting. Even if Chase was low on the totem pole, permits for high explosives weren't handed out to companies that employed criminals.

So, no, he wasn't exactly like the guys from her past.

Jane snapped from her thoughtful daze and scowled at her reflection in the black computer screen. "Nice standards there, Jane Morgan. Clean underwear and no felony record." Her reflection glared at her, stern and disapproving. Her neck was straight. Her shoulders rigid. Her nostrils flared with outrage. Until she suddenly slumped in defeat. "I'm a fraud."

Fraud she might be, but she was damn good at maintaining the illusion. When a car door slammed in the parking lot, Jane snapped straight, banged on the keyboard to bring her computer out of sleep mode and jumped right into the report she'd been working on the day before.

The door opened and she expected to look up and

see Mr. Jennings walking in. What she didn't expect was the man who'd visited her dreams the night before.

But she was cool Jane now, the impenetrable fraud, so she merely raised an eyebrow. "Good morning, Mr. Chase."

"Hello, Miss Jane," he countered.

She almost laughed at his joke, and what a disaster that would have been. If he knew she found him charming, he might ask her out again. She didn't allow her expression to budge. "What can I help you with?"

He held out the folder he'd tucked under his arm. "See? Safe and sound. I'm the soul of responsibility."

"Mmm-hmm," she murmured, trying to hide the way he was wreaking havoc on her concentration. His sleeve had inched up, revealing more of the tribal tattoo on his left arm. "Thank you."

"So…" he said.

She jerked her eyes up from his arm.

"Have you thought any more about it?"

"About what?"

"Going out to dinner with me?"

"No," she answered as if it were the honest truth. Actually, it was. Dinner hadn't entered into her thoughts even once.

"Come on." He smiled at her, his wide mouth curving into a very handsome grin. His dark blue eyes sparkled. "Just dinner."

"No, thank you."

"Why not?"

"You're not my type." The bald-faced lie fell smoothly from her tongue.

"You sure?" He glanced toward his arm, and Jane felt her pulse leap.

Oh, my God. Had he looked at his *tattoo* when he said that? She felt her face heat despite her best efforts to suppress the betraying flow of blood. He'd seen her looking.

But those could have been looks of horror, she told herself. They'd meant nothing. *Nothing.*

Her pulse wouldn't listen to her. It gathered speed. Chase smiled and put one hand on her desk to lean closer. His gaze fell to her mouth, and she could feel herself breathing too fast.

Last night as she'd boxed, she'd imagined her trainer was Chase. She'd imagined him grabbing her, his hands sliding across her damp skin, his mouth descending with a growl....

Oh, God, her masquerade was crumbling around her. What if she let Chase—

Her cell phone rang, breaking the man-spell she'd fallen under. Jane looked down to the phone, and the display was a bucket of cold water dumped over her head. "Mom" it read, the backlight glowing red in warning.

She stared at it for a moment, skin cooling as each second ticked by. "Yes," she finally answered him, "I'm sure."

"Sure about what?"

"I'm sure you're not my type, Mr. Chase, but thank you very much for the invitation."

Though his face fell, Chase didn't look the least bit angry. In fact he pulled a business card from his back pocket and handed it over. "All right, then. Call me if you change your mind. That's my cell."

"Thank you." She meant to drop it in the trash. She really did. But as Chase turned and walked out, Jane tucked his card into her purse. Then she turned off her cell phone and stuck that in her purse, too.

She was working, and the world of rough men and burned-out cars and bad mothers could go to hell.

"I'M SO GLAD YOU DECIDED to meet me," Lori Love said. "God only knows how long I'll be sitting here." She pushed one of her brown curls behind her ear and set her elbows on the bar.

Jane smiled. Lori and Mr. Jennings were very seriously involved, and Jane seemed to have gained a friend in the deal. Still, they weren't really the type of friends to hit the town together, mainly because Jane didn't hit the town. She glanced around the dark hotel bar. "I don't know why you agreed to meet Mr. Jennings here."

"Oh, I'm smarter than you think. Quinn's at a business dinner at The Painted Horse. I refused to go, but I'd already agreed to that damn city council party at eight. So we're meeting in the middle. I get to avoid the boring dinner but still participate in free drinks afterward."

"Congratulations." Jane raised her empty martini glass in salute.

"Why aren't *you* coming to the party?"

"I wasn't invited." Jane looked up in surprise when the bartender put another drink in front of her. Apparently he'd noticed her waving the glass around. "Oh, thank you."

"Please come with us," Lori said. "It's downstairs

in the ballroom. You can keep me company while Quinn talks shop."

Jane considered it for a moment. A party. Drinks. Eligible, appropriate men. Professional and educated. The party would be the perfect place to meet the kind of man she needed to meet, but the thought of doing that tonight, of being professional and conservative and reserved... Jane glanced down at her drink and found it empty.

"Sorry, but you're on your own," she said. "No work for me tonight."

"Damn," Lori muttered. "Hey, did you read that book-club book yet?"

Jane had talked Lori into joining the monthly women's group at the local bookstore. "I did. It was really thoughtful and deliberate."

"Ugh. I thought it was depressing," Lori said. "I didn't make it past chapter six, when she went back to her suicidal husband. I dropped it and picked up one of my dirty books instead. The book-club meeting is right before my trip anyway. I'll be busy."

Jane felt a sharp stab of envy. Lori was building a life for herself, too, but it had nothing to do with trying to make herself respectable. Lori was stretching her wings, reading erotic novels and going back to college and traveling to Europe by herself. But Lori had been the good girl her whole life. She'd been responsible and respectable. Jane didn't have that kind of past to fall back on, so she pretended to like depressing books that educated women recommended.

Another small act of fraud that added to Jane's growing feeling of unease.

Lori nudged her. "I've still got that box of naughty stories with your name on it."

Jane considered the offer for a moment. She'd turned Lori down flat a few weeks ago, but maybe dirty books would be a good outlet for her now. She'd found herself ogling her trainer during that boxing session the night before, and Tom was 100 percent gay. But gay or not, his shoulders reminded her of Chase's.

"Maybe?" Lori said with a cheeky smile, but then her eyes shifted and the smile turned to a bright grin. "Hey, Quinn."

Quinn Jennings slid up to the bar next to his girl-friend. "Hey, Lori Love," he answered, his deep voice sinking to a purr.

Jane nearly blushed to hear it. Here was living proof that a good, intelligent man could throw off sparks with the right woman. Jane didn't *have* to settle for safe and boring. She could find safe and spicy, just as Lori had. Then again, Quinn Jennings had never made Jane perk up and take notice. He wasn't her type. Just as Greg hadn't been her type and neither had the dentist she'd dated before him or the veterinarian before that.

"Hi, Jane," Quinn said. "Are you coming with us?"

Lori took his hand. "Nope, she's going to stay here and get sloppy drunk."

The couple laughed at the idea, probably unable to imagine Jane being anything less than dignified. Little did they know.

Quinn muttered something about contributing to the cause, then tossed a ten-dollar bill onto the bar. "Another one for her," he called.

"Oh, no, Mr. Jennings. I don't—"

But he was already pulling Lori toward the door. "I'll see you Monday, Jane. Stay out of trouble."

The drink arrived, and what could she do but drink it? Fifteen minutes later she was cradling Chase's card in her hands. He had a business card, so maybe he wasn't just a ditchdigger. Maybe he was a supervisor of some sort. "W. Chase," it said. His first name must be something horrific. Something like Worthington or Wessex.

Just Chase he'd kept saying, as if he were embarrassed to be called Mister. And he was right, of course. It didn't suit him.

Jane glanced up, accidentally meeting the eyes of some guy two stools down. When he smiled and rose from his seat, she bit back a groan. She wasn't in the mood. Not for him, anyway.

"Hi, there," he said. "My name's Dan."

"Hi, Dan." Jane didn't offer her name. He was cute enough, and he was wearing a suit and tie, but he wasn't her type. None of these guys was. She was hopeless.

"Do you live here in Aspen?" the guy was asking.

"Mmm-hmm."

"I'm here on business. It's a beautiful place."

"Yes, it's lovely." God, why was he even coming on to her? She was wearing her ivory suit and her glasses, not to mention her pulled-back hairstyle. She'd designed herself to look uptight and unapproachable. Maybe she just looked lonely and desperate. An easy lay.

Dan leaned his elbow against the bar. "Can I buy you a drink?"

"No, thank you. I'm meeting someone here."

That finally drove him off. As he sauntered away, Jane watched his back, thinking that he looked rather…petite. About the same height as her, with the same slight build as Greg.

Jane was five-eight and curvy. Was a big man too much to ask for?

She looked at the card again. Chase. He was big. He turned her on. And for whatever reason, he'd asked her out. He clearly wasn't the marrying type, but did that mean she couldn't just use him for a good time?

Mr. Jennings had dated a lot of the wrong women before he'd found Lori. He hadn't taken any of those relationships seriously. Why shouldn't Jane do the same?

And it was almost her birthday. Still, it wouldn't be smart to sleep with someone from her professional world. It wouldn't be smart at all, but it would be a heck of a birthday present.

Didn't she deserve one night of hard, primal sex with a *real* man? Just one tiny, delicious detour on her journey to a respectable future? No one knew about her past. No one could point and say, "That girl is just as trashy as she used to be."

Jane took out her phone. "You're tipsy," she tried to warn herself, but that only made her feel better about what she was doing. "This is a bad idea," she breathed. "*Really* bad. But I'm tipsy."

Finger shaking, Jane turned on her phone. She reached to press the first number, but she didn't do it. She set the phone down on the bar. She took a deep breath. And then it rang.

"Oh, jeez," she muttered, slapping a hand to her chest. Saved by the bell. Except that the screen was flashing "Mom" again, and that couldn't be good.

"Hello?" she answered.

"Oh, Jane, thank goodness! I've got awful news. Just awful!"

"Mom, what's wrong?" Her heart leaped.

"It's Jessie!" her mom wailed.

"Oh, no. What's happened?"

"He never came home and I've tried calling you all day. But, oh, my God, I finally heard something. Your brother is in *jail!*"

"Oh." Jane's heart began to slow. "I see. For what?"

"I don't know. All I've heard are rumors. He hasn't called home. I don't know what's going on!"

"Calm down. He hasn't called home because he knows Dad is going to kill him." Glancing around, she lowered her voice. "He was probably picked up for possession. You know he gets high, Mom."

"Will you have your boyfriend find out where he is? Somebody said it might be Pitkin County."

"Are you—" Jane snapped her mouth closed. *Are you crazy?* she'd meant to say. "Mom, it's Friday night. There's nothing to be done now."

"But he'll be there all weekend if we don't—"

"Mom," Jane said sharply. "Calm down. If he hasn't broken down and called you, then he's probably okay. If he doesn't get in touch before the morning, I'll do what I can, all right?" But damned if she was calling Greg.

"But…" Her mother's voice faded away.

Jane felt her heart twist with worry. "Mom, is Dad there?" Her stepfather, Mac, was solid as a rock. Her mom would be fine as long as he was home.

"Yes, he's here."

"All right. What did he say?"

There was a long pause. Her mom's voice fell to a

whisper. "He said we should let Jessie cool his heels until he got the…nerve to call home and ask for help."

Clearly Mac had used harsher language than that, but Jane just nodded. "Okay. It's going to be fine, Mom. He's twenty-one years old, and if he's starting to get into trouble, a few days in jail will be good for him."

"It…it just doesn't seem right." Her voice went hoarse with tears.

"No, it's not right," Jane muttered before she said goodbye and hit End. It wasn't right that no matter how hard she tried, Jane couldn't get away from this life. The life of courthouses and bail bondsmen and visits to jail. It didn't matter how good she was at her job or how hard she worked. All it took was one phone call and Jane Morgan was right back in the trailer park.

She picked up the business card and looked at it one last time.

Yeah, she was spiraling, all right. Might as well enjoy the damn ride.

CHAPTER THREE

AH, CHRIST. Chase slapped down the visor of his truck in a burst of panic. He'd forgotten to shave.

"Shit," he muttered at his reflection, swiping a hand over his prickly jaw. He popped the visor back up with another curse. There was no time now. Jane Morgan had called and asked him to meet her. Even the quick shower had been a risk. He'd half expected to come out of the bathroom and find that she'd left a message calling it off. Now that he was only steps away from the bar he wasn't turning back.

He wasn't sure what was going on, but he damn sure wanted to find out. Chase slammed the door of his pickup and rushed across the street to the bar.

It took a few seconds to spot Jane. She sort of...blended in to the background. Despite it being Friday night, her hair was still pulled back into a tight bun. She still wore her pricey-looking white suit. As he watched, she took off her glasses and rubbed her eyes. Jane was getting sleepy. He was about to miss his chance at a date.

Chase pushed through the mingling crowd and stopped next to her table. "Hey, Jane."

"Oh!" she yelped, slipping on her glasses before she pushed awkwardly to her feet. "Hello."

"I'm really glad you called."

"I…just…I had your card." Her hands gestured helplessly, so Chase waved her back to her chair.

He glanced down to her glass of water. "Can I get you a drink?"

"Um…sure."

Chase caught a waitress's eye, and the woman sauntered over with a grin that faded when he tilted his head toward Jane. She ordered a martini and looked surprised at his request for a Coke.

"Aren't you going to have something?"

"No, I don't drink."

Her eyes flew wide behind the glasses. "Oh! I'm sorry. I'll cancel mine, then, and—"

"Hey, it's no big deal."

She shook her head. "I don't want to be disrespectful or—"

"It's no problem. I'm not an alcoholic, so you don't have to worry that you'll push me off the wagon. My dad's a big drinker, and I thought it'd be better if I never started down that road."

Jane looked doubtfully down at her water.

"Seriously!" He laughed. "You know I work in construction, right? I guarantee my friends can throw back a hell of a lot more alcohol than you can. So drink up."

Her drink arrived as if on cue. "Well…" She picked up her martini with a bemused smile. "All right. Cheers, then." Still, she took only a tiny sip.

"So why did you call? Not that I'm objecting." When a blush climbed her face at his words, Chase grinned. A blush was good. Very good. The modest Miss Jane did like him, despite her earlier words. There was something about her that made him want to… mess her up a little. He'd never been interested in a woman like her before, but for some reason her coolness fascinated him. And this new nervousness pushed heat through his skin. She'd probably never even been alone with a guy like Chase.

Jane took another sip of her drink and swallowed hard. Her pearl earrings glinted softly, as if warning him of her modesty. "It's my birthday. On Sunday, I mean."

"Oh, happy birthday."

"Thanks. So I just thought, um… Well."

Chase blinked at the sudden blush in her cheeks. "What? You thought I'd make a good *birthday present?*"

"No!" she cried. "Of course not! That would be… No, I just thought I'd…celebrate."

But that hot red burn belied her words. He'd been half joking, but now…

Jesus Christ, was he supposed to be the present she gave herself for her birthday? Chase wasn't sure how he felt about that.

No, wait. He was sure after all. It felt pretty damn fine with him.

Jane finished her drink in one gulp.

"So," he ventured, suddenly unsure what to say. All he could think about was the fact that Jane really was looking for a good time, and that good time apparently involved him. Still, she couldn't possibly mean to be so forward. Maybe she thought they'd hang out tonight and go on another date on Sunday.

Chase cleared his throat. "How's work going?"

"Fine. How's the business of blowing things up?"

He grinned. "Pretty damn fun. Not that I get to blow

things up very often, but when I do, it's a rush. You wanna see a blast sometime? Maybe next week?"

"Oh." Her soft mouth made a lovely little O. He noticed how perfect her skin was and wondered what it would feel like if he dragged his fingers across her cheek. Though her eyes had brightened with interest, she shook her head. "I can't."

"Think about it. I'll call you next week."

He ignored the way she frowned. She might be shy, but she'd called him. She *was* interested.

"Chase, I don't want you to take this the wrong way, but…"

"Shit, did I screw up already?"

"No, I just want to be clear about something." Jane sat up a little straighter, though he wouldn't have thought that was possible. She always looked stiff. This girl needed some serious relaxing, and he'd be happy to show her how to get down and dirty.

"I'm not, um…" She cleared her throat again. "I just got out of a relationship, so this isn't… This is casual."

"Casual."

"Yes. Temporary."

Chase wasn't sure why he felt a little twinge of hurt. After all, he'd asked her out while still riding an adrenaline wave. He hadn't thought about much more than the challenge of getting her out for a drink, and then a little more. "Okay. Duly noted. I asked you out because I thought we might have fun, that's all. No pressure."

She smiled, her eyes flashing happiness. "Good. Have you had dinner?"

"Yes. Have you? I'd be happy to—"

"I'm good," she blurted.

So she didn't want dinner or a relationship. Was he losing his mind or did that leave only one possibility? "Let me buy you another drink," he offered, the only thing he could think of.

"No, but thank you." Her eyes fell to the table. "One more thing. I wouldn't normally go out with men with whom I have a working relationship. I mean, I wouldn't normally do this at all, but…"

"I'm happy you're making an exception."

"I trust you'll be discreet?"

"Oh, of course." Chase tried to shake off the feeling he was being interviewed, but Coke sloshed over the rim of his glass when he picked it up.

"If you breathe a word of this to anyone, I'll have to deal with come-ons and crude remarks. I can't have that in my workplace."

"No problem. You can trust me."

"Good." She nodded, her mouth serious. "Can we go to your place, then?"

His throat spasmed, choking off the soda he'd been swallowing. The Coke tried to escape another way, burning toward his nose. Chase coughed in a desperate attempt to retain some dignity, but he couldn't stop his eyes from watering. "What?" he managed, swiping at the tears. Despite his theorizing, he hadn't convinced himself that Jane had called him for sex. He was feeling more sure by the second.

Jane didn't answer. She'd regained her composure, perhaps because he'd lost his, and now she sat in her normal prim pose, hands clasped and resting on the table in front of her.

"Why?"

She frowned at him over those little black glasses. "Why do you think?"

The noise in the bar seemed to grow louder, making it hard for Chase to think. Of course he knew *why,* but…

Chase didn't normally jump into bed with any woman who showed interest, but there was some sort of *spark* between them. Something that made him want to throw caution to the wind. Since he'd met her yesterday, his interest had built minute by minute. Hour by hour. And now, even though they hadn't even had a first date… Now he felt an urgency overtake him. She didn't seem like a woman who propositioned men. This wasn't likely to be an open-ended offer. Chase was working within a limited time frame.

And it *was* her birthday. Almost.

Hell, this was every man's dream, wasn't it? A woman asking permission to jump his bones? Jesus, his little fantasy about showing the uptight secretary a good time was unfolding in front of him like a puzzle unlocking. It seemed way too good to be true.

Too good to be true…but Jane was watching him, waiting, eyebrows raised.

"Let's go," Chase said, holding out a hand as he stood. If this sweet little secretary wanted a good time, Chase was damn sure going to do his best to give her one.

JANE STOOD and smoothed down her skirt as Chase threw a couple of bills onto the table. Her knees shook. She'd never done this—not as an adult, anyway. But here she was, taking a man home for meaningless sex. Well, not to *her* home, but still.

When Chase grabbed her hand, she realized it was

the first time they'd touched. She also realized that his skin sent flashes of electricity sizzling along her nerves. His hand was hot and big and rough around the edges. He felt like a *man*. Her weak knees shivered.

He led her out of the crowded bar and across the street to his truck. When they reached the passenger door, Chase stopped and turned to face her with serious eyes.

"This isn't something weird, is it?"

"What?" The tipsiness she'd been comforting herself with made it hard to figure out his strange question.

"I don't look like your dead husband or anything, do I?"

"What are you talking about?"

He watched her, his fingers sliding more deeply between hers. "You said you've never done this before."

"I haven't." Not recently anyway.

His eyes narrowed to glittering slits as his gaze dropped to her lips.

Before she could think what to say, Chase dipped his head and pressed his lips to hers. She wasn't ready for it. Strange, considering she'd propositioned him just a few minutes before. But she wasn't expecting the taste of him right at the moment, his lips brushing over hers.

His mouth was nothing like his hands. His mouth touched her softly, a gentle pressure, testing her, feeling her out. When her shock wore off, Jane finally responded. She parted her lips a little, pressing into him, and Chase took the hint.

A shock of warmth against her bottom lip revealed itself to be his tongue, touching briefly before drawing away.

"Mmm." She sighed, angling her head in encouragement. He tasted her again, teasing her until she followed his tongue with her own.

Oh, my. His work-roughened hand slipped around the back of her neck as he pulled her closer. Chase's kiss became deeper, deeper, until Jane found herself clutching his T-shirt and hanging on tight. His tongue thrust slowly. There was going to be no jackrabbit action in this man's bed. This was a careful, controlled assault.

The shivering in her knees climbed higher, shaking through her thighs. As if sensing his work was done, Chase brushed his lips over hers one last time before pulling away.

"Well," he murmured. "Ready to go?"

Jane nodded. "Definitely."

The truck beeped, the locks popped open and Chase reached for the door handle. "After you, Miss Jane."

She flushed a bit at the reminder of who she was to him, but that didn't stop her from climbing up and snapping the seat belt into place. This was a bad idea, but Jane wasn't really a good girl and she never had been. She'd been faking it for ten years without a slip. Ten long years.

Frankly, it was a miracle she'd lasted.

Now she was tipsy and he was hot, and she wanted to drop the good-girl act for a few minutes. Or hours.

Chase slipped into the driver's seat and flashed her a wicked smile. "I don't know what's gotten into you, Jane, but I definitely like it."

Finally she could respond to that grin exactly the way she wanted to. Jane smiled and slanted him a look from the corner of her eye. "Just drive."

"Yes, ma'am."

She felt the looks he kept aiming her way as he drove, as if he found her impossibly intriguing. Amazing how an offer of free sex could monopolize a guy's attention.

Jane squeezed her thighs together, thrilling at the darts of pleasure that resulted. The dream she'd had the night before had gotten her body primed for pleasure. Now just that one kiss had her squirming.

Thank God she'd put on sexy underwear that morning. She didn't always wear lacy bras and panties, but it was one of the small pleasures in her life. Sexy lingerie. A tiny concession to her true nature. A secret beneath her professional clothing. It was a secret she wanted to let Chase in on. Quickly.

She hid her body beneath perfectly tailored clothing, because otherwise she drew too many eyes. Her curves had drawn attention from the time she'd hit puberty at eleven. The wrong kind of attention for a young girl, but wrong was just what she was looking for now.

"My place is just around the corner," Chase said, breaking the silence.

Only two blocks from Main Street. Wonderful.

"Are you cold?" he asked. Even though she said no, he pushed the Up arrow on the climate control system. "Music?"

She shook her head and he dropped his hand. They had nothing in common, nothing to talk about, but Chase seemed determined.

"Do you live here in town?"

"Mmm-hmm." His big hand was sitting right there next to her hip. She wanted to pick it up and put it on her knee, maybe run it up the inside of her thigh so she could feel his calluses rasp against the softest part of her body.

They turned onto a narrow side street, and Jane held her breath in anticipation, counting the seconds until Chase slowed and pulled up to a three-story building. His brow furrowed. "I'm not sure my place is clean."

Jane opened the door and hopped down before he could back out of this. If he backed out, she'd never get the guts to do it again. Clutching her purse, she met him at the driver's side door, thoroughly enjoying the way his body kept on rising as he stepped onto the driveway and stood straight. God, he was big. "I'm not a neat freak," she lied. "It's no problem."

He unlocked the door to his condo and stuck his head in to look around before swinging it open. "Good news. It looks okay."

It actually did look okay. A bit bachelor-pad, what with the flat-screen TV complete with multiple gaming systems. But it didn't smell funny and there weren't pizza boxes lying around. Just a few newspapers and a coffee cup…plus one pair of muddy steel-toed boots. Why, oh, why, did those make her heart pitter-patter when fine Italian loafers made her lip curl?

She had an illness. Hopefully, sleeping with Chase would work like an immunization. Tetanus shots lasted only ten years. Perhaps degrading sex had the same rate of effectiveness.

Jane wandered toward the black bookshelves while Chase turned on more lights and picked up the papers. Unsurprisingly, the shelves held DVDs instead of books. Hundreds of DVDs. She peered closer. There were action movies, sure, but they were outnumbered by big award winners. Movies like *Being John Malkovich* and *Atonement*.

"This was a really good book," she murmured, running her finger along the edge of a case.

"I don't read much."

She didn't feel a smidgen of surprise at that. Her family had never had books around either.

"So," he said, the word fading into silence as he walked toward his small kitchen and opened the fridge. "I've got a couple of beers in here. You want one?" He was jangling his keys nervously, so Jane decided she'd better give him a task. When she asked for ice water, he looked relieved.

They could draw this out with drinks and awkward conversation, or they could skip all the pretense. Jane moved to the stereo system and the iPod connected to it. She scrolled through the songs, looking for something that fit her mood.

Before Chase had even shut off the faucet, Jane found the perfect album and hit play. Then she turned the volume up and let the bass beat drown out the voice of the woman she was now. Tonight she was going to embrace the bad girl who lurked deep inside.

CHAPTER FOUR

WHEN A HARD LINE OF BASS began to pulse, Chase frowned and turned toward the window, imagining some kid driving by with his speakers blasting. But no, the sound was too clear for that. He glanced at the stereo Jane was moving away from.

"I'm sorry. Did I leave…that…?"

But Jane wasn't rushing back to find the stop button. She was walking toward him slowly, white suit jacket sliding down her arms. The brown shirt beneath it was silky and sleeveless, but not fitted enough to reveal much more.

"Too warm?" he asked.

"Yes," Jane answered. Apparently she was way past warm, because she stopped in the middle of the room and reached for the bottom of her shirt, not even pausing before she whipped it over her head. "You were right."

"Oh?" He couldn't say more than that. His throat was closing up as his eyes sent images to his brain.

She reached for the side of her skirt and unzipped it. "I do want you as my birthday present. Is that insulting?"

The skirt dropped. Chase felt his eyes bulge. Holy shit. Jane Morgan, Miss Prim and Proper herself, was fucking *stacked*.

He'd been right to doubt his suspicion that she was plump. She wasn't plump at all. Her waist was tiny and taut. It curved down to rounded hips, hugged by white lace panties. There was more white lace cupping her full breasts. Naked, she looked less like a wallflower and more like Jessica Rabbit. Especially when she reached up and tugged her hair free of its bun. She shook it out, and waves of glossy brown suddenly curved over her shoulders.

The glass slipped in his hand, and he barely caught it in time. Chase set the water down with a clunk.

"Is it?" supersexy Jane asked.

"Huh?" Her thighs were tight but more than full enough to be womanly.

"Is it insulting that I want you as my present?"

"No. No, it's not." In fact, his dick was showing interest in being the main showcase of the gift exchange. He'd seen a porno movie like this once. The serious-looking secretary who was suddenly overcome with lust that transformed her into a sexpot. Chase glanced at the door to be sure no camera crew had arrived.

No, they were alone. The bass line thumped. Jane stepped closer. When he realized that he was standing in his kitchen like an idiot while a half-naked woman beckoned from the living room, Chase moved toward her.

He remembered that kiss as soon as he got close to her. Then he put his hands on her shoulders and found that her skin was even softer than it looked. Holy God.

As he lowered his head, she rose to meet him. This kiss was anything but a tentative exploration. Her tongue met his and slid hard against him as he ran his hands down her back to get his first taste of her curves.

Jane snuck her hands beneath the back of his shirt and started her own exploring. The combination of her hot, soft skin beneath his hands and her fingers sliding over his back had him aching hard within seconds. She pressed closer as if encouraging his arousal, angling her mouth to take him deeper.

Deeper. Oh, hell yeah, he wanted to get deeper.

Sliding his hands lower, he slipped beneath her underwear and found his fingers curving over the most beautiful ass in the world. Not that he'd seen it yet, but it was round and firm and high and it fit his hands like a fantasy.

He spread his fingers wide and pulled her tight against him. When he heard the rasp of his stubble against her chin, Chase lifted his head. "I'm sorry. I forgot to shave."

"No," she murmured. "It's perfect." Proving that she meant it, Jane dragged her open mouth down his jaw to his neck and sucked at his pulse.

Before he knew it, she'd pushed his shirt up and was trying to lift it over his head. Chase helped her out, even if that did mean giving up his very pleasant holding place.

"Oh, God." She sighed. "Look at you."

"Me?" he scoffed, meaning to turn her around to get a view of that ass, but Jane was busy tracing his collarbone with her tongue and he didn't want to be rude and interrupt. Her wet mouth dragged to his shoulder, where she sucked and bit a path over the wide black swirls of his tattoo. Chase closed his eyes and let her explore, though his hands itched to get back to her skin. He closed them to fists as she sighed against his shoulder and slipped around to his back.

"You are so sexy," she whispered. He felt the tip of her tongue touch the nape of his neck and Chase shivered. Though he wanted her back in front of him, he let her continue her exploration just for a moment…just long enough for her to run her hot tongue all the way up his neck.

"Jesus." Sparks of pleasure slipped down his spine. He spun around and slid his hands around her small waist. "You're fucking gorgeous, Jane."

"Thank you," she answered politely, for some reason sinking away from him. It was so impossible that it took a moment for his mind to register that Jane Morgan was going to her knees.

"Jane," he moaned, thinking he should protest. But his body seized control of his mind and shut it down with brutal efficiency. Jane was on her knees before him, little black glasses still perched on her nose, and she was reaching for the button of his Levi's.

He'd fallen into some sort of alternative dimension. Been sucked into an X-rated video game. Nothing about this night made sense. Nothing about this current image made sense, but Jane's fingers were sure and quick, and soon enough she was tugging his zipper down and slipping her hand into his jeans and past his underwear.

Her fingers slid against his bare dick and his breath hissed between his teeth. His whole body tingled with anticipation. He was completely off balance, with no idea what might happen next, and that sense of surprise seemed to push all his blood closer to the surface. Just the faint pressure of her fingertips on his shaft felt like the best sexual experience he'd ever had. And Jane was licking her lips as if there was more to come. Much more.

She tugged his jeans down a little and slipped his dick free, her hand curled firmly around the base. And then, just to complete the fantasy, Jane smiled up at him as if she had just unwrapped the best birthday present in the world.

JANE TRIED NOT to let her hand curl too tightly around his cock. She didn't want to squeeze too hard and scare the man, but good Lord, he was painfully gorgeous. Thick and hard and swelling even bigger as she watched. The head was wide, but the shaft was even wider.

Her sex pulsed with every beat of her heart. *This* was a man. With his rough hands and tattoos and thick erection. Her body *needed* him.

She stroked him slowly, taking in the shape and weight of him. Her mouth watered as she traced a fingertip around the flared head.

"Jane," he murmured again, and she glanced up at him with a smile as she slipped her glasses off. Then she pressed a chaste kiss to the tip. The muscles of his stomach jumped.

Still smiling, she closed her eyes and tasted him. Just a taste, just a slow swirl of her tongue around the head. He smelled of soap and tasted faintly of the salty fluid that glistened at the tip. "Mmm," she purred as she parted her lips and pressed a wet kiss.

Then she took him inside her mouth.

"Ah, God," he groaned. His hand stroked her hair, the calluses catching faintly at the strands. Jane gave herself up to her lust and slid him deep. She licked and sucked him until he was fully primed, until his hand shook against her temple and his breath rushed from his lungs. She wanted more, wanted to keep going, but she couldn't risk him finishing this way. She had plans for this man, and they didn't involve sleepy cuddling.

After one last lick, she set him free. "Ready?" she asked.

His eyes opened, but the pupils were wide and distant. "What?"

Laughing, she stood and tilted her head toward the hallway.

"Oh." He pulled up his boxer briefs and half-zipped his jeans. "I was ready before. Now I'm incoherent."

"I noticed."

Chase arched an eyebrow and took one of her hands to tug her toward the bedroom. "You break a man down and then you mock him? That's cold."

"Or hot."

"Yeah," he agreed with a smile. "Or hot."

When they crossed the threshold of his bedroom, Jane was still laughing, but he took care of that by pulling her into his arms.

His naked belly touched hers and his arms circled her waist as they kissed again. He was an excellent kisser, even more so now that he was turned on and losing control. The thrusting of his tongue got Jane even wetter than she had been.

She felt the slide of his hands up her back, felt his fingers work briefly at her bra before the straps fell free. Jane inched away and let it slide down her arms.

Power coursed through her as she watched his reaction. Men liked her breasts. They were large, a full size D, and she could see Chase's appreciation in the widening of his eyes and the parting of his lips. She shouldn't feel powerful because of that. Men liked breasts. She hadn't accomplished anything admirable by shrugging off her bra, but Jane still raised her chin and arched her back and reveled in the lust in his eyes.

"Damn," he breathed, starting to reach for her, but Jane put her hand to his naked chest and pushed him back until his legs touched the mattress. He sat down hard, still gazing up at her breasts.

Jane toed off her heels, then pushed down her lace panties.

"Damn," Chase repeated, this time with a smile. "You should be arrested for hiding under all those clothes, Miss Jane. You look like a wet dream walking."

"Oh, yeah? So you think it'd be a good idea to show a little cleavage to the surveyors every morning?"

"Um… Okay, you're right. Stay buttoned up."

She curved her hands over her breasts and squeezed lightly. "What about the contractors? You think they'd like the view?"

"Yeah, I think I'm gonna buy you some baggy cardigans for your birthday."

Laughing, she sauntered toward the bed. She'd forgotten that Chase was funny as well as sexy.

"Seriously," Chase breathed, pupils dilating again as she drew near, "I had no idea."

"So why'd you ask me out?"

He glanced up. Briefly. "I thought you were cute in an intimidating kind of way."

She stopped before him and put her hands on her hips. "And now?"

"Now I think you're hot as hell…in an intimidating kind of way. Come 'ere."

His hands curved around her waist and pulled her between his knees. The stubble on his jaw dragged over the curve of her breast before she felt his mouth close over her nipple. Wet heat pulled her tight inside. Though she tried to twist her hands into his hair, Jane found that it was too short, and she had to settle for spreading her fingers over his head and pulling him closer.

His hand closed over her other breast and squeezed the nipple hard.

Gasping, she let her head fall back as he licked and sucked. Suddenly his other hand was between her thighs, the edge of his fingers sliding over her sex.

His sharp gasp cooled her nipple and Jane bit back a laugh. She'd just gotten waxed last week, and he couldn't have suspected that. But she was glad she had, because she could feel even the smallest movement of his roughened fingers against that tender skin. Her amusement vanished when his thumb brushed her clit.

Oh, God, yes. She was so turned on. Like nothing she'd felt with any of her recent boyfriends. This was wrong. Wicked. She didn't even know his first name. And that was why she loved it. Being bad had been her favorite hobby years ago, and it seemed she still had the knack for it.

He stroked her, his fingers sliding easily over her wetness, delving deeper, rubbing tension into her belly. Jane set one knee on the bed, then the other, straddling his legs and forcing him to lie back.

Scooting higher, she pressed her knees on either side of his hips and leaned down to kiss him. When his hand slid up her thigh and found her sex again, she whimpered. When he pressed a finger slowly inside her, Jane moaned and tilted her hips.

He felt so good as he slid in and out, in and out. She sucked his tongue and groaned in encouragement. The encouragement worked. Chase eased another finger in, stretching her tight.

"Oh, God," she moaned. "Oh, yes. Yes."

"I want inside you," he murmured.

Biting her lip, Jane nodded. She wanted it, too. His thick shaft and smooth head. All of it. She eased off the edge of the bed as he toed off his shoes and dug in the pocket of his jeans for a condom. He'd come to the bar prepared. When she saw the wrapper in his hand, Jane pulled the jeans down his legs and tossed them aside.

Finally he was naked, and the rest of his body finished the glorious picture he'd presented before. Nice. Very nice.

Jane climbed back on and took the condom from him. Biting her lip in concentration, she carefully rolled it on, giving him a few extra strokes while she was at it. But she didn't linger. She was too darn horny to wait any longer, so she pushed up and positioned herself right over his cock.

Chase held his shaft steady and spread one hand over her hip to ease her slowly down. At first he slipped easily in, but when the thickest part of him reached her, Jane held her breath at the pressure. She didn't want to breathe or think or even sigh. She just wanted to feel.

"You okay?" he rasped.

Nodding, she lowered her hips another inch.

"Oh, Jesus," he groaned, grabbing her hips with both hands. He eased her up, then down again, sinking himself deeper.

She was panting now, giving up any attempt to hold her breath. A few moments later she'd taken him all the way, and her sex was too full and too tight…and it felt glorious.

Chase's blunt fingers dug into her hips.

She waited a moment, letting herself adjust. She hadn't had a man this big in a long time. And he looked like her custom-made personal fantasy, stretched out beneath her. The black whorls of his tattoo wrapped around his arm and curved over his shoulder. She knew now that the tattoo spread over his shoulder blade before climbing up his spine. God, he was lovely. Hard and strong.

He watched her carefully, face serious and waiting. When she squeezed the muscles of her sex, air hissed through his teeth, and Jane smiled. He was powerful, but sensitive, too, like a muscle car precision-tuned to respond to the slightest bit of pressure.

Jane rolled her hips, rising at the same time before easing down. Oh, God, *yes.* She set the rhythm, working herself against his rock-hard shaft.

His hands left her hips and rose to cup her breasts, his thumbs dragging hard over her nipples. Jane arched her back, rolling her hips.

"Ah, Christ," he groaned. "You've got muscles everywhere."

"Pilates." She sighed, dropping her hips harder against him.

He rose to meet her, driving deep, pinching her

nipples hard. Her soul swelled inside her, pushing out until her body felt too small.

This was who she was. She wasn't a cold, controlled businesswoman who didn't need a man. She was a hot, needful thing who reveled in using and being used in turn. This was who she really was, deep inside. A woman proud of her big breasts and curvy ass. A woman who thrilled at inspiring easy lust in strange men.

She took him faster; her hips fell harder.

"Fuck!" he growled. His arms wrapped around her and the world shifted, and suddenly Jane found herself on her back.

If she'd thought him deep before, she'd been mistaken. Now he slid deep and true and hard, pounding into her.

"Oh…" She sighed. "Oh, yes." She dug her nails into his ass in case he wasn't listening.

He fucked her harder, nothing shallow or fast about it.

Chase hooked his arm under her knee and pulled her leg higher. Suddenly he was hitting the exact right spot. A spot she'd forgotten about in the past few years.

"Chase."

His back grew slick under her grasping hands. His hips slapped into her.

"Yes," she panted. "Yes. *Yes.*"

Finally that familiar pressure began to build high in her sex, and every brutal thrust rubbed against it. "Chase!" she screamed, pulling him closer, knowing she was scratching him and not caring in the least. She was too busy coming her heart out, her hips jerking hard against his thrusts.

She was still distant, floating high above herself, when he roared and drove into her one last time…and then all she could feel was her heart pounding and her breath rushing from her tight throat and his limbs sliding slick and sweaty against hers.

Wow, her mind whimpered. Oh, wow. Just…*wow.*

He was breathing even harder than her, his forehead pressed into the mattress next to her ear. Aware now of her clutching fingers, Jane relaxed her hands and smoothed them over his back. His breath hitched. She pressed a tiny kiss to the edge of his tattoo, hoping he wouldn't notice and mistake it for attachment.

That had been…amazing. Unbelievable. Sure, she'd wanted some sort of sexual miracle. She'd wanted him rough and big and dirty and, most important, good in bed. But there'd been a small chance he could've been just as awful in bed as Greg.

It was a chance she'd been willing to take. And it had paid off in spades.

Chase slid his arm free and let her leg fall back to the mattress. Slowly, slowly he slipped out of her body before rolling to his side with a groan.

Parts of her ached. Parts that hadn't ached in a very long time. Jane quietly stretched, listening to her muscles sing. Oh, yeah.

"Jane?" Chase whispered.

She tilted her head toward him.

"Damn. That was… Damn."

"Yeah." She smiled. "Thank you."

"No, thank *you.*"

Well, on top of everything else he was polite.

"Are you hungry?" he asked. Hungry? Before she

could shake her head, he nodded. "I'm starving. I'm going to jump in the shower and then I'll make us a snack. Stay there."

Jane felt a twinge of stark regret. She didn't want to get up yet. Her muscles were still warm and melting. And Chase was being surprisingly...sweet.

He pushed up from the bed and walked toward the bathroom.

"Chase?"

He tossed a smile over his tattooed shoulder. "Yeah?"

What could she say? *You're amazing? You're wonderful? I'm sorry for what I'm about to do?* Jane cleared her throat. "Thanks for celebrating my birthday with me."

Chase winked. "You're pretty fucking welcome. I'll be right back and we can celebrate again if you want."

Letting her head sink to the mattress, Jane sighed. Where did he get so much energy? She'd never seen a guy so wide-awake after sex, and he was putting a crimp in her plan.

The shower started. The bathroom echoed with the sound of his whistling. Whistling? Jane frowned at the ceiling. He should have just rolled off her and started snoring. Then she could have gotten out of here without the guilt that was twisting through her chest.

"Crud," Jane groused, but as soon as she heard the shower door thud closed, she got up, pulled on her clothes and walked out.

"Thank you, Chase," she whispered as she closed the door. It had been a lovely fantasy, but now she had to get back to her real life. Or her fake life. Whatever it was, Chase didn't fit into it.

CHAPTER FIVE

THERE WAS NO QUESTION about it. Her real life sucked donkeys. And her brother was an asshole.

She winced at the uncharitable, vulgar thought about the little boy she'd spent countless hours babysitting. He'd been a sweet kid. Too sweet. Their mother had let him get away with murder, hiding his transgressions from his father.

But apparently the police didn't think he was cute. He hadn't been released. And on top of that, Jane was spending her Saturday at her parents' house, watching the sheriff serve a search warrant.

She snuck a peek at her stepfather, who was leaning against the kitchen counter, looking as if he didn't want to be in his own home.

If her mother had made Mac aware, he wouldn't have let Jessie get away with things like shoplifting gum from the gas station or lying to his teachers about why he hadn't done his homework.

But Mom had always loved bad boys, of course. And her enabling love had let Jessie grow up into a slacker who figured he could charm his way out of anything. If it wasn't for the large and very intimidating presence of his father, Jessie probably would have been a complete waste. As it was, he at least pretended to try to find a job.

But now the deputies were getting ready to search Jessie's room and the rest of the basement. They hadn't gotten access to the rest of the house, anyway, and that just might save her stepdad's sanity.

Mac crossed his arms, face red and eyes narrowed. He'd backed into the kitchen, separating himself from everyone to help control his temper, a gesture Jane recognized. His appearance was frightening and his temper was real, but he'd spent the past twenty years doing everything he could to stay out of prison. His quiet anger filled the room, but he didn't give it a voice.

Her mom, on the other hand, cried loudly, hands clutching the warrant. "But he didn't do anything!" Her conviction was incredibly real considering she had no idea why the cops were there.

They were from the county sheriff's department, but the warrant had come from Aspen. At least the family knew where Jessie was being held now—right in Jane's backyard.

"All right," Jane said to the female deputy keeping her company, the one making sure she didn't destroy any evidence. Her mother had her own personal keeper and the biggest deputy was stationed near the kitchen, eyes on Mac. "Please tell me what he's been charged with."

"He was arrested by the Aspen P.D., ma'am. You'll have to contact them."

"Of course," she muttered. "Mom, let me see the warrant."

A crash sounded from the basement, and Jane threw

a concerned glance at Mac, who took a deep breath and turned to face the wall. Her mother sobbed.

"Mom, please keep it down. Dad is upset enough, all right?"

Her mom nodded and sniffed hard, trying to control herself.

"I'm going to read the warrant, and then I'm going to try to get in touch with someone at the Aspen police department, okay? Now that we know where he is, we'll be able to find out the charges, no problem. It's all public record. And they must have set bail already."

"I know." Her mom sighed. Of course she did. They were all well versed in the ins and outs of the justice system.

The warrant was enlightening. The police were searching for stolen goods that related to an ongoing investigation. The belongings of two women were listed: purses, credit cards, cash and licenses.

Crud. An ongoing investigation. Not good. Jane looked at the hunched shoulders of her stepfather and cringed. Mac was going to be past furious.

"Do you know about the stolen-goods investigation?" Jane asked the deputy.

The woman gave her an impassive look. "You'll need to contact the Aspen P.D., ma'am."

"Yes, I got that, thanks."

She waded through the last of the scarce information in the warrant before shaking her head. "This is ridiculous," she muttered. "Jessie's no thief."

As if on cue, a deputy emerged from the basement staircase with a big plastic bag. It wasn't empty.

Mac's mouth tightened. "Call Aspen," he growled,

causing his guard to shift nervously. Mac's brown hair was peppered with gray, but he still looked dangerous as hell. His green eyes shot daggers at the cop, and his big arms warned that he could back his rage up with power. The blue-black stains of the tattoos on his arms gave a warning, too—one any cop would recognize. Here was a man who'd spent a good part of his life in prison.

Jane dialed information and turned to face the corner for a small sense of privacy. The black lacquer end table was polished to a shine and reflected her own anxious face back at her.

She'd lost her adventurous side over the course of the past few hours. Now she was pale and plain again, her mouth pinched, her forehead creased with worry. She looked like a woman who'd never enjoyed so much as a decadent dessert, much less a big animal of a man.

As she spoke to the receptionist at the police department and then got transferred to another desk and then another, Jane watched her own face grow tighter, her features twisting into fear as she talked.

By the time she hung up, her reflection had gone blurry with angry tears.

"Mom," she whispered as she turned to face the room. No one heard her. Another deputy passed by on his journey from the basement to the vehicles parked outside. "Dad," she said.

Mac lifted his head and looked at her.

She swallowed hard and lifted the phone a little, as if that would explain her horror.

"What is it?" he asked.

Jane shook her head and swallowed again, finally getting her throat clear enough to speak. "Jessie… I got through to a detective in Aspen. He said…he said that Jessie was stopped for speeding and suspicion of driving under the influence. He was arrested for possession of marijuana, and when they searched the car they found stolen credit cards. Several of them. He's been charged with multiple counts of theft…and felony grand larceny."

Her mother groaned. Mac spit out a curse. And all three deputies in the room moved their hands toward their guns.

For nearly twenty years Jane had managed to steer clear of anything even resembling a jail or a prison. She'd even avoided seeing friends in the hospital, because the ugly floors and echoing halls reminded her of uniforms and shackles. She wasn't sure quite how many hours she'd spent in prison visiting rooms as a child, but it had been way past the point of too many.

Jane Morgan's twenty-year reprieve was over. She was heading right back to where she'd started.

IT SMELLED OF CEMENT. Not a bad smell, she supposed, unless one had to live with it for years at a time. No grass, no flowers, no baking cookies. Not even utilitarian things like exhaust or freshly cut wood. At least when they went out to the yard in winter they could smell the sharp freshness of falling snow.

The last time she'd been in a visiting room, she'd been too young to understand the horror of this. At the time she'd been more concerned with the itchy lace on her new dress and the frightening appearance of her mother's newest love interest.

But now the sadness of the place fell upon her like a

wave. The Aspen police department was clean and modern, but that didn't change the brutal truth. Some of these people would be leaving after a few hours behind bars. Some would be here for a couple of years, serving sentences for minor crimes. And for some, jail was just a way station on the way to state or federal prison.

Please don't let that be Jessie.

A loud clank echoed through the small visiting room, and Jane looked up to see Jessie shuffling out in an orange jumpsuit, his eyes bright with anxiety. "Hey, sis," he mouthed as he took his seat.

"Dad's not here?" he asked as soon as Jane picked up the phone.

"No, it's just me."

"Okay, good."

"Jessie, what the hell were you thinking?"

"I don't know." His blond hair flopped over his brow when he shook his head.

"If they've found stolen goods in Dad's house... He's a convicted felon, you idiot!"

"I didn't think it was that big of a deal. I got pulled over for speeding, and the cop found some..." His eyes darted to the side and he leaned forward as if they weren't separated by thick glass. "He found some pot and a few credit cards, okay?"

"Not your cards, I assume."

"No," he said sullenly.

"If they think Dad's involved in some sort of identity-theft ring—"

"It's nothing like that, all right? I just lifted a few purses from Ryders."

"You're a selfish idiot!"

He stiffened. "I'm sorry. I needed some cash, all right?"

"And some credit cards?"

He shrugged, the same expression on his face that he'd worn when he'd been suspended from sixth grade for a week. Sullen anxiety.

"Why didn't you call us? Bail was set on Friday!"

"It doesn't matter," he muttered. "Sixty thousand is too much and Dad won't pay it anyway."

Well, he was likely right about that. And Jane probably wouldn't front the bond money either, because lately Jessie was just the type to say "Screw it!" and head off for a vacation in Mexico.

"Is there anything else you need to tell me? Anything else they might have found in your room?"

"No, nothing. They keep asking me about some girl, but I've never heard of her."

The hair on the nape of her neck stood up. "What girl?"

"Some girl named Michelle something. She must've had her purse stolen."

"Did you take it?"

"I don't know. Maybe."

Jane lost her last thread of patience. "Well, how many purses have you stolen, Jessie?"

"I don't know. Like fifteen or something. Girls put them on the floor at Ryders when they want to dance. They just leave them there like fucking idiots."

Fifteen? The contents of fifteen purses would easily be worth more than a thousand dollars, making the crime a felony. "Oh, yeah. *They're* the idiots. Have they assigned you an attorney?"

"They gave me some papers to fill out for a court-appointed guy."

"Don't talk to the cops unless he's present. I'll do my best to find you a good lawyer by Monday, okay? And I'm going to try to find out more about this Michelle. *Don't say anything else.*"

"All right." He flinched when the one-minute bell sounded. "Tell Mom and Dad I'm sorry, all right?"

"I will. But you'd better start thinking about what you're going to do when they release you. Dad's not going to let you back in the house."

He nodded and the tip of his nose turned red as if he was holding back tears. "I'm sorry, sis. Honestly. I didn't mean…" One of the cops began to approach from the other side of the room.

"I love you, Jessie."

"Yeah, me too." The officer took the phone from his hand and hung it up. Jessie's eyes were damp, but he put on a crooked smile as the guard grabbed his elbow to urge him up.

She tried to catch the man's eye, but he didn't look at her. She was no one. Just some piece of trash involved with a criminal. She remembered that, too. The way the officers would look through her and her mother, or—worse—glare at them or shake their heads in disgust.

Jane hung up the phone and pushed numbly to her feet. It was Saturday afternoon and she had to find Jessie a better lawyer. Her mom couldn't do it. She played possum in the face of trouble—she always had. And her stepfather wasn't the type to work the phones and puzzle out a problem. He was strong and steady and worked with his hands.

Jane was the one who lived in Aspen. She was the one who'd been dating a man in the D.A.'s office.

She'd hardly spent any time at home for the past few years, had tried her best to separate herself from them without giving them up entirely. Maybe if she'd spent more time with Jessie he wouldn't have turned into a thief. Maybe if she hadn't turned her back on him, he wouldn't have thought it was okay to steal money from careless women.

But whatever he'd grown into, he was still her brother even if she'd never consider introducing him to her friends. He was her brother and he still had a good heart…and she'd help him if she could find a way.

CHAPTER SIX

CHASE CLUTCHED the steering wheel hard. He breathed deeply. Counted to twenty. But every time he glanced toward the Jennings Architecture office, fury rose in his gut.

His first reaction when he'd stepped from the bathroom on Friday with a stupid grin of anticipation on his face…his first reaction had been confusion. Then, once he'd realized Jane was gone, he'd jumped straight into abject worry.

A woman out walking by herself in the middle of the night? He'd paced for a few minutes, then pulled on jeans and rushed out to look for her.

Nothing. He had no address. She hadn't left so much as a note, and her phone call showed on his cell as "blocked," something he hadn't had the attention span to notice when she'd called and invited him out.

With no way to contact her, Chase had stayed awake for hours worrying. The next morning, when the newspaper hadn't reported any injured or dead or missing women, Chase had let his worry turn to anger.

Unbelievable. He'd been used.

Okay, he'd known he was being used, but he hadn't known he was being *used* used.

Chase shifted, rolling his shoulders back. He felt… strange. Uneasy. As if someone had slipped something into his drink and, well…taken advantage of him.

Ridiculous, of course. He'd been fully aware and more than willing the whole time. But he'd thought they were having a genuinely good time together. And then she'd yanked the rug out from under him. While he'd still been naked and basking in the afterglow.

In Chase's opinion, that had been uncalled for, and he deserved an apology.

The digital numbers of the dashboard clock jumped from 8:14 to 8:15 a.m. Jane was late. He'd arrived before eight on Friday and she'd already been working. Suddenly his worry was back, though he tried to beat it down.

Jane Morgan was fine. She was just a stone-cold bitch.

His mouth twitched at the lie. No. She wasn't cold. She'd rocked his fucking world on Friday night, and if he was being honest with himself, that was part of the reason he was so pissed. When he'd stepped out of the shower and toweled himself off, Chase had been downright giddy. Exhausted, but giddy. Like a goddamn little girl.

"Shit," Chase muttered, running a hand over his eyes.

At the very moment he decided to salvage his pride and drive away, a car turned into the lot. A little white BMW zipped past him, Jane Morgan at the wheel. She didn't glance in his direction. In fact, she seemed totally lost in thought, brow furrowed as she pulled straight into a space and jumped out of the car.

By the time Chase got his door open, she'd already unlocked the office and slipped inside. Being late probably didn't sit well with a girl like Jane.

And the sight of her, all prim and proper again in a dark gray suit, wasn't sitting well with Chase. She looked the way she always did. Unruffled. Unmoved. Cool and composed as she turned on lights and moved toward her desk. She looked as if Friday night had never happened.

Until Chase walked through the door.

Jane's eyes flew wide as she swung toward him. "Oh!" she yelped. "What are you doing here?"

She sounded so absolutely incredulous that Chase felt a jolt of fury. "Seriously?"

"Well…" He watched her gather up all her shock and will it away to nothing. It took only a few moments before her expression settled into calmness, and she was prim Jane again. "Yes, I'm very serious. What can I help you with, Mr. Chase?"

"Look at my face, Jane. I'm not in the mood for this. You took off in the middle of the night. While I was in the *shower*."

"Er…" Her face stayed impassive, but she had the grace to blush, anyway.

"First of all, I was terrified something had happened to you."

She shook her head, drawing his attention to the way she'd rolled her hair under at the nape of her neck. "What do you mean?"

"I mean that you were out walking in the middle of the night!"

"It wasn't the middle of the night. It was nine-thirty. In Aspen." When he opened his mouth to cut her off, she raised a hand to stop him. "I only walked the two blocks to Main Street, and I had a can of mace with me. I grabbed a cab as soon as I reached The Lodge."

He crossed his arms. "And how was I supposed to know that?"

A flicker of confusion crossed her face, and Jane dropped her hand. "I'm sorry."

"Secondly," he growled, uncrossing his arms and moving forward until his thighs hit her desk, "that was really fucking rude, Jane."

"I…I suppose it—"

"Kind of cruel, as a matter of fact."

"Cruel?" she whispered.

"I was okay with being your little birthday gift to yourself. Use me. Fine. But I don't appreciate being treated like a worthless piece of garbage afterward."

"I'm sorry. I…I thought you'd be glad I was gone."

"Now, that's just a lie, Jane. If you thought I'd be glad, you would've stuck your head in my bathroom and said, 'Thanks for the ride, stud. I'll call you some-time.' Instead you waited until I'd turned my back and then snuck away so that you wouldn't have to speak to me after you fucked me."

That brought more color to her cheeks. He felt a moment's happiness that he'd gotten to her, and then the unthinkable happened. Jane Morgan began to cry.

Not really *crying,* Chase scrambled to assure him-self. Her eyes just got a little…wet. She sniffed.

"Oh, shit," he muttered. "I'm sorry."

"No, you're right." She sniffed again and swiped at her eyes. "I was beyond rude."

"Okay, but I shouldn't have said that."

"You have every right to be mad. I was…I told myself it was okay because you were a man, but it wasn't okay. It was unkind. I'm sorry. I'm really sorry."

"All right, apology accepted. I didn't mean to make you cry."

She put her shoulders back and took a deep breath, seemingly calming herself, but a tear still escaped and slipped down her cheek before she swiped it impatiently away. "I had a tough weekend. It's not your fault."

"Bad birthday?"

"Oh, boy," she said on a laugh, but the laugh turned into a little hiccup.

"Aw, Jane," he murmured, edging around the desk to pull her into his arms. He half expected her to resist, but she stepped into him and pressed her forehead to his shoulder.

"I'm okay. Really." She actually sounded a little better. He'd expected her to break down, but she took a few breaths and relaxed. "All right," she whispered, but she didn't push away.

"Tell me nothing bad happened to you."

"No, nothing. I'm just stressed out and tired. I had trouble sleeping last night."

Good. Now he could enjoy the chance to touch her. He recognized the scent of her shampoo already. It had been imprinted permanently on his brain on Friday night. "I'm glad you're okay."

"Thank you. I'm really sorry, Chase."

Chase was busy with thoughts of the last time he'd touched her, so it took a moment for the noise behind him to register. He was just lifting his head when Quinn walked past.

"Hey, Chase," Quinn muttered. "Morning, Jane."

Jane jumped back, jerking violently away before Chase could drop his arms. Inhaling sharply, she slapped a hand over her mouth as if to stifle the sound, her eyes flying to her boss's back. But Quinn walked on, head down, totally absorbed in the papers in his hand. A few seconds later he disappeared into his office and closed the door.

"Oh, my God," Jane whispered. "Chase, you've got to get out of here. Oh, *God.*"

"All right, all right. I'll go." He held up his hands to appease her, but she backed away. "But you owe me another date."

"I certainly do not—"

Quinn's door opened. He stuck his head out, brow furrowed with harsh suspicion when his eye fell on Chase. He glared at Chase for a moment, then his eyes slid to Jane.

"Jane? Is everything okay here?" He sent Chase another dark glance, as if she needed a hint.

"Yes, sir. I'm sorry. Everything's fine."

"You're sure?"

"Yes, Mr. Jennings."

Quinn took a moment to look between them again, eyes narrowed. "All right. If you're sure you're okay…"

As soon as his door closed again, Jane snapped, "Get out!"

"Absolutely, as long as you agree to dinner."

"I specifically said… Okay, *fine!* Just go."

"I need your number."

Jane snatched up a Post-it note and scribbled on it before shoving it into his hands. "Out. *Now.*"

He smiled. "I'll call you."

She was growling when he left, but Chase wasn't

the least bit worried. That girl was hot. And he wanted more time with her, despite the way she'd treated him. He'd enjoyed the hell out of being used…up until the part where she'd snuck out as if he was a gigolo she didn't want to pay.

Next time he'd tie her up before he took a shower.

Grinning in anticipation, Chase slammed his truck door and headed out to the morning's site. If only there'd been an explosion scheduled, he would've been in a perfect state of bliss.

"THE POLICE ARE OBVIOUSLY trying to draw this out. They're looking for something bigger, but your brother claims to have no idea what it could be."

Jane nodded at the grandmotherly woman behind the desk. She didn't look like a defense attorney, and maybe that was a good thing. She certainly seemed sharp and aggressive.

"The charges are ridiculous. Felony grand larceny will never hold up. I've filed for a probable causes hearing. We'll hear soon."

"You haven't found out anything more about this Michelle woman?"

"No. You thought you remembered the name from the search warrant?"

"I think I remember Michelle, but not the last name, and my mom threw the warrant away so she wouldn't have to look at it. Shouldn't you be able to get another copy?"

"I should have it today. As to who she could be… Jessie says that one of his friends is dealing. He wouldn't say who or what, but apparently a girl OD'd a few weeks ago. He's worried it has something to do with that, but swears he's never sold drugs. Maybe one of his friends is trying to pin something on him."

Jane felt her heart speed to a panicked pace. "Oh, God."

The attorney held up a steady hand. "That's just Jessie's mind turning. There's absolutely no evidence of anything, one way or another. The cause hearing will happen soon. They'll have to show the rest of their hand and that will work to our advantage."

"Is there something I can do in the meantime? Anything?"

"Just be patient. And be ready for my call if you want to be at the hearing."

Her stomach turned as she wondered who the prosecuting attorney would be. "I don't think I can. Is it important that I be there?"

She nearly slumped with relief when the woman waved a dismissive hand and shook her head.

Jane hurried out of the attorney's office, trying not to look guilty. Even respectable citizens had attorneys. And even excellent office managers occasionally snuck out of work at four forty-five if the office was empty.

Mr. Jennings hadn't asked about Chase. He'd sent her a few questioning looks throughout the day, but that was the extent of it. And he wouldn't have asked why she needed to leave early either, but she'd still wanted to avoid the conversation.

The knot in her stomach eased a tiny fraction as she stepped out into the spring air and felt it cool her cheeks.

The attorney seemed competent, at any rate. Levelheaded. Patient.

But Jane wasn't feeling patient. She was feeling guilty. And that guilt was demanding action. There had to be *something* she could do. Even something small like comforting her mother.

As she drove toward her parents' house in Carbondale for the third day in a row, the gorgeous scenery of jagged mountains and new leaves blurred as she considered the horror that had happened in the office that morning.

First she'd realized how awful she'd been to Chase. He might be a big tattooed bruiser, but he wasn't trash. And even if he had been trash… Well, trash had feelings, too. Jane could attest to that.

And then… Then somehow the past few days had all caught up with her. Standing there in front of Chase, feeling ashamed for how she'd treated him, that moment of weakness had allowed fear and anxiety to bubble through the cracks in her shield. For a moment she'd been just a girl whose little brother was in big trouble. She'd felt helpless. The next thing she'd known, she'd been wrapped in his arms, crying.

It had felt good. His arms were strong and his skin was so hot. Jane had gone from being horrified by his presence to snuggling him within the space of one minute.

She shook her head as the highway shot past canyon walls. A semi rocketed past her, shaking the car, but her whole world seemed to be shaking right now, and Jane didn't even wince.

It had been idiotic to think she could hook up with a guy she'd met at work and keep it totally separate from her professional life. And now she would have to go on a date with him.

"Crud," she whispered.

Crud, because it was supposed to have been a one-time thing.

Double crud, because she really, really wanted to do him again. And if they were going on a date, she'd have the perfect opportunity.

This wasn't her anymore. She didn't date men whose jobs involved shovels and sweat.

But she felt a need to make up for how she'd left him on Friday. More guilt. She should have known he'd worry. Chase seemed like a nice guy. He'd certainly been nice about being her birthday present.

Jane suddenly found herself smiling as she remembered his crazy theory that she was a young widow in the throes of grief. But as she drove over a rise and headed down the other side, her smile froze. At the bottom of the hill sat Ryders. Chrome glinted off dozens of motorcycles parked in the lot. Broken glass shimmered in the gravel.

Ryders was the biker bar where Jessie liked to hang out...and was his favorite crime scene, apparently. Jane was pretty familiar with it herself.

As she passed the bar, a greasy-looking guy walked out, his arm around a woman whose leather vest covered only about 45 percent of her breasts.

Trash, Jane immediately thought, then winced and shook her head. She knew it was wrong to judge people based on appearance. She knew it was a defense mechanism, but that didn't stop the hostility she felt toward women who wore leather cut down to their belly buttons. It was a knee-jerk reaction to her own sordid past, and she didn't know how to let it go.

She wanted to let it go, because she knew every time she judged someone else, she was really thinking of herself. It wasn't healthy.

Seconds later a bike roared past, speeding around her. The driver looked a lot like Jessie, and Jane felt a shock at the quick, sharp thought that he'd been exonerated and released. It wasn't him. He didn't own a Harley, first off. Second, he hadn't been released from jail.

But that brief moment of surprise shook loose an idea, and Jane hit the brakes and pulled over onto the shoulder to turn the car around. Jessie and his friends hung out at Ryders. Maybe she could find out who was dealing. Maybe she could get the name of the girl who'd OD'd.

She eased into a narrow space at the very edge of the lot. She locked the car, then checked the handle just to be sure. Conscious of what Jessie had freely admitted to, she tucked her purse tightly under her arm and crunched across the gravel to the blank wood door. There were no windows here. No one wanted to hang out at a well-lit bar.

The sun was still shining, but inside it was dusk. Murky dusk. All Jane could see were neon beer signs. She stood there blinking for a while, hard rock music skipping through her brain while she waited for her eyes to adjust. Slowly the bar came into focus, looking exactly as it had when she'd let her breasts hang out here fifteen years earlier.

And just like before, all the men were staring at her. Jane doubted it was for the same reasons they'd stared then. Back then, her bleached, spiky hair and heavy makeup had shouted for attention. Now she looked like a woman who'd stumbled into the wrong place.

Setting her jaw, Jane walked toward the largest group of bikers.

CHAPTER SEVEN

WRIST BALANCED on top of his steering wheel, Chase narrowed his eyes against the setting sun and glanced down at his phone. He hadn't called Jane yet, so he had no idea why he kept checking to see if she'd left him a message. It made no sense. Then again, Jane had been the one to call on Friday.

He would've liked to pretend he was letting her stew. Making her sweat a little. Truth was, his dad had called and put the kibosh on any thoughts of going out with Jane tonight.

Dad had called with his normal message. "Hey, son! You haven't stopped by to see me in a while. Why don't we have dinner?"

But Chase was fluent in his father's secret language. What he meant was, "I'm out of money and I need beer. Buy a case or two, and some cigarettes, and bring them to my house. And if it makes you feel better, bring sandwiches, too."

His stomach used to burn when that phone call came, but not anymore. He'd finally started reading up on dependency and enabling relatives. There was no beer in the back of his truck. Just groceries.

He slowed to make the corner at Ryders, but before

he'd quite completed the turn, his head stuttered to the side. Amid the bikes and pickups in the Ryders lot sat a shiny white BMW.

Lifting his foot off the accelerator, he let the truck slow for a moment so he could stare at the car. But after a few heartbeats, Chase burst out laughing. The idea that Jane would be at a biker bar...

"Oh, Christ," he gasped, wiping his eyes. Fucking hilarious.

Ten minutes later he'd pulled up to his father's trailer, identifiable amid the rows of similar trailers by the Green Bay Packers flag flying above the door. They'd never lived anywhere near Wisconsin. Another thing Chase would never understand about his dad.

"Hey, Dad," he said as he pulled open the screen door.

"Billy!" his dad called, waving from his recliner.

"I brought fried chicken. You hungry?"

"Sure. Sure. I'm hungry. Let's pop open a beer and have dinner."

He fought not to roll his eyes. "I don't drink, Dad. And I didn't bring any beer. Just dinner."

His dad's eyes flew to his for a brief moment before they slid away. "Oh, all right. That's fine, I guess. We'll just have dinner. I sure would appreciate it if you could grab me a few beers before you head back to Aspen, though."

Chase felt his heart beat harder, but he shook his head. "Let's just eat."

"Sure!" his dad said brightly, but Chase saw the resignation in his eyes. Chase hadn't brought beer last time, either. The gravy train was over.

One piece of chicken later, his dad's eyes started

wandering around the trailer. "Well, all right," he said, as if they'd just eaten a four-course meal. "Thanks for the food."

At least he wasn't a mean drunk, Chase thought as he grabbed another piece of chicken and chewed. His dad had never been a mean drunk, but maybe it would've been easier if he was. Chase could've just moved on and left him behind.

As it was, he felt he couldn't leave him behind. Chase's last serious girlfriend had accepted a job in Utah and asked Chase to come with her. They'd been at an important crossroads in the relationship. A move to Utah would have meant a house together, a path toward marriage and serious plans. But Chase had said no. He couldn't leave his father alone.

It had been Chase's decision, but he'd been furious when his girlfriend had packed up and driven away. At the time, he'd been self-righteously sure he'd been right and she'd been heartless. But that surety had since drifted away and he could see he'd let a good relationship go without a fight.

His dad slapped his hands against his knees, calling Chase's attention back to him. "All right then, Billy."

Resigned, Chase packed up the box of chicken and put it in the fridge, then put the rest of the groceries away while his dad paced across the small living room, sliding a thumb nervously across his bottom lip, brow lowered in concentration.

"Bye, Dad," Chase said. He got a wave in reply. Before the screen door had even closed behind him, he heard the beep of the phone being dialed.

"Hey there, Debra!" his dad said cheerfully. "You

up for a game of Scrabble tonight? I've got the tiles if you've got the drinks."

Debra was the sad old lady who lived two rows over. Sometimes Chase found her passed out on his dad's couch. Better than the bed, anyway.

Trying not to let his relief bloom too large, Chase escaped to his truck and took off. He slammed his palm against the stereo button, relieved that he'd loaded a few good CDs in. Usually he listened to his iPod, but today he didn't have the patience to scroll through songs. He needed immediate relief, and the complicated guitar riff provided that.

When Ryders came into view, he managed a smile. He even glanced at the BMW as he passed, still smiling. As he reached the highway, a movement in the rearview mirror caught his eye. A woman was being pushed out the bar door, her arm in the grasp of a big bruiser.

Not really an unusual sight at Ryders.

Chase turned the corner and drove on, but his eyes got narrower the farther he got from Ryders. The reflection in the mirror had been too small to make out many details, but she hadn't looked like the typical biker chick. She'd been wearing…glasses? Yeah, she'd definitely been wearing glasses. And a sensible gray suit. Then there was the BMW to consider.

"No way," Chase insisted to himself. No way was Jane Morgan at Ryders. She was a hotel-bar kind of girl. Maybe even karaoke on a wild night.

But his foot eased off the accelerator.

"It wasn't Jane." His voice sounded sure, but Chase was remembering the way she'd licked his tattoo.

Could it be that Jane had some sort of…bad-boy fetish? Was he just the latest notch on her bedpost?

That was ridiculous, right?

"Right," he said aloud. And then promptly threw his truck into a gravel-tossing U-turn.

The engine roared as he sped back toward the bar. If it was Jane… Well, then maybe she'd come to Ryders looking for him. It seemed like the kind of place he might hang out. If he drank. Except she knew he didn't drink. He did like to play pool, though, and it wasn't as if he'd never set foot in the place.

Oh, great. Now he was being a little girl again. Awesome.

His shoulders had tied themselves into knots by the time he started down the hill toward the bar. Halfway there, he could see that the white BMW was gone.

Aware that he was treading very close to a certain line, Chase popped open his phone and dialed her number.

"Drop it, Chase," he ordered himself as the phone began to ring. This was ridiculous. It hadn't been Jane, and it was none of his business even if it had been. "Drop it."

Suddenly the line opened up and Jane answered. "Hello?" Even on the tinny connection, he could hear the strain in her voice.

"Jane, it's Chase. I don't want to pry, but did I just see you coming out of Ryders?"

Silence stretched between them for several heartbeats before she spoke. "Um…Ryders? No! Of course not. No."

He frowned. It seemed as if her correct response would have been *What's Ryders?* "Well, I was driving past and I was sure I saw you. It's kind of a rough place. Are you in some sort of trouble?"

"No, I…" She cleared her throat in a quick little cough. "No, I'm fine, of course. Everything's fine. No big deal."

What the hell? Chase took the phone away from his ear and glanced at it. Now she wasn't even denying it. "Jane—"

"I'm sorry," she interrupted. "I've got to go."

He grabbed at his last chance. "I was hoping to take you out to dinner tonight."

"Oh, I can't. Not tonight. I've got something to do."

"Tomorrow, then?"

"I'm not sure about tomorrow either. Things are a little crazy right now. I'm not trying to blow you off, though. Really." She was starting to babble now. "I'm not backing out. Maybe later in the week everything will be better."

There was nothing he could do but give in gracefully and let her hang up. Nothing he could do tonight, anyway.

PACING ACROSS her stepdad's living room, Jane wanted to stomp her feet and pout, but she was grown-up and reasonable now, so she crossed her arms tightly instead. "You had no right to do that."

Mac crossed his arms, too. "Oh, yeah?"

"I wasn't doing anything wrong, Dad!"

"Right. Crawling around a biker bar asking questions about a crime. That seemed like a good idea to you?"

"I—"

"Going to Ryders looking like a damned plain-clothes detective…that seemed like a good idea?"

She felt about sixteen again, complete with the pouty chin. "I told them I wasn't a cop."

"Well, great. I'm sure they were fine with that. That's why Arlo called me and told me to haul my ass over there and get you out."

Her anger dropped a notch, but the space it left filled up with frustration. "I'm trying to help Jessie. That's all."

"You can help by calling up that boyfriend of yours at the D.A.'s office and getting some information."

Jane threw her hands up. "Dad, I broke it off with him."

"Can't you at least call the guy?"

Oh, God. What was she supposed to say to Greg? *Hey, guess what? I'm not the woman you thought I was. I was raised in a trailer and my brother's been arrested for theft and drug possession. Can you help?* She held back a shudder. "I'll go to him if I need to, but right now we've got to tread carefully."

"Agreed," he muttered. "So don't go back to Ryders again. If there's any questions that need asking, I'll ask."

Jane shot him a doubtful glance. Sure, Mac would be a good tool for intimidation, but he'd made clear that Jessie had made his own bed and would have to lie in it. He wasn't inclined to help, but Jane needed to do something.

She figured she could gather up bits and pieces of information, and if anything solid came up, she could turn it over to the police.

But Mac was right about her appearance. She did look like a cop. Right down to the conservative black heels. "Have you heard anything new?" she asked.

He slipped the faded bandanna off his head and

rubbed a hand over his graying hair. "I talked to Arlo," he growled. "He didn't know anything about Jessie snatching purses, obviously, or he would've beat the shit out of him for causing trouble with the customers."

"What about…" She swallowed, afraid to bring up the subject. "I, um…I heard Jessie's been hanging out with a dealer."

Mac's whole face shifted into a terrifying scowl. "That little shit. He's got some nerve living in my house and hanging out with that kind of trouble."

"You hadn't heard anything at all?"

He shook his head, his hoop earrings catching the faint light from the kitchen. "Arlo would've told me if Jessie was getting mixed up in ice. And I doubt he was dealing himself. They don't usually hang out in pairs."

She nodded, then put a hand over the ache in her stomach. "I wish I knew what the police suspect. Maybe we're just being paranoid."

"Maybe."

Jane reached out to put a hand on his arm. Her fingers looked pale against the crude lines of his tattoos. "Are you okay?"

"Yeah, yeah," he said, shrugging. "Hey, your grandma wants to see you." He was obviously hoping to distract her from her sympathy, and it worked.

"Oh, God," Jane groaned. Grandma Olive was a woman Jane could barely handle on a good day. "That woman isn't even related to you. I don't know why you let her keep hanging around."

Mac shrugged again, his dominant mode of communication when he was upset, then peered out the window as a car drove past.

"Where's Mom?"

His shoulders tightened. "She went to see Jessie," he muttered.

Tires crunched on the driveway and Jane walked to the window to see her mom pulling up. "I'm sure…" Jane started before realizing that Mac had left. The door to his small office clicked shut just as the front door opened and her mom came in, face blotchy from crying.

Jane pulled her into a hug. "You saw him?"

"Yeah. He looked good." The weeping started again, so Jane squeezed harder.

"It's all right, Mom. We'll get him out. The new attorney seems really good."

"Thank you so much, baby. Mac and I will try to pay you back for—"

"No. I want to do this." She needed to do this, because then she could continue with her fraud and still feel like an almost-decent daughter even though she kept her family hidden. She'd pay for the attorney, and get Jessie out of this mess, and then everything could go back to the way it had been.

Her mom sniffed. "Okay, I'll go get dinner ready. It's chili. I hope that's okay."

"Thanks, Mom. That sounds really good. I'll be there to set the table in a few minutes."

Her mom rushed for the kitchen while Jane walked quietly to Mac's office door and put her ear to it. Nothing. She knocked and eased it open. "Mac? Are you okay?"

"Fine," he growled.

She sat in the folding chair at the corner of his metal desk. "Dad."

His jaw stiffened, but he said nothing. He acted

tough, but the idea of his son in jail was clearly too much for him. Mac wouldn't go visit Jessie, but he'd sit here and worry about him all the same.

"We'll get him out."

"Maybe he needs to be in there."

She thought of all the years Mac had spent in prison and touched his forearm briefly. He hadn't become her stepfather until she was seven. She loved him, but she hadn't spent her early years curled up on his lap, so they weren't touchy-feely, but he seemed so lonely today. "You refused to go see him?"

His face twisted in fury. "He put himself in this position. He knows better. Goddamn it, he *knows* better. And if he were here right now I'd knock him into the wall."

She nodded.

"After I got out, I promised your mom she'd never have to sit in another prison waiting room again. I wanted something better for her and for you kids. I tried my best to raise him right."

"This is his fault, not yours."

"I let him get away with too much. If he gets out, things are going to change."

She nodded again and put her hand over his, thinking how often he'd emphasized to Jessie that he expected more of his son than he'd made of himself.

Jane swallowed back the threat of tears. "You saved me, you know. You saved me, Mac."

He shook his head. "I let it go too long."

"You were a good father to me, and you've been good to Jessie, too." His hand tightened to a fist. "Mom's getting dinner ready. Are you coming out?"

"I don't know if she wants me out there. She's pissed."

"You know she never stays mad long."

Mac shrugged, staring down at Jane's hand on his.

If Jessie went to prison, it would kill Mac. No question about it. She wouldn't let him be broken like that, not after what he'd done for her.

She could still remember that moment when he'd come to pick her up at that Denver police station. The sight of his strong arms pushing open the scarred doors to rescue her from a terrifying night. She'd felt such relief to see him, but her fear had remained. Fear and shame and regret and defiance. Still, she'd never once thought Mac would hurt her. Her fear had been the disgust she'd see in his eyes.

"I love you, Dad," she said, and then she left him alone with his worries because there was nothing more she could do. Not until tomorrow, anyway.

HE'D HAD NO REASON to stop by Jennings Architecture that day, so Chase had restrained himself. Restraint had seemed especially important considering his plan for that night. Following her from work would be crazy. Insanely creepy. But if he just happened to drive by Ryders again… Well, if he saw a white BMW, he'd pop in and look around.

Only because Jane had seemed awfully upset about something.

Granted, he hardly knew the woman, but he *had* slept with her, which meant he probably knew her better than most other people. They were friends of some sort. Intimate acquaintances, at least. And he could go to a bar if he wanted to. It was a free world.

The fact that he had to justify it to himself wasn't a good sign.

Still, he threw on his sunglasses and headed out. It was seven when he pulled up, the same time it had been yesterday when he'd driven by. And lo and behold, there was a white BMW parked in the lot, on the north side this time.

His heart beat hard at the sight, telling him how nervous he was. Chase ignored it and pulled in next to the car. "I'm just trying to help," he muttered as he walked heavily toward the door.

He thought he'd spot Jane as soon as he walked in. She'd blended in at that Aspen bar, but there was no doubt she'd stand out here. He glanced around the crowded room, trying to spot her. Nothing. He looked again.

Well, shit. She hadn't been lying at all.

Still, Monday was dollar-beer night, and the place was packed. Jane could be here, waiting in line for the bathroom or something.

Chase ordered a Coke and squeezed into a seat next to the wall as a new song began to blast from the bar speakers. Guitar riffs jagged through the air. A few minutes passed, and he was beginning to feel pretty sure that Jane wasn't in the place.

On the other hand, he was actually starting to have a good time. Not being a drinker, bars weren't on his to-do list very often, but one of his favorite songs was playing, the mood of the crowd hadn't progressed past rowdy fun and there was a gorgeous female ass gyrating right at the edge of the crowd of dancers.

Propping his back against the wall, Chase sipped his

Coke and watched the show. That tight, round ass was just barely concealed by a denim skirt that stopped close to the top of her thighs. Those thighs were pretty damn nice, too, the muscles tightening in time to the music. They reminded him of Jane's thighs, and the thought made Chase smile. Considering the way Jane had loosened up in his apartment, he might even talk her into doing a little dance for him if he was lucky enough to get up close and personal again.

Aware that a nice ass was distracting him from watching for Jane, Chase let his eyes roam over the room again. He knew a few people here. One of his part-time employees was parked near a giant inflatable beer can, his arm around a friendly woman. The guy manning the far side of the bar was someone Chase had gone to school with. And the giant who'd just walked in was known to everyone in the Carbondale area simply because he was so tough that people edged away from him: Big Mac MacKenzie. Still, he wasn't a bad guy. Chase had bought an old bike from him ten years before and Mac had treated him more than fairly.

Mac seemed to be looking for someone, too, as he stood frowning in the doorway for a while before he headed to the back.

Chase finished his Coke and glanced back toward the hot dancing girl. She leaned into a young guy whose hair hung in waves past his shoulders. She was up on her tiptoes, her legs longer, her skirt shorter. "Nice," Chase murmured, popping a piece of ice into his mouth.

He watched the girl's lips as she yelled something into the guy's ear. Nice lips. They were full and luscious just like Jane's, only painted a deep, shiny red.

As she spoke, her eyes cut toward the bar, and Chase sat up too quickly, swallowing a large chunk of ice.

She had eyes just like Jane, too.

He swallowed hard, feeling the ice squeeze down his throat. "Wait a fucking minute…" Jane's ass, Jane's thighs. Jane's mouth and eyes and… "Oh, Christ," he breathed as she turned on her heels and he caught sight of her front. Jane's breasts, too, barely hidden by a pink spaghetti-strap tank top. And there was, without question, no bra under there.

Jaw dropping, Chase rubbed his eyes, hoping to clear up his faulty vision. But no, when he looked again, it was still…*Jane?* Jane in a short skirt and heels and a flimsy little shirt? Her hair hung in a straight fall, nearly to the middle of her back. The glasses were gone, and if her occasional squint was any indication, she hadn't replaced them with contacts.

He squinted a little himself, just to be sure it was really her. It was, though he wouldn't have recognized her if he hadn't seen her in sexy underwear and no glasses a few days before.

Jesus.

Shock had muffled his brain for a moment, but as her identity settled into his head, Chase's mind nearly exploded.

Why was Jane dressed like that? Why was she in Ryders? And *why* was she letting that biker dude stare at her tits?

She frowned at something the guy said, then leaned over to shout into his ear again. Chase found himself leaning forward as if he might hear. As if some shouted conversation on a dance floor could unravel this mystery.

It was a fetish. It must be. Some weird bad-boy thing. She was trolling for big greasy men with tattoos. Men she could use and throw away and never think about again.

Men like Chase.

He was scowling so hard that his head started to ache, so Chase rubbed a hand over his skull and tried to shake it off. Whatever. It had been only one night, and Jane had been pretty damn clear that she was using him. Hell, maybe he'd been the start of this fetish. Maybe he should be flattered.

But flattery had never made his gut burn like a phosphorus fuse.

While he was frowning at the pain, Jane's friend waved another guy over. Within a moment, Jane had snuck her arm beneath the man's black leather jacket and wrapped it around his waist. The two men spoke for a long minute while she stared intently at the floor, looking more as if she was taking mental notes than planning a date.

The first guy nodded and disappeared, and Mr. Leather Jacket put his arms around Jane's shoulders and pulled her smack against him, rocking his hips in time to the music. Jane rocked, too.

Chase stood up to leave. This girl was too crazy for him. He set his empty glass on the bar, vaguely wondering when he'd managed to crunch through all that ice. Shoulders heavy with sudden fatigue, he made his way toward the door, staying close to the wall and far from the dance floor.

He couldn't help one glance back, but he regretted it when he saw Leather Jacket's meaty paw resting over the curve of Jane's ass. "Best of luck, brother," he muttered.

Hand on the door, Chase was turning away when he caught a rush of movement at the corner of his vision. The rush was moving toward Jane.

He froze, fingers spread wide against the scuffed wood, and watched Big Mac clear a ruthless path through the crowd. He didn't have to push people to the side—everyone simply parted like a field of grass. Everyone but Jane.

Mac lunged right at her, his hand closing around her upper arm in an iron grip. The music still roared. Chase couldn't hear what they shouted, but they were definitely arguing as Mac swung Jane around to face him. Her leather-clad dance partner backed away, hands held high in appeasement.

For a few brief seconds the alarm that had been twisting tight in his neck started to relax. Jane didn't look frightened. She didn't even look surprised. And Chase suddenly realized why she wouldn't be. As Big Mac MacKenzie tugged Jane away from the dance floor, it registered in Chase's brain that *Mac* was the one who'd pulled Jane into the parking lot the night before. She was his girlfriend maybe. Big Mac's crazy, sleeping-around, drama-loving girlfriend. Probably they both got off on it.

Unbelievable. Chase's brain was tumbling.

But as he watched, Jane snapped her arm free of Mac's grip, shaking her head. The big man's eyes narrowed with fury as a flush crept up his face. As he swung back toward Jane, Mac's hands tightened into massive fists. His lips twisted into a snarl.

Adrenaline jumped into Chase's veins with the force of a tidal wave. He surged forward, hoping to reach Jane before those fists landed on her. He wasn't going to make it. He was still twenty feet away.

But instead of hitting her, Mac wrapped his arms around her body and simply picked her up and carried her toward the door. Toward Chase. Her feet kicked wildly, stiletto heels landing on the man's shins like a rapid-fire gun.

Chase finally reached them, and dug his fingers into Mac's elbow. "Get your fucking hands off her, man."

"Excuse me?" Mac shouted.

"I'm not going to stand here and watch you abuse a woman. Get your hands off her *now.*"

"Chase!" Jane gasped. She gave up her fight and hung limply in the man's grip.

Mac growled, "Mind your own business," and tried to shove past him toward the door. But Chase tightened his hold, and Mac finally let Jane's feet drop to the floor.

"I told you to mind your own business."

Chase kept his weight on the balls of his feet and his arms loose at his sides. He hadn't been in a fistfight in a couple of years, and Mac was one big bastard. But as long as he didn't land a surprise roundhouse punch, Chase would do okay. He just had to be ready. "And I told you to leave the woman alone. If you wanna knock somebody around, try it on me."

"Chase," Jane panted, reaching a hand out to flatten it on his chest. "Don't. It's okay."

Mac growled, "Get back," putting his hand against Jane's shoulder as if he'd push her, and Chase lost it.

He knocked the man's hand away and grabbed a handful of his shirt to yank him off balance. The large fist that flew at him was easy enough to spot, anyway, and Chase almost dodged it in time. No broken nose, but his ear exploded in pain before he managed to get in a good jab to Mac's gut. The crowd shouted approval.

"Stop!" Jane screamed. "Stop!"

Chase shoved Mac away and got his fists up high enough to block another punch. Jesus, Mac was fast for a big guy.

They circled each other as the crowd formed a dense ring around them. "Back up, Jane," Chase muttered.

"No. Stop it. Please, Chase… He's not going to hurt me. I swear." Suddenly she was sliding in between them, blocking their fight with her own body.

Chase dropped his hands and backed up.

"Take it outside!" someone roared from the bar.

"Yes," Jane urged. "Let's go outside. Please." She stepped closer and nudged him toward the door. Chase moved, but he kept his eyes on Mac, just in case. His ear was still throbbing Tom-and-Jerry style, as if it were four times its normal size and pulsing like a siren. He kept moving outside until he was a good fifteen feet from the doorway.

Jane followed him through the front door and walked out onto the gravel to wait, arms crossed and lip caught between her teeth. Her arms pushed her breasts higher, showing them off.

Chase dragged his gaze away, though it cost him a few drops of sweat to manage it. He eyed Big Mac for a moment before looking back to Jane's barely there outfit. "What the hell's going on here, Jane?"

Her arms tightened around her body. "Nothing."

"Nothing." He let his eyes slide down. "So this is just how you like to party?"

Her cheeks flamed and she dropped her arms. "No."

"You like guys who treat you this way? Put their hands on you?"

"No!"

"Then why would you hook up with a guy who'd knock you around? You need to get in touch with a therapist or something. This is sick."

She shook her head. "It's not what you think."

"What is it, then?"

Jane pressed her red lips together, stubbornness written in every line of her face.

Mac grunted and shook his head in disgust. "I can't listen to this. She's my daughter."

Jane's cheeks paled, while Chase felt his face twist in undiluted confusion.

"Huh?"

Mac repeated the same strange words. "She's my daughter."

His *daughter?* Chase looked from Mac to Jane and saw absolutely no resemblance. Then again, Mac's facial hair might be throwing him off. "Your daughter?"

"Yes."

When he met Jane's gaze, she stared hard, her eyes shimmering with anger. "This is a personal family issue," she bit out. "It has nothing to do with you." She shifted, drawing his eyes to her legs.

"Sorry, but I'm really confused."

Mac shrugged. "I don't have time for this, damn it. I've got a customer coming to the shop in ten minutes. Jane, keep your ass out of that bar and stop acting like a goddamn fool."

She rounded on him. "I have every right to be in

there. One of his loser friends has gotten him into this trouble."

"This is your grand idea for helping Jessie?" Mac scoffed while Chase tried to follow whatever the mysterious topic might be. "You put on a short skirt and a barrelful of makeup? What's that supposed to accomplish?"

"It's supposed to accomplish getting them distracted enough to talk to me."

Mac threw his hands in the air. "I don't want to have to worry about you, Jane! I've got enough to worry about."

Her face fell. "I'm sorry."

"Stay out of that place, Jane." He sighed. "I'll talk to Jessie's friends, okay?"

"They're scared of you."

"Yeah, and somehow I think the threat of my fists could be more effective than the promise of something else from you."

Chase wasn't so sure of that, but he held his tongue, because Mac was her dad. His brain was still stuttering over that one. Big Mac MacKenzie was Jane Morgan's *father?*

Jane muttered something too low to hear while Mac turned toward Chase. "I guess I should thank you for trying to defend my boneheaded daughter."

"Yeah. Sure." Chase took the hand he offered.

"Next time I won't hit you."

He arched an eyebrow. "Next time I won't hit *you.*"

"All right, then." Mac's mouth turned up in what could have been a small smile. "Jane, if you go back in, Arlo's gonna call me, so don't bother."

Her jaw edged out as if she wanted to pout, but she

gave Mac a hug before he left, whispering something in his ear. Chase tried to gather his thoughts, but they were like bouncing footballs, jagging left or right before he could grasp them.

"I'd better go," Jane muttered as Mac walked away.

Chase glanced up at the night sky. "You're kidding, right? You're gonna leave me hanging like this? Jane…what the… Big Mac is your *dad?*"

"Stepdad."

In high school Chase had known one of the Mac-Kenzies, but her name hadn't been Jane. She'd been a pale blonde with a world's worth of problems and a love of thick black eyeliner. Had Big Mac remarried?

Jane was squirming, ready to get away, and the squirming was rather pleasant in her current attire. She looked at the door of Ryders, squinting a little.

"Have you had dinner?" he asked.

"I don't have time for a date tonight, Chase. And I've got to…" She swept a dismissive hand down her body. "My clothes."

Yeah. Her clothes. "I'll take you back into Ryders for a burger if you'll promise to tell me what's going on."

Her eyes screamed suspicion. "Why?"

"Because you want to go back in and I want to know what the hell you and Mac were talking about."

She cocked her head, studying him. Her red lips glistened. "Arlo will call Mac."

"I'll talk to Arlo."

"You know him?"

He shrugged, trying to play it cool. "Sure."

"All right. I'll have a burger with you. But this counts as our date."

Relief swept through his gut. If she'd refused, he wouldn't have gotten any sleep tonight. His mind would've raced for hours, trying to figure out exactly who Jane Morgan was and why she was going under-cover at a biker bar. "Deal. But you stay with me. No wandering off on your sting operation or whatever the hell it is."

He surprised a distracted smile out of her before she made a beeline for the door. Her toe caught on the threshold and she stumbled a little.

"You can put your glasses on if you like. I don't mind."

"They clash with the toe ring."

Chase glanced down. With the visual bounty on display, he hadn't noticed the silver toe ring. And he forgot it again when she took his hand and pulled him toward an empty booth. The tank top stretched thin across her breasts, revealing the whole lovely curve of plump flesh. His mouth watered in memory.

"Okay," he murmured as she slid into a booth. "Wait right here. I'll talk to Arlo. You want a drink?"

She shook her head and Chase rushed off to assure Arlo that he'd assumed responsibility for Jane. The bartender seemed relieved to hand over the burden and happily donated two Cokes to the cause. Chase added a couple of burgers to the order.

"All right," he murmured as he slid into a seat opposite Jane. "Spill it."

CHAPTER EIGHT

Jane tried to hide the shaking of her hands by wrapping them around the glass he handed her. She was totally exposed. Physically, yes, but it was more than that.

For years she'd ignored the background static of her life, pretended that she was simply somewhere else. In high school she'd put her head down and plowed through her classes, ignoring the insults of the boys she'd once chased and the girls who'd never liked her. She'd smiled her way through graduation when her mom had worn a tube top that prompted catcalls from her classmates. After school she'd dyed her hair back to its natural brown and changed her name and taken a job in Aspen, and that had been the end of it. She'd been done.

Except that it wasn't done. Jane had started over, but she hadn't gone far enough.

She should have moved to Denver. New York. London.

Why hadn't she gone farther?

She knew why. Arrogance. John McInnis Architecture had been her very first job. It had been a stepping stone. A way to save money for college. But she'd been good at it. Really good. She'd worked her way from file clerk to receptionist to personal assistant to

Mr. McInnis. It had been invigorating, being good at something. Being respected. Being deferred to. Pride had filled her like a drug.

She'd worked for Mr. McInnis for three years before he'd retired and recommended her to help start Quinn Jennings's new office. Then her fate had truly been sealed, because Mr. Jennings had given her a small stake in the company as a starting bonus. Her transformation had been complete. She'd become a business-woman. An office manager. A *partner.*

And if she occasionally ran into people from her old life, it didn't matter. They didn't see her. She wasn't that girl anymore. She'd let herself be lulled into thinking she was safe. The static had been reduced to a faint hum. The sound of a television turned on in the next apartment.

Until now.

Chase watched her patiently. She didn't want to tell him. But even dressed as she was, he didn't seem to recognize the truth about her. He didn't point and call her a slut. To him, *this* person was the disguise.

She took a deep breath and blurted out, "My brother Jessie's in trouble."

"Jessie," he said, frowning, as if he'd never heard of her brother. Thank God.

"He's in trouble and I'm trying to help him out of it."

"What's going on, Jane?"

She bit her lip, thinking. "You can't tell anyone."

"I'm the soul of discretion."

Jane glanced nervously around. Jessie's two best friends were still there, living it up, totally uncon-cerned with their friend's incarceration. What jackasses. They were a little blurry to her, but she could clearly see the way they laughed and pushed each other and hooted at every girl who strolled past. Within thirty seconds of approaching them, Jane had been propositioned in the least appealing way. *Hey, you ever taken it from both ends at once?*

Good God. There wasn't an ounce of subtlety between them. They didn't seem capable of stealing car stereos, much less dealing drugs.

"My brother Jessie's been arrested. I think the police are trying to set him up for something he didn't do."

"Seriously?"

"Yes. I was hoping his friends might know something. Or I thought they might give something away. They're obviously Dumb and Dumber."

Chase craned his neck to see where she was looking. "Those two guys you were dancing with?"

"Yes."

"You want me to see if I can strike up a conversation?"

Did she? Jane considered his offer carefully, but the further she moved down this insane path, the more ridiculous it seemed. She'd clearly come here tonight out of a crazed need to do something. Anything. Even if it meant dressing up like a floozy and flirting with losers and pissing off her stepdad.

A distracted waitress slapped two plates on the table and hurried away.

Jane sighed. "No, thanks. Mac was right. This was a stupid idea and I don't know what I'm doing here. I'm tilting at windmills."

"You're what?"

"Flailing. Uselessly."

Chase ignored his burger and reached for her hand. "This is why you were so upset yesterday, right? I wish you'd told me. I'll help if I can. You seem a little out of your element."

Did she? Well, that was really nice of him to say. "Thank you."

He let go of her hand and reached for the greasy burger. "So why do you suspect the police are setting him up for something?"

"They found him with stolen goods, but they're asking him questions about a woman he doesn't know."

"That's it?"

She shrugged and pushed a French fry around on her plate. "Innocent people get convicted all the time."

"You think so?"

Yeah, she sure did.

Jane finally took a bite of her burger. Salt and fat flooded her tongue, an abrupt reminder that she'd skipped lunch today. Her body went limp with relief. Maybe she hadn't been thinking clearly. She hadn't slept well since Saturday. She'd been skipping meals to make phone calls and do research. Now she was trying to help her brother by starring in a bad movie about the good girl who goes undercover.

How utterly idiotic.

Her eyes burned with sudden tears, but Jane simply closed them and chewed. Every bite left her feeling a little stronger, a little more clearheaded. She couldn't trust the police or the D.A. to treat her brother fairly. But there had to be a better way than this. There had to be.

"Hey, are you okay?" Chase asked.

"I…" She opened her eyes, praying that no tears had escaped her control. They hadn't. "I think I am, actually. Thanks."

"So you don't want me to escort you around the bar in hopes we can overhear a criminal confession?"

Jane narrowed her eyes. "Are you making fun of me?"

"Only because you have hamburger grease on your nose."

"Oh. Crud."

"Also, you look very cute, dressed like that and saying things like *crud.*"

"Shut up," she demanded, though she was laughing when she said it. And just a few minutes ago she'd been on the verge of crying. Maybe it was the comfort food. Or maybe it was Chase. He was the human version of comfort food. Bad for her. Delicious. A physical reminder of her past. Warm and filling. *Relaxing.*

He reached toward her with a paper napkin and swiped at the end of her nose.

"I'm a mess," Jane groaned.

"No, I got it."

"I mean I'm a *mess.* A real mess."

"No way. You're the most together person I've ever met."

"Clearly I'm not."

"Jane," he scoffed. "You're smart. You're calm. You're professional and capable and a total office badass. You scare big construction guys into behaving like frightened schoolgirls, and you're what? Thirty?"

"Twenty-nine."

"Sorry."

She waved off his cringe. "I'm not professional and capable now."

He flashed a grin. "No, but you are pretty amazing."

Jane automatically glanced down to her chest, then looked up to find his eyebrows rising.

"That's not what I meant. But, um…bravo."

"Oh, God." Mortification heated her cheeks to instant fire.

Chase burst out laughing, and suddenly Jane was laughing, too, leaning against the table and laughing and trying to keep her cleavage from becoming indecent exposure, all at the same time.

She was on a date at a biker bar with an inappropriate guy. She was eating a greasy hamburger in slutty clothes while her brother was in jail. And she was having fun.

Jane started on her fries. When she looked up a few moments later, she found Chase frowning at her plate. "What?"

"I'm trying to figure out your fry selection process."

"My what?" She laughed.

"Your selection process." He gestured toward her plate. "You're picking through those fries like you're looking for something specific. What is it?"

"Um…" She looked down at the fry she was holding. She'd never thought about it before, but she supposed she did have a fry hierarchy. "I like the short ones first. They're perfectly crispy but tender on the inside. Then the long ones. Still crispy on the edges, but maybe too soft toward the middle."

"Then what?"

"Then I move onto the long fries with narrow,

crunchy ends. If you break the ends off, they're fine. After that, it all breaks down according to my desperation. How do you choose fries?"

"Me?" He leaned forward, eyes narrowing with concentration. "I study the pile…"

"Mmm-hmm."

"And then I eat all the ones on top first. The ones on the bottom come last."

She rolled her eyes. "That's pitiful. You've got no standards."

Chase shrugged. "I like my fries like I like my women—hot and ready to be eaten."

"Oh, God." She managed not to spit out her mouthful of fries, but after a quick sip of Coke, she looked at Chase and found him wiggling his eyebrows suggestively. Then she was lost. She laughed so hard she snorted and had to hope the sound was lost in the guitar solo screeching through the speakers. They were protected a bit by the high backs of the booth, but not nearly enough. She might not have outgrown her taste for men like Chase, but she'd definitely outgrown her love of guitar rock.

Once her laughter died, she threw a hopeless look toward Jessie's friends. She hated to walk away from this scheme, but knew she had to. "You want to get out of here?"

"Now?" Chase asked. "Well, I'd file an official complaint about the length of this so-called date, but I'll give you a pass, considering."

"I'm sorry. I just want to go home and change."

"It's fine," he said. "Let's get you out of here."

She took his hand thankfully and let him lead her

out. Even over the music she heard one of Jessie's friends shout, "Hey, babe, where ya going?" Chase squeezed her hand tighter—offering comfort or just feeling pissed, she couldn't tell.

The darkness surprised her when she stepped outside. It was later than she'd thought, and Jane was damn grateful for Chase's presence when she was forced to stroll past a rough-looking group of guys. These were real bikers, not guys who liked to ride Harleys on the weekend. She recognized the skull insignia on the jackets, marking them as a gang from Grand Junction.

The men stared at her bare thighs but didn't say a word, and Jane didn't protest when Chase walked her across the dark parking lot toward her car.

"Jane, what are you planning to do?"

Her shoulders tightened. She had no idea what she was going to do. Who could she turn to for advice? Chase was the only one who had even a clue who she really was.

They stopped next to her car, and Jane cleared her throat so she could speak past the rising anxiety. "No one knows about my family, Chase. I…" Disloyalty was an ugly feeling, but she wasn't going to deny her flaws. "I love them, but I'm not like them. I don't want anyone to know. I don't want my brother's legal problems affecting my career."

"I won't say a word."

She glanced up at him, wishing he could help her in some way. Wishing she were the kind of person who knew how to ask for help.

"You can trust me," he said.

She shook her head against the warmth of his words. "I hardly even know you."

Though his expression was hard to make out in the dark, his shoulders cast a big shadow when he shrugged. "You know what you know."

Well, that sort of meant nothing, but he was still right. So far, he'd been a really good guy, despite his tattoos and boots and fascination with explosions. He might not recognize *Don Quixote,* but he did know how to worry over a woman's safety.

Jane crossed her arms and leaned against the door of her car. "You don't know anything about the law, do you?"

He was quiet for a moment. His boots scraped against the gravel when he shifted. "Not much, no. My dad was a cop a long time ago."

"I don't know what to do." Saying it should have made her feel weak, but somehow she felt a little better. Or maybe that was the way Chase's shoulders got bigger when he shifted toward her.

"I can't say I know, either, but you've got to have at least one person you can talk to."

"Like you?"

His head cocked to the side. "I already know your secret, and you clearly need to bounce ideas off someone. I can be the person who says, 'Maybe going half-dressed to a biker bar isn't the best way to help your brother.'"

She reached out her hand to give him a scolding little shove, but he didn't move. Chase was solid, in more ways than one. And Jane was tempted in more than one way, too. "I don't want to be accused of leading you on...."

"You mean if you reach out to me I might think you're my special gal and make a pest of myself?"

She smiled. "Something like that."

"I'll try to control myself."

Hard music leaked out of the bar, offsetting the romance of the starry sky above her. The night might be beautiful, but the setting was dark and seedy.

She thought of the way Chase had confronted Mac, with bared teeth and clenched fists. The threats he'd snarled as he'd tried to protect her, a woman he barely had a connection to.

"Is your ear all right?" she murmured, reaching toward his head. She ran a finger down his temple, afraid to touch the injury itself.

His voice dropped a notch. "I think I'll be okay."

His stubble rasped against her fingertips, and the feel of it sent shivers deep into her skin. It was dark and he was big and rough. She didn't even need to think of what he'd done to her last Friday night; she was wet already just from the sight of his wide body looming over her in the faint neon glare of the bar.

Curving her hand around the back of his neck, Jane pulled him down, happy to note he didn't need much pulling.

His hands spread over her shoulders as if he'd been thinking of touching her for a while. His lips pressed hot and hungry against her mouth. The taste of him was a shot of adrenaline. Every nerve in her body sprang to life, and now she was *definitely* remembering what they'd done on Friday.

When his tongue plunged into her in a familiar rhythm, Jane knew she had to have him again. Had to. It wasn't desire, it was *need*.

Everywhere he touched was naked skin. Her shoulders, arms, back. His hands moved restlessly over her, calluses adding just the right friction. Jane snuck her hand beneath his T-shirt to feel his skin, too, and in the dark it was as if they were naked already, clasped together, arching and sighing.

His groan rumbled into her as his mouth angled deeper. She moaned her own encouragement when one of his hands slipped down the front of her shirt. He cradled the weight of her breast, thumb stroking over her nipple. Oh, yes. Oh, *man.* He deserved a reward for his initiative.

Jane rubbed her hand over the front of his jeans, pressing against the bulge there. Apparently he was surprised, because Chase jumped in shock, bumping his nose into hers.

Laughing, she stroked him, then snuck her other hand down the back of his jeans to press her nails to his tight ass.

"Christ," he hissed, fingers tightening on her breast. His free hand swept up her thigh. The skirt was too short to provide any barrier at all, and Jane didn't even have time to draw a breath before he plunged his hand into her panties and slipped his fingers along her wetness.

"Yes," she whispered. "Yes."

He pushed one finger in, the pressure arching her back along the curve of the steel behind her. She fumbled blindly for the button of his jeans.

"Not here," he rumbled.

"Yes, here."

"I'll take you home."

"No." The button finally gave in to her clumsy hands. "I can't wait. Please."

"Not *here,*" he insisted, but she wanted it here. She wanted it in a parking lot, in public, against a car with the background music of a trashy bar as the soundtrack. She wanted to be used, wanted to feel that cheap rush of need and desperation.

"Jane," he said, "Anyone could—"

She stopped his stupid argument by wrapping her hand around his naked cock. The words died a rough death in his throat. "Fuck me, Chase. Right here."

"Goddamn it," he groaned as she stroked him. Despite his curse, he plunged another finger into her and kissed her to stop her sharp cry.

The truck next to her suddenly chirped, its lights flashing briefly. Jane gasped, but Chase didn't react. "Get in my truck," he growled.

"I don't want to go—"

"I'll fuck you here if that's what you want, damn it. Get in."

His crude words thrilled her, and Jane let him move her the few feet to the passenger door of his truck. She followed him in and slipped off her panties so she could straddle him. While he was still sliding on a condom, Jane nudged the straps of her tank top off and pushed it down to bunch at her waist before climbing atop him.

She took him deep and true with one hard drop of her hips.

"Christ," he whispered, his hands squeezing her arms too tight.

Needing to feel the way he filled her, Jane didn't move for a moment; she just closed her eyes and breathed. The music filtered through the windshield, muted but still there. A pack of bikes roared out of the parking lot. She opened her eyes to find their head-lights flashing close enough to make her breath hitch. The close call made her sex beat harder.

Jane squeezed her thighs and began to ride him.

Chase drew in a hard breath. "God, you're beauti-ful." The neon limned his face in red.

She rose slowly, marveling at the length of him as she slid up, then filled herself with him again. "You're perfect, Chase. Just perfect."

His mouth closed over her nipple, cutting off her ability to speak. She could only groan and sigh as he gripped her hips and set the pace he wanted.

This wasn't the first time she'd had sex in the parking lot of Ryders. As a teenager she hadn't been wise or choosy, and she'd gotten more stupid with every wine cooler she'd finagled from the wolves at the bar. So no, this wasn't her first time being used in the parking lot of Ryders, but it would clearly be the best. Because Chase was the kind of guy who took his pleasure in pleasing a woman. He wouldn't try to get by with a quick finish and halfhearted "Thanks, babe." He meant to make her come, and Jane meant to oblige him.

She pressed one hand to the roof of his truck for leverage, and slid one hand between their bodies to rub her clit as she rocked her hips.

"Jane," he groaned. "You're the hottest thing I've ever seen."

She was. She was hot and slutty and she didn't care who might walk by and see her doing Chase in his truck. When she heard a conversation drift to her ears from only a few dozen feet away, her sex tightened with excitement. She rubbed herself faster, and Chase surged up to meet her hips.

"Fuck yeah," he urged.

"You like it?" she whispered. "You like watching me ride you?"

"I like watching you ride me, and I like watching you finger yourself, and I'm gonna love watching you come." He cupped her breasts and squeezed her nipples.

"Oh, God, yes. Chase…don't stop. Don't."

He jerked his hips up to meet her.

"Yes. Just like that. Oh, Chase, just like that." The world rolled over her, pulling her deep beneath a black wave. She couldn't stop her scream. She couldn't. She screamed and pressed her fingers hard to her clit as her hips shook against his. The hard pulse of her sex made her feel even more filled with him. Stretched and taken.

As the spasms faded, her heart beat even harder. Chase wasn't done yet. He'd fallen still, his eyes glittering in the faint light as he watched. "Feel better?" he murmured, a smile curving his lips. A drop of sweat traced its way down his jaw.

"Definitely," she sighed.

He lifted her, sliding himself free so he could turn her around. Jane rested her forearms against the dashboard as he lowered her back down to take him again. She put her head to her fists and whimpered as he guided her hips up and down, sliding even deeper than he had before. The muscles of his thighs tightened to steel beneath her.

She pictured his view like a movie, the way her ass tilted down when she sank onto him, the way he spread her cheeks when he lifted her up. His breathing got quicker and rougher. He loved this. Loved it. And that made her feel stupidly cherished, just as it had when she'd been a damaged young girl.

Now she knew the difference between lust and affection, but his carnal appreciation still filled her up inside. She still thrilled to every gasp as he took her. And when he groaned and shuddered and surged hard into her, Jane smiled at her clenched fists and sighed with a kind of pleasure she hadn't found even with her own climax.

She was an animal with him…and she loved it.

CHAPTER NINE

CHASE'S HANDS were still shaking when he woke up the next morning. Or he felt as if they were. But when he snapped open the paper to read it, the print held steady. So he wasn't shaking, he was just…weak.

Jane Morgan had ruined him. Ridden him hard and put him up wet. He might never recover.

Mentally he was even worse off. Who was this girl? If pressed, he would've guessed Jane had been educated at an East Coast prep school or something. Instead, she was the stepdaughter of Big Mac MacKenzie, an ex-con who sold and customized motorcycles for local bikers. She held herself like a woman in complete control of her structured world, but she'd urged him to do her against a car, fully exposed to anyone who might walk by.

And he didn't remember Mac having any daughter named Jane.

Chase frowned down at the paper, seeing letters but not words. Chase had lived in the next town over, so he hadn't known much about the family. The only daughter he'd heard of was named Dynasty, and Jane couldn't be more dissimilar. But Jane had said she was a stepdaugh-ter, and there was a good chance that Mac had been married before. There could've been two or three or six stepsiblings wandering in and out of that house.

Whoever the hell Jane was, he couldn't stop thinking about her. She was intriguing as a sexy librarian, and she was damn hot as a barfly, too.

His body perked up at the thought of her, but Chase just sighed and shook off the images flashing through his mind. He likely wouldn't see her today and there was no point getting worked up.

He tossed back the last of his coffee and headed out to the hotel site. There'd be no blasting today, but he could get out there with a pickax and maybe get his muscles back to solid form. Two hours later he was pouring sweat and bleeding from a few tiny cuts in his arms where flying shards of stone had nicked him. White dust coated every inch of his clothing. He felt great, and the corner of bedrock was as perfectly angled as it would get.

He was solid again, and strong enough to dare a phone call to Jane. He tossed the pickax to his site supervisor and tugged his phone from his pocket.

"Hey," he said softly when Jane answered. "How are you? Did your brother get his hearing?"

"Yes, some of the charges were dropped." She sounded exhausted. "He's now charged with possession, which we expected, and felony possession of a financial device, which I was hoping he'd avoid."

"But nothing unexpected."

"No, not yet. But…" Tension dragged her voice to a rough pitch.

"What is it?"

Her silence radiated uncertainty and distrust, but she

took a deep breath and spoke very softly. "His attorney finally got her hands on the search warrant. The stolen goods listed belonged to two women. One of them is missing and the other one…the other one was killed three weeks ago."

"Shit," he muttered.

"He didn't do it," she rushed on. "He couldn't have. Jessie might be a slacker and a thief, but he's no murderer."

"Okay. All right. They haven't charged him with murder or assault or anything like that, right?"

"No, nothing. But they clearly suspect him."

Chase rubbed a hand over his hair, afraid he was about to make a big mistake. "Look, you need help, right?"

"I… Maybe. I mean, yes. Yes, I need help."

"I want to offer to introduce you to someone."

"Who?"

"My dad."

"Your dad?"

"He was an investigator with the state police." Chase felt his jaw tighten over the words. That had been a lifetime ago, but his dad had been good at his job. He'd just gotten caught one too many times with an open beer in the car. The state police had been forced to let him go. "It would be complicated."

"Um, because of the…"

"The drinking, yeah. He's highly functional as long as you catch him before three. His mind's still sharp. If you can get him copies of the police and evidence reports, he might see something. Something important. He used to be amazing at seeing things other people couldn't see."

"Chase," she whispered. "I don't know. I don't want to cause any trouble for you."

"I wouldn't offer if I didn't think I could handle it. If you really think Jessie's innocent..."

"I do. He's no angel, obviously. At best, he's a thief, but he's got a good heart. If this investigation goes too far in the wrong direction... It happens all the time, Chase."

"Then I'll ask my dad to help. All right?" He waited. He'd hesitated to offer, knowing it would force him and his dad to spend time together. But now Chase held his breath, hoping she'd say yes. He wanted to help wipe that lost look from her eyes.

"Okay," she finally breathed. "Okay, ask him. I'll see what I can get as far as reports."

"Good."

"Chase...thank you. Thank you for helping me."

He hung up and swiped a hand over his brow. His dad wouldn't be up before ten, so Chase had at least another hour to convince himself this was a good idea. Maybe he could fool himself by then.

As SHE HURRIED OUT of the police station, Jane was sure she could feel people staring at her. Ridiculous, of course, but it didn't stop her neck from burning. She breathed a sigh of relief as she stepped outside and hurried down the steps.

"Jane!" a man called. Her pulse leaped with fear that a police officer was about to pull her back in and click on a pair of handcuffs. She hadn't done anything wrong, but she was associated with a murder suspect, after all.

Just as she started to look over her shoulder at the glass doors of the station, a hand clasped her elbow. "Oh!"

"Jane, how are you?"

She found herself face-to-face with a man she hadn't seen in months. "Oh, Mitch. Hi."

The wind blew his blond hair over his forehead and Mitch pushed it back, offering her a sheepish grin. "I was just thinking about you, Jane. How've you been?"

"Great!" She said too brightly, fighting the feeling that she'd been caught. "Wonderful."

Apparently he'd gotten to know her well in the weeks they'd dated, because he frowned at the tone of her voice and glanced up to the building behind her. "What are you doing here?"

"Traffic ticket," she blurted out.

His gaze dropped to her hands, and she realized she was holding a thick sheaf of papers. Not exactly the paper trail associated with traffic tickets. Mitch was a dentist, not a lawyer, but that didn't stop the doubt from darkening his eyes. "What—"

"I've got to go!" She started to turn.

"Wait, I wanted to ask… I thought we could grab dinner sometime. Spend a little time catching up."

"Oh, Mitch, I don't think I can."

His brown eyes crinkled when he smiled. "Think about it?"

"I'm sorry, Mitch. I appreciate the offer, really. But I just started seeing someone else." She was using Chase for sex—she might as well use him as an excuse, too.

"Darn. All right. Well, let me know if it doesn't work out."

"I will. Thank you." As she walked away, Jane fought the urge to break into a run. Her panic made no sense. He had no idea why she'd been in the police station. He wasn't a danger to her. Mitch was a great guy. So great that she couldn't figure out why she'd broken it off in the first place.

When faced with the perfect man—the perfect man looking for a real relationship—Jane ran. She ran as if her life were in danger, even though these were the men she sought out for dating. But when talk turned to kids or marriage or a trip home to meet the parents, panic spun her down.

Yet that was what she had always *wanted*. A successful, stable husband. A beautiful home in a perfect neighborhood. Children playing in a green yard.

No trailers. No visits to jail. No revolving door of felon stepfathers. No moving from prison town to prison town. No secondhand clothes or old cars or parents you were embarrassed to let your teachers meet.

Jane took a deep breath and kept her pace slow and steady. Mitch was just the kind of man she meant to marry, so why did the sight of him wrap a tight band around her chest?

When her phone rang and she saw Chase's number, that band snapped free with such suddenness that breath flew into her lungs. Because she was waiting to hear about his dad, obviously. Not because he was thinking about her as that phone chirped. Not because he was waiting for her to pick up, wondering if she was there.

"Hello?"

"Jane. Hi. My dad's on board."

"Oh, good. I'm so glad. I'll pay him. Is that all right?

The lawyer said that hiring an investigator is pretty common, so I want to be sure your dad is compensated."

"Sure. He wants you to get copies of the arrest report, and any reports the women might have filed when their purses were stolen. Also, any evidence about their deaths, of course. Do you need help? This sounds like a lot."

"No, I just got his arrest report, and his lawyer has already filed motions to release all the information about evidence. I'll go back and see if I can find anything on the women."

"What time do you want me to pick you up?"

She glanced at the plain silver face of her watch. Ten-thirty. "Going through the reports may take a while. And I should really stop at the office. I took a personal day, but... And your work. I don't want to get you in trouble." She meant to offer to wait until five, but her urgency stopped the words from leaving her throat. *Please don't make me wait until five.*

"I can leave early. How about two-thirty? Is that too late?"

"No! Thank you. Chase, you've been so nice to me. And thank you for last night." Silence greeted her words, letting her know she needed to replay them in her head. Oh, God. "I mean, thank you for your help at the bar!"

"No, thank you. Really."

Jeez. Hadn't this happened last time? This polite appreciation for a devastatingly dirty act? "I... Okay. Well, I'll see you at two-thirty." She gave Chase her address and hung up.

Flustered and distracted, she rushed into her office

and began hurriedly sorting through the mail on her desk. Her personal life was fluttering out of control, and she couldn't stand the thought that her work life might be sliding, too. If she could just keep Jennings Architecture running smoothly, it would act as a cap, keeping her secrets dark and hidden. Everything would be fine. She would be fine.

"Jane?"

She jumped up from her seat, hand flying to her chest. "Good morning, Mr. Jennings!"

"Jane, what are you doing here?"

"I just wanted to be sure everything was in order for the rest of your day, sir."

"I'm fine. Don't worry about me. If there's something going on in your life, take as much time as you need. You've earned it." He put his hands in his pockets and stared at the floor for a few seconds before glancing up at her. "*Is* there something going on?"

She really didn't want to lie to him, especially when his eyes were warm with concern. "Mr. Jennings…"

"I'm worried about you, Jane. Yesterday you sent me an e-mail that had two typos."

She gasped in genuine shock.

"I know," Mr. Jennings said with a solemn nod. "I called Lori to find out if she had any idea what was going on."

"I'm sorry, Mr. Jennings. I promise I won't let this affect my work again. I—"

"Oh, come on, Jane. I'm not worried about the e-mail. I'm worried about *you*. But just tell me to back off if it's none of my business."

Her cheeks were on fire—she was sure of it.

"All right, the framers are starting on my house today, so I'm going to take Lori up to see it. Will you lock up when you leave?"

"Yes, of course. You've got your keys? And your phone?"

He nodded, but she noticed that he patted at several pockets before leaving. A lump growing in her throat, she watched him go. Quinn Jennings was like a brother to her. The kind of big brother she would've picked for herself if that kind of thing were possible.

She'd never had a big brother to look out for her. It had been just her and Jessie, and for a while there, she'd loved being a big sister.

For so many years it had been just Jane and her mom. She'd never suspected her new stepfather would be released from prison and show up on their doorstep with all his belongings stuffed in one duffel bag. Neither had her mother, or she would never have married him. That sort of defied the purpose of a lifer husband.

But Mac had been released on a technicality and everything had changed. Big Mac had been intimidating as hell, and Jane had spent months waiting for her mother to send him on his way. But he'd stayed, and then suddenly there'd been a little brother.

Jane had thought of Jessie as her pet. She'd held him and fed him, and had once tried to tie a leash around him. She'd even led Jessie into her room and let him nap on her bed while she did homework. The truth was, she'd helped to spoil him rotten as much as her mother had.

But then she'd hit puberty, and her little brother had

been the last thing on her mind. She'd been a horrible sister from the moment she'd turned twelve. Neglectful and distant and self-obsessed. She'd contributed to his problems. But if she could help him now, maybe everything would be okay.

Jane glanced at the phone. A good sister would call her ex-boyfriend D.A. no matter what. A good sister wouldn't hesitate. But Jane was hesitating.

Snatching up the phone before she could talk herself out of it, she dialed Greg's number.

It rang a few times, and she was greeted by a moment of silence before Greg said, "Jane?"

"Greg. Hi." Her tongue dried out so fast it nearly stuck to the roof of her mouth.

"I'm glad you called."

"You are?"

"Yeah, I'm… Look, I'm sorry for what I said in the restaurant. It was out of line."

Oh, thank God. He wasn't mad anymore. Maybe this wouldn't be so hard. "You had every right to be angry. I shocked you. I'm really sorry."

"Why don't we get together tonight and talk about this more? I miss you, Jane."

"Greg—"

"I've never taken anyone home to meet my parents. I wouldn't have planned that if I hadn't been considering a future with you. I'm not ready to give you up without a fight, Jane."

Oh, God. A horrible thought popped into her head, expanding until it filled her skull and pushed every rational thought out. What if she took him back? Just for a little while? Just until her brother was exonerated?

She could find out who was leading the case, how the investigation was going. She could even hang around his office and listen for little tidbits of information.

"Please?" he whispered. The real emotion in that word shocked her out of her madness.

"I'm sorry, Greg. I'm sorry, but I can't." Her hands shook with the horror of what she'd been contemplating.

His breath left him in a long sigh. "Just think about it," he muttered.

Feeling awful, knowing she should say no, Jane kept her mouth shut, unable to take that last step to cut their bond completely.

"What were you calling about, then?" he snapped in a much colder voice.

"Um, I had a question. Do you know who's been assigned to the Michelle Brown case?"

"Michelle Brown? Why?"

"I…" She couldn't say it. Her stomach rolled at the thought. *Because my brother is a suspect.* "I know someone who knew her," she blurted out. "I told them I'd see what I could find out."

"Not another one," he muttered. "I think that girl was friends with half the people in Aspen. The D.A. has the case right now. I seriously doubt he'll assign it to anyone else."

"Should I be nervous? Is there a killer out there stalking young women?"

"Well, you're ten years older than Michelle was, Jane," he said drily, clearly meaning to be snide. "But no, I wouldn't worry too much. I can't reveal anything else, but we may have the guy in custody already."

Although she was sitting down, a wave of dizziness

descended over her. He must mean Jessie. He must. "You think you've caught him?"

Greg cleared his throat, and his voice became sharper. "I'm not saying we caught him, okay? Don't go spreading that around. I'm just saying that these kinds of people are usually involved in other criminal activities. It's likely he's already in custody for some minor crime."

"Like what?" she pressed.

"Look, I've got to go."

"Wait… How will you know it's him? Did someone see him at the scene? Is there—"

"Jane, I can't give out that kind of information. What the hell do you think you're doing?" Suspicion rang clear in his voice.

"Nothing. I'm sorry. I was just curious."

"Yeah, well, if you were my girlfriend, maybe I'd consider talking this out with you." He left it at that, clearly waiting for some sort of response.

"I'm sorry, Greg—"

"Don't," he said stiffly.

She snapped her mouth shut and listened to him take a deep breath.

"Please don't say it again, Jane. I just…" The last word broke a little, as if he were getting choked up.

Jane squeezed her eyes shut, hoping he wouldn't cry.

"Just think about me, all right?" he rasped. "You can't just walk away from me like this."

When she didn't answer, the line went dead. Hating herself, Jane set the receiver down. She hadn't accomplished anything and now she felt worse than ever.

Jane sat next to Chase in the passenger seat of his truck. The same seat they'd had sex in last night. Good Lord. Chase felt a fluttering in his chest. The weakness was back again.

"Okay," she said. "Any ground rules?"

"With my dad?"

She offered a reassuring smile.

Chase glanced toward the trailer. "No, he's easy enough. He's a happy drunk. Just do me a favor and don't offer to run out for beer."

She nodded, but neither of them made a move to leave. "When did he start to drink?"

"A while ago. He was a detective in Grand Junction when I was a kid. He always drank to unwind, but then my mom died, and…"

"I'm so sorry, Chase. I didn't know."

"It was, uh, kind of horrible." He gave a nervous laugh, avoiding her eyes. "It was just a routine surgery. An appendectomy. She had a bad reaction to the anesthesia…and then she was gone."

"Oh, no! How old were you?"

"Nine. He started drinking more, but it was all right for a while until he lost his job, and then…" He dared a look and found Jane with her hand pressed to her mouth and tears shimmering in her eyes. "Don't cry!"

"But it's so sad."

"Oh, come on." He pulled her into his arms and listened to her sniff against his shirt, trying not to give in to the tightness in his own throat. Even twenty-five years later, he still missed his mom so much. "Don't make me cry, all right? You only like me because I'm a big slab of meat. I can't show any weakness if I want a chance to sleep with you again."

"Oh, stop it. It's sad."

"It was sad. Yeah." He kissed the top of her head before he realized what he was doing, but Jane didn't pull away at the show of affection, so he tucked her tighter beneath his chin. If he had to use his pitiful past as a lure, that was fine. He wasn't above it. He wanted to touch her, constantly. And there was so much of her he hadn't touched.

"Chase?"

"Hmm?" The skin of her neck was so soft under his fingers.

"Are you using the story of your broken childhood to make a move on me?"

"Maybe."

She shoved him away, her mouth fighting a smile.

"Hey, I didn't plan it, but I'm sure my mom would want me to be happy, right?"

"You're horrible!" she cried, slapping his arm, but she was laughing now instead of crying, and the tightness was gone from his throat. And for the first time in this long week, Jane looked peaceful.

He ran the back of his knuckles over her cheek just to feel the way the muscles bunched there when she smiled. "Are you ready? We should get in there before he makes it through his first six-pack."

The smile faded and she reached to move his hand, but her fingers lingered against his for a long while. "I'm ready. Are you?"

"Sure." Chase's heart sank as he stepped out of the truck, but he kept his smile in place anyway. It wasn't her problem. Still, he was relieved when his dad answered the door on his best behavior. He'd showered and put on clean clothes. The living room of the trailer looked decent.

"Hey, Dad. This is Jane Morgan. Jane, this is my father, Peter Chase."

He could see Jane's pleasant surprise as they exchanged handshakes and small talk. His dad even got her a glass of lemonade before he got out a notebook and pen and they each took a seat around the kitchen table. It was cozy and normal. Chase watched her laugh at one of his dad's jokes, and it was a little like a slow-motion scene in a movie. He wanted to pause the video and leave it stopped for a moment.

But the scene kept playing out, and the shaking of his dad's hands betrayed a flaw in the story. So did the circles under Jane's eyes and the stack of police records set before her.

"Mr. Chase, I'll pay you for your time, of course. Is fifty dollars an hour fair?"

His eyes lit up. "It's more than fair, Ms. Morgan. But let's be sure I can help you first. Why don't you tell me what you know, and we'll take it from there."

Jane told him the whole story, with some details that Chase hadn't heard before, and when she got to the part about the women whose names had come up during the investigation, his dad sat up straight.

He asked questions about who'd said what, and where she'd seen the names, and what she'd found out about the women.

Chase hadn't seen him this interested in anything besides beer in years.

"How sure are you?" his dad asked Jane. "How sure are you that your brother had nothing to do with this?"

Jane sat forward, all her coolness vanishing. Her mouth tightened with fierceness. "I know he didn't do it. Not because I see him through rose-colored glasses, but because I don't. He's a pothead and he's lazy, and apparently he's a thief, as well. But Jessie has never been mean. He's not cruel. He's not an angry person. When he was twelve, my dad found a dead dog behind the garage, and Jessie threw up before he got within five feet of it. Killing someone or something…it's not in his nature. He was always the kid bringing stray cats home, even if he wasn't interested in taking care of them afterward."

Chase wanted to touch her, put a comforting hand on her shoulder, but this was more important than what he wanted. He watched his dad nod thoughtfully. He'd opened a beer when he sat down, but Chase suddenly realized he hadn't touched it during the conversation.

"All right," his dad finally said. "All right. You've got my attention. I'll be happy to look over the file after I get in touch with your brother's attorney."

"Thank you." She sighed, a long breath leaving her deflated. She drew a white envelope from her purse and slid it across the table. "Here's your first payment. Please let me know if there's anything else you need. I put the attorney's card in there, too, and my phone number, just in case. Thank you, Mr. Chase."

"Call me Peter. I'll be in touch."

Chase cast a worried eye at the envelope, wondering how much money was in it and how long it would take his dad to spend it. But this was part of what he'd taken on when he'd decided to introduce Jane to his father. He couldn't protest now.

CHAPTER TEN

"Your dad was really sweet."

Chase nodded. Yeah, his dad was a nice guy. He always had been. "Thanks. He seemed really excited about the files."

"He's not convinced Jessie didn't do it."

"He's still a cop."

"Good. That's good."

She stared out the window at the creek that ran alongside the road. Her face had that distance it had when she was sitting behind her desk.

Chase screwed up his courage. "Should we go to dinner?"

He glanced away from the road again and found her still staring out the window. Clutching the steering wheel, he looked back to the highway. Ah, well. Meaningless sex was all it would be. A guy couldn't get too upset about that.

"Chase…" she started, just as her phone began to beep. "Crud." She snatched it up and flipped it open to read the text message. "Oh, no!"

"What? What is it?"

"Grandma Olive. Mac says she's in the county hospital. I've got to go."

"What's wrong?"

She shook her head. "He just said he can't use his cell phone in the emergency room and she's okay. I don't know what's wrong. Will you take me?"

Chase had already slowed and started the turn back toward Carbondale. It took only ten minutes to get to the hospital, and he followed Jane into the E.R. at a run.

It wasn't a big building, and they both spotted Mac in his bandanna and black leather jacket at the far end of the E.R. at the same time.

"Dad," she panted when they got close. "What happened?"

"Who's that?" a reedy voice called from behind the curtain. "Dynasty? Is that you?"

Jane rushed forward and pushed the flimsy blue material aside.

"She just cut her finger," Mac said. "She's fine." He shook his head at Chase. "Crazy old coot."

Chase watched Jane approach the old woman, whose silver hair was wound up in a tight bun on top of her head. Her grandmother had called her *Dynasty*. Weird. She was senile, maybe. Or half-blind and mistaking Jane for a sibling. Though even Jane's coloring was the opposite of Dynasty's. And the old woman's eyes were clear and sharp as she spoke to Jane. She didn't look confused. Or crazy. Or even the least bit vague.

A strange tightness crept over Chase's skin as he looked at Jane. She was back to her expensive, conservative clothes and elegant heels. Her thick hair was tamed into a French braid and her glasses hid her big brown eyes.

"So," he said to Mac, his eyes still on Jane, "she's changed a lot." *It can't be,* his brain scoffed. *She can't be.*

"Yeah," Mac answered, neither confirming nor denying Chase's insane suspicion. And the suspicion truly was unbelievable.

She can't be.

He finally met Mac's eyes and took the plunge. "She even changed her name."

One corner of the man's mouth rose. Chase waited for him to laugh and ask what the hell he was babbling about, but Mac just inclined his head.

Jesus. Chase shifted and glanced toward Jane again. She seemed to be engaged in a hushed argument with her grandmother. Well, hushed on Jane's part. The grandmother offered a loud "Oh, mind your own beeswax, Susie Q!"

No one could change that much. Plus, the old lady had just called her Susie Q. Grandma was clearly not all there.

Still, he decided to try subtlety one last time. "Why'd she do it?"

A thoughtful grumbling sound rose from Mac's chest.

Chase felt his shoulders bunch, waiting.

"She decided she didn't want to be Dynasty Alexis anymore. Can't say I blame her."

Dynasty.

Dynasty Alexis MacKenzie. Holy shit. *Dynasty.* His hands went numb as his heart churned unevenly.

"The name was the least of the changes, thank God."

He hoped the horrified shock didn't show on his face. "Sure. Of course."

"She's amazing." Mac nodded to himself. "We're really proud of her. But…" He raised an eyebrow in warning. "I wouldn't bring all that up if I were you. She doesn't like to talk about her past."

Chase nodded. Of course she wouldn't want to talk about it. She'd been… Well, there wasn't a polite word for what she'd been.

"Jesus," he breathed. He could vaguely remember her—spiky hair bleached pale blond, eyes smoky with black eyeliner. And, now that he thought about it, almost the same body she had now, though she'd kept all of it way out in the open back then.

He remembered the first time he'd met her. It had been a wild party, and young Dynasty had been the wildest of all. She'd perched on his lap, her beer in one hand and his thigh in the other. He'd been seventeen years old, and the feeling of her hand stroking his leg while he snuck peeks at her unbelievable cleavage… Chase had been throbbing hard within seconds. Dynasty had laughed and asked if he liked her. He'd slid his hand softly over her bare knee in answer. Oh, hell yeah. He'd liked her a lot. Especially when she'd started pressing little kisses to his neck, her hip rocking sweetly against his erection.

He'd been in heaven for ten minutes, anticipating the kind of fun they would have when they moved to one of the back bedrooms. In fact, he'd been issuing just that invitation when Terrell James had leaned in and whispered the bad news. "That's Big Mac's daughter, man. She's thirteen."

Even now his stomach plummeted in remembered panic. Thirteen. *Thirteen!* He'd been headed for his own troubled youth at that point, but he hadn't been that far gone.

In a panic, he'd meant to slide her gently off his knee, but it had veered toward a push.

She'd squeaked, "Hey!" her red mouth plumping into a pout.

"S-sorry," Chase had stammered. "Uh. I just saw my girlfriend come in." He'd felt like a dick saying it, but Dynasty had been unaffected. She'd shrugged and flounced off, and five minutes later she'd been perched on another boy's lap. The next time he'd looked around, Dynasty—and the boy—had been gone.

And now she was…*Jane?* Unbelievable.

"Who's that?" a voice called, pulling Chase out of his cloud of confusion. He looked up to find Grandma Olive pointing a finger at him.

"He's with me, Grandma," Jane said.

"With you? Well, ain't he big as life and twice as natural."

Jane rolled her eyes.

"He doesn't look like he'll be starring in one of those little-blue-pill commercials anytime soon, if you catch my drift."

"Oh, for God's sake," Jane muttered over Chase's shocked laugh.

The old woman's eyes sparked with life as she gestured with her bandaged hand. "He reminds me of your grandfather."

"He's not my grandfather," Jane snapped. "And you seem to be fine, by the way. I'm going to call Mom and tell her not to worry, then I'm going to find your doctor

and see if he'll give you a prescription strong enough
to knock you out."

"Don't be sassy!"

"Oh, *I'm* the sassy one," Jane huffed as she took out
her phone and hurried toward the far doors.

"You there," the grandmother said to Chase, jerking
her head to the side to call him over.

"Yes, ma'am?"

Her eyes narrowed as he drew closer. "You're a big
one, but you look kind of dumb."

"Uh…" What the hell was he supposed to say to that?

"Well, there you go."

Chase blinked and smothered the urge to yell, "Am
not!"

"Do you have a job, at least?"

This was solid ground, anyway. "Yes, ma'am. I own
my own company."

"Hmph." She eyed him suspiciously. "What kind
of company?"

"Excavation, ma'am."

Her eyes narrowed even more. "You look scared.
You're not scared of an old lady like me, are you?"

"A little," he answered honestly.

"Ha!" she barked. "I like you. What's your name?"

He relaxed a bit, wondering why he was so happy
that she liked him. "My name's Chase."

"I'm Mrs. Olive MacKenzie, Dynasty's grandmother." Her approval seemed to temper her sharp
tongue and they chatted about her garden for a while
until Jane returned and said it was time to go.

"And Grandma Olive," Jane said, "let somebody
else cut the limes next time."

"Young lady, I was making margaritas before your mother was born. I'm sure as hell not going to stop now."

Jane shook her head. "Come on, Chase." She walked toward the door, but Olive put her hand on Chase's arm to stop him.

She waved him closer and Chase leaned obligingly down. "Don't bring her home knocked up."

"Oh… God. Okay."

He lurched away while she smiled serenely.

Jane grabbed his arm and hurried him toward the door. "What did she say to you?"

"She told me not to knock you up."

"Good Lord."

Chase couldn't stop himself from laughing. "Your grandma's a hoot."

"That woman is not my grandmother." As they emerged into the parking lot, the wind hit them like an unfriendly hand. Swollen clouds gathered on the horizon.

"She's Big Mac's mother?"

Her eyebrows rose in exasperation. "She was married to Mac's father for about nine months before he died. Then she just never went away."

"She doesn't have any kids of her own?"

"Oh, she's got a son, but he doesn't speak to her anymore."

"Why?" he asked, shocked that a man would do that to his mother. He'd give anything to have his mom back.

"Grandma Olive told her son that his wife dressed like a blind whore."

"Ouch."

"Which might have been forgivable if she hadn't announced it during a toast at their wedding reception."

"Yikes." A horrible thing for the old woman to have said, but Chase found himself snorting with laughter.

Jane's lips were pressed tightly together, but he could see that she was about to burst out laughing herself.

"You have to admit she's pretty funny."

"All right," Jane answered. "I'll give you that. But the woman made my life a living hell when I was a teenager."

Chase tried to imagine Grandma Olive in the same room with young Dynasty Alexis and shuddered. It would not have been a peaceful pairing. "Well, she likes me," he said proudly.

Jane sent him a sideways look as he opened his truck door for her. "I guess Mac's tattoos have finally worn her down. A few years ago she would have ordered you to go scrub that nonsense off your neck or get out of her sight."

"I take it Grandpa didn't have any ink?"

"No," Jane said. Her eyes glittered with mischief. "But she'll go on and on about what a nice round bum he had if you ask her."

"She would not!"

"*Au contraire.* She says you could bounce a quarter off it. Tight as a drum and perfect for gripping."

Chase slammed her door, then shot her a glare when he slid behind the wheel. "If I think of Grandma Olive the next time a woman digs her nails into my ass, I'll never forgive you."

She finally let her laughter free, and it was a beautiful thing. Rich and husky and full of naughtiness. Damn, she was sexy. But he still couldn't reconcile her with that troubled young girl. If he'd had to guess what had happened to Dynasty, he would have envisioned her walking down a very ragged road. High-school dropout. Kids with different fathers. Drinking and drugging and a parade of useless men.

He'd graduated high school when she was only fourteen. When had she cleaned up her act? And why? He didn't dare ask her. She didn't seem to realize that he was Billy Chase. Hell, she might not even *remember* Billy Chase. And if she did...

Jane was clearly a woman who'd separated herself from her past. She wouldn't appreciate a stroll down memory lane.

Now that he knew her secret, Chase felt as if he should be closer to understanding her, but instead he felt his grasp on Jane Morgan slipping away. She was more of a mystery than ever. And he was more fascinated than ever.

He didn't ask about dinner again. He simply drove back to Aspen and pulled up to his favorite Thai restaurant. When she didn't protest, Chase felt sadly thrilled, and he had to wonder if Jane was even harder on his self-esteem than she was on his body.

Oh, hell. He wasn't complaining. Yet.

JANE'S MOUTH WATERED at the unrelenting scent of spices that permeated the restaurant. She'd forgotten lunch again, and though she should have insisted Chase take her home, she couldn't bear the thought of throwing together a healthy tuna salad with fat-free dressing. She needed spice and heat and the richness of coconut milk. She needed curry. And chicken satay. And maybe just a few spicy shrimp, as well. And, most of all, she desperately needed a mai tai.

She had no idea if Chase's father would be able to help, but somehow she felt lighter, as if she'd left part of her burden behind along with those files. Chase had warned her not to expect anything from his dad until tomorrow, because he'd start drinking early and simply fade away as the evening wore on. But somehow that was freeing, too, knowing that she'd hear nothing tonight. She could let it go for a few hours and simply wait.

But the waiting revealed her exhaustion, not to mention her gnawing hunger.

When the satay arrived, Jane jumped on it, wondering if Chase would notice if she took three skewers and left him with two. *Someone* had to eat the odd one out. Probably he'd be too polite to mention it. Way more polite than a guy with tattoos on his skull should be.

The peanut sauce was a wave of flavor in her mouth, and Jane sighed as she swallowed the first bite.

"So," Chase said, "how did Mac become your stepfather?"

Even the pleasure of the sweet sauce couldn't stop her stomach from freezing. "He married my mother," she answered coolly.

"Yeah, I got that part. Did your parents get divorced?"

"Yes." She piled slivers of cucumbers on the chicken before taking too big of a bite. *I'm busy here, buddy. Can't talk.*

"How old were you?"

Jane took a long drink of her mai tai and shivered with relief. "I was two." She grabbed a shrimp that set her mouth on fire, and had to gulp down a bit more of the drink.

"Wow, that's really young."

"Have you tried the shrimp? It's perfect. This place is amazing."

"It's my favorite restaurant. Aside from that burger place off Main. They use thick-cut bacon. Man, do I love bacon."

Smiling, she sucked at her straw, startled when it started gurgling. Lifting the glass high, she glared at the last traces of pinkened rum.

"Another?" Chase asked.

"Yes, please," she answered immediately, determined to keep the muscle-melting feeling progressing. For the first time in days her tension was gone. Actually, it hadn't been days at all. She'd felt pretty melty after sex with Chase in his truck.

She reached for another shrimp and realized there was nothing left on the plate but a lettuce leaf. Her disappointment floated away on a smooth river of rum.

"So did your dad stick around?" Chase asked as the waitress delivered their entrées and another mai tai.

"No." She took a big bite of red curry and chased down the heat with mai tai. Heaven. Spicy Thai heaven.

"He left?" Chase asked.

What were they talking about? Oh, right. Her sorry excuse for a father. "He was in prison." She took another bite and another drink.

"Oh…I see."

"No." She was slurping at the bottom of the glass again. Where in the world had all that mai tai gone? She set it down and started to laugh. "Chase, you couldn't possibly see. My mother was… Jesus, I don't even know what she was. Let's just say that my childhood was spent moving from prison town to prison town."

"Following your dad?"

"No, he stayed in one place. My mom collected lifers."

Chase shook his head, fork paused halfway to his mouth. "Lifers?"

"She was a prison groupie. She married guys in prison. Four of them, to be exact. All of them men she met after they'd been sent to the big house. You are looking at the tender outcome of a conjugal trailer visit." She put her hand to her mouth. "Oh, my God, did I say that out loud?"

"Yes," Chase murmured, voice quiet with shock.

His slack face made her giggle. And then it made her collapse with laughter. "Oh, boy," she squeaked. "Your expression is priceless."

"Your mom *collected* prisoners?"

"Oh, yeah. Like pound puppies." She wiped her watering eyes. "It was quite a colorful existence for a kindergartner, let me tell you."

"Jane," he said, his face falling from surprise to worry, "how often did you move?"

She shrugged. "Whenever she got tired of visiting that man, she'd start writing to another. My dad was the first, though, so I guess that makes him special. God, is it hot in here? Whew. I'm hot."

"I think it might be a combination of liquor and curry."

"Oh, crud. Really? That's embarrassing. Not as embarrassing as going to school with the children of your stepdad's prison guards, though. Can you imagine?"

"No," he said over her snort.

She took a deep breath and tamped down her laughter. "I don't know why I told you all that."

"It might have to do with that first drink you sucked down."

"Maybe," she agreed, just before regret hit her smack in the face. "Chase, I'm sorry. I wasn't thinking. About the drinks."

He rolled his eyes. "Not that again. It's fine. Get falling-down drunk. I promise not to call AA. And while you're tipsy, is there anything else you want to get off your chest?"

Alarm sank deep into her bones. One more drink and maybe she'd spill it all. Not just the bad stuff her mother had done. That was easy to lay out on display. Her childhood had hurt, but it hadn't been her fault. She'd been blameless…until she'd turned twelve and started making her own mistakes.

"Jane…"

"Nope," she lied. "That's all I have. Everything else about me is unremarkable. Boring. No need to ply me with more drinks." Which was unfortunate. For a moment there, she'd considered getting seriously blitzed.

Chase's head tilted slightly as he looked into her eyes, a furrow appearing between his brows. Fear wormed into her stomach at his look of confusion, but she talked herself down. He'd grown up in Grand Junction. He knew nothing, and she wouldn't tell a soul.

Still, the puzzle turning behind his eyes scared her.

"What?" she asked.

"You just…" His eyes fell to the table. "You confuse me."

"No, I'm simple," she insisted. "This stuff with my family might be complicated, but I'm not like them. I'm different."

"Is that why you're with me, Jane?"

"I'm not with you."

"Yeah, I got that. I mean, is that why you're having a fling with me, instead of dating like a normal person? Because I remind you of them?"

Her mind rolled, turning over, picking up speed. She knew what it was, but she couldn't say it. She couldn't say, *That's who I really am. A woman who needs a big, rough man. A sad young girl who needs to be used so that she feels wanted. Someone who believes a man's not really a man if he doesn't have scars on his hands and dirt ground into his jeans.*

She couldn't say that, because now she was a woman who believed in refinement and education. She built relationships on respect, not on physical attraction. She measured a man's worth by his ambition and intelligence and bearing. Not by the way he handled himself in a fistfight. Not by the width of his shoulders.

"Maybe I'm having a midlife crisis."

"You're twenty-nine."

"Right. I'm twenty-nine. I'll settle down soon. Get married, have kids. So before I turned thirty, I thought I'd find out what it was like to walk on the wild side."

"Oh, really?" he huffed.

"Yes."

He didn't add anything more—he just watched her—and for some reason his silence made her squirm. Jane breathed a sigh of relief when the waitress approached and left the bill on the table. Change of subject. "Let me get this."

"No, I got off pretty easy on our so-called date. I was having trouble living with myself."

Yes, she'd been a cheap date. Burger, Coke, screw in the truck. That made her think of just how fun it had been to feel cheap. Maybe he'd make her feel cheap again tonight. Like old times. She attempted to slide him a seductive look, but it disintegrated into a yawn.

"Come on, Jane," he said, reaching for her hand as he stood. "You look like you're about to slide to the floor."

"No, I'm fine," she insisted, despite the way her knees swam when she rose. "I'm getting my second wind."

"Mmm-hmm. How many hours of sleep did you get last night?"

She smiled flirtatiously. "You're not telling me I look tired, are you?"

"You look exhausted. You've got dark circles under your eyes, you're yawning and two mai tais nearly put you under the table."

"Did not," she scoffed. But when he helped her up into his truck, Jane melted into the seat. Okay, maybe she was exhausted. And tipsy. But she didn't want to be dropped off and left to drag herself to bed. Being tipsy seemed like the perfect excuse to have sex with Chase again.

It still seemed like a good idea when she blinked awake a few minutes later and found Chase opening the passenger-side door. "Hey," she breathed, stretching awake.

"Your keys?"

She dug around in her purse and handed them over, thoroughly enjoying the way he took control. He slid her off the seat and walked her up to her door as if he owned the place. Despite another yawn, she was already anticipating what they'd do once they got to her bed. Sure, she'd meant it to be a one-night stand, but the man transformed her body, as if she were Sleeping Beauty awakening from a long, dry slumber.

Chase guided her through the door. "I'll call as soon as my dad gets in touch."

"Hmm?" She spun back toward him, one hand reaching for the wall to steady herself.

"Get some sleep, Jane."

"But it's six-thirty."

"Right. Sleep for twelve hours and get a fresh start tomorrow. It'll be good for you."

"But—"

"Good night, Jane."

She was still staring openmouthed at the door when she heard him drive away. Trying to puzzle out what had happened turned out to be too much work, so Jane took Chase's advice and just went to bed.

CHAPTER ELEVEN

JANE MORGAN WAS LOSING IT. She was losing it, and she was losing it *at work.*

This couldn't be happening. She was a master at her job. An impervious wall of professionalism and knowledge and absolute control. Jane *was* her job. It was the best part of her, and that had been a comforting thought until now.

"I'm sorry, Mr. Jennings," she said again. "It's got to be here somewhere."

"It's really no big deal. You probably already sent it to Edward."

"No!" She realized she'd raised her voice—actually yelled at her boss—when he took a step back. "I mean, no sir, that's not possible. I never, ever send out files or sketches or blueprints without making a copy first. Never."

"Okay, but I—"

"Oh, my God," she yelped. "What day is it?"

"Um…I think…" He looked up to the ceiling, waiting for his mental calendar to spit out an answer. "Thursday, maybe?"

"Thursday," she murmured. "Thursday the fifteenth." Her fingers hovered over the files for a moment before they clenched into sudden fists. "Thursday the fifteenth. Seven-thirty breakfast meeting with the head contractor for the Gramercy job." Air pressure pressed into her. "I didn't… I didn't remind you. Did you miss the meeting? Please tell me you didn't miss the meeting."

"It's okay." Mr. Jennings held up his hands and took a sidestep toward his office door. "No big deal. He called and I apologized and we're meeting for lunch tomorrow."

"You have lunch with Edward Cohen tomorrow!"

"Just change it," he said, and darted for his door. "Ed won't mind. It's okay." The latch clicked softly closed behind him as Jane's heart beat faster and faster.

She was disintegrating. Every piece of herself that she'd so carefully constructed was peeling away like ancient wallpaper. First she'd slept with the type of man she'd assiduously avoided for ten years. Then she'd cried at her workplace. She'd been caught in an embrace by her boss. Then the typos. The getting drunk over Thai food. And now…now the lost project proposal. And worst of all, she'd caused Mr. Jennings to miss an important meeting. She'd embarrassed and inconvenienced him. She'd failed.

Her purpose in this office was to keep exactly that sort of thing from happening. It was the reason Mr. Jennings had brought her in. It was why he paid her well and told her he couldn't live without her.

This job was her confidence and her pride and her self-worth. The only thing in the world she was good at. Without this job, she was just a girl with a high-school diploma and an expensive wardrobe. She would *not* let this slip away.

"Where is it?" she muttered, glancing one last time through the open file drawer. The proposal didn't stick its head up and wink at her, so she slammed that drawer and moved on to the next.

"It's got to be here. It's got to." At some point her brain poked her in the back of her spinning head and told her she could reconstruct most of it from Mr. Jennings's computer files, but that wasn't the point.

Fifteen minutes later Jane was at the last cabinet, hands shaking as she flipped through every single file, when she found it. She found it. Filed under *E* for Edward, instead of *C* for Cohen. "Oh, thank God," she breathed, clutching the proposal to her chest.

"Jane?" a female voice asked from the front door.

"I found it!" Jane said as she swung toward Lori Love.

"Good! That's really great." But Lori didn't seem to understand just how much relief Jane was feeling, because her voice sounded downright strained.

Jane got up from her knees, still clutching the papers to her chest. "Sorry, I lost something. Whew. Now I have to order a basket of cookies for a contractor. Contractors like food, right? That should smooth things over. Mr. Jennings is in his office, by the way. I'll let him know you're here."

"Wait," Lori said. Her brown curls swung when she let the front door close behind her. "I'm here to see you, Jane. Quinn called me. He's worried."

"There's no need to be. It won't happen again. I'm mortified, but—"

"Jane."

She shut her mouth in response to Lori's serious tone.

"You remember how screwed up my life was last year?"

"Mmm-hmm."

"So when I tell you I can recognize the signs of a woman falling apart, do you think you can trust that?"

Hmm. This was a more difficult question to answer, because Lori was obviously about to point out that Jane was falling apart. "I suppose it depends on the woman."

"Jane." Lori was a no-nonsense kind of girl and her voice made clear she wasn't interested in coddling Jane.

"Yes?" She wanted to hold the papers for a little longer, but she made herself set them neatly on her desk before wiping her sweaty hands on her chocolate-brown skirt.

"*You* are falling apart."

Unwilling to answer, Jane cleared her throat and took a seat.

"If you want privacy, you know I have no problem with that, but know that if you want to talk, I'm here."

"Thank you." She folded her hands in her lap and waited for this to be over. Her ears rang as if her blood pressure was skyrocketing.

Lori didn't give up. "Last year I was quietly drowning in front of everyone and I refused to say a word. Obviously I won't argue with your right to take the same route. Are you drowning?"

"No."

"Would you tell me if you were?"

"No."

"Okay. I won't ask any more questions."

Mr. Jennings stalked out of his office. "I will."

"Quinn," Lori said sharply, but he aimed a glare in her direction before sliding it toward Jane.

"Has Chase done something to you? Is that what's going on? Is he abusing you?"

Jane gasped in horror. "No!"

"Well, all this started that day I walked in on you two, so pardon me if I'm suspicious. Did he force himself on you, Jane? Because I'll—"

"No, absolutely not. Chase isn't the type to— We're not really— It was just a hug!"

"Oh, yeah? You two are friends? You're in the same wine-tasting club or something?"

Jane clenched her teeth and narrowed her eyes at him. "I apologize for my inappropriate behavior that morning. If I'd acted with propriety you wouldn't be prying into my business right now, and this conversation could have been avoided."

Lori muttered, "Snap," and raised an eyebrow at her boyfriend. "I think she just told you to mind your own business, sweetie. Which was exactly what I was going to say."

But Mr. Jennings wouldn't give up. "This guy is like, six-five, and has tattoos on his neck!"

"Yowza," Lori said, her eyes flickering in surprise. "But that still doesn't mean anything. I doubt anyone would've expected Quinn Jennings to date an auto mechanic. Opposites attract."

"No," Jane said. "Chase and I are not dating. In fact, I just broke it off with a gentleman who—"

"Are you pregnant?" Mr. Jennings interrupted. "Is that it?"

"No!"

"Because if you are, I'll support you in every way possible. Whatever you want to—"

"I'm not pregnant! And I am not a living, breathing episode of *Jerry Springer*, so whatever else you might suspect, please keep it to yourself! I have the right to use my personal time however I like, and I'm under no obligation to discuss my life with you. It's none of your business."

His brown eyes darkened with sudden hurt, as if they were bruising right before her eyes. "Of course it's not," he said. "Of course. I apologize."

Oh, God, he looked so sad. "Mr. Jennings—"

"No, I'm sorry. I shouldn't have pried. Anyway, I've got to go check on the framers, so I'll see you later, Lori." He pressed a distracted kiss to his girlfriend's cheek and headed for the door. "Jane, take as much time off as you need," he murmured as he left.

She stared miserably after him, wondering how she could be so cruel to a man who treated her so well. Then again, that seemed to be her specialty these days.

"Don't worry about him," Lori said. "It doesn't matter how much respect they have for women, men still think they need to fix things for us."

"I'm fine, Lori. Honestly. I've just got a few family problems that I don't want to discuss. Will you tell him that?"

"Sure."

"Thank you." Jane felt her throat burn with sorrow for the pain she'd caused Quinn Jennings.

"And you wouldn't let a man treat you badly, right, Jane?"

Lori's eyes made clear that she was offering help if

Jane should need it. Jane shook her head, but truthfully, she'd once reveled in being treated like dirt. Now she did it only on the weekends.

No, she scolded herself. Chase might be a fling, but he hadn't once treated her like dirt, even when she'd deserved it.

"I promise you I'm not being treated badly by anyone. That's not what this is about."

"Okay, good." Lori smiled, transforming herself from cute to adorable. "So then this big guy with tattoos is someone who's treating you *right?*"

"Out," Jane snapped, pointing toward the door.

"Fine, fine. I've got to track down my grumpy architect anyway. I'll take some Starbucks up to his lot. You want anything?"

Jane shook her head, holding her breath until Lori walked out and disappeared from view. Then she snatched up the phone and dialed Jessie's lawyer to beg her for new information. This balancing game was too much. She'd thought she was strong, but she was cracking under the first signs of strain.

"I was just talking to your investigator," the lawyer said.

"My investigator?"

"Mr. Chase. He's here in my office. We're going over the arrest records and putting together a list of questions to ask Jessie when I see him this afternoon. I normally don't bring in an investigator unless it's a capital case, but he's been very helpful."

"Oh, good!" Jane glanced at the clock. It was only 9:00 a.m. and Chase had warned her that his dad never got up before ten.

"As a matter of fact, I'm going to put him under contract with a confidentiality agreement, if that's all right with you. Same rate you're paying him, but it'll be billed under the firm's charges."

"Great. That sounds wonderful."

"The prosecution floated a lower number for bail. It's thirty thousand, which is still pretty damn high—another indication that they're trying to build a bigger case."

Thirty thousand. That would be three thousand up front and the full thirty thousand on the line if Jessie decided to skip town. She couldn't do it, not with all the lawyer's fees, as well.

"Thirty thousand," she repeated.

"Jessie already told me that your dad won't pay it," the lawyer said. "I'm going to work on getting it reduced further. So don't worry. Jessie's fine for right now, and he understands where we are."

Jane thanked her and hung up.

Thirty thousand. She couldn't afford it. If he bailed on her, she could lose her condo. But now she was remembering when Jessie was thirteen and he'd call and ask if he could hang with her for the weekend. Most of the time she'd put him off. What if she hadn't? What if she'd taken him under her wing instead of putting all her energy into running from her past? What if she'd thought of Jessie sometimes, instead of just herself?

Vowing to look over her savings as soon as she got home, Jane put her head down and got back to work. She responded to e-mails and sent out blueprints and set up a whole flurry of automatic e-mail reminders to keep Mr. Jennings on schedule. Something inside her clicked back into place.

I can do this, she assured herself. *I can.*

Two hours later Mr. Jennings returned, offering her a halfhearted smile. She stood, wanting to reach out and hug him, but holding herself back. "Mr. Jennings, I apologize."

"No, I'm sorry. I shouldn't have pushed you like that."

"I…" She thought of how he'd reached out to her. How Lori had reached out. She thought of how she pushed people away and kept them at a safe distance, because it couldn't be the real Jane that they liked. It was the woman she'd created with smoke and mirrors that people wanted to know. "Mr. Jennings, I…I do consider you a friend."

His smile stretched to a relieved grin. "I'm glad."

"But I don't really…" She shook her head, hands gripping each other for comfort. "I don't really know how to do that. Right now I'm having some family problems. That's all it is. I don't want you to worry. I'm fine."

"Okay, good."

"If I need anything, I know I can come to you or Lori, and that means so much to me. Thank you."

Before she could brace herself, Mr. Jennings stepped forward and wrapped his arms around her. "You're like a sister to me, Jane. I care about you."

Panic exploded through her. Not because she thought he meant something inappropriate, but because he didn't. He honestly respected her. He loved the woman she pretended to be, and that made something deep inside her ache.

If he knew the real her—the brash, angry girl who'd grown up in half a dozen trailer parks—he wouldn't be so sure of his opinion. And Lori wouldn't want

Jane anywhere near her boyfriend, much less cuddled in his arms.

"Maybe someday you'll call me Quinn," Mr. Jennings said, seemingly unaware of her turmoil. "That's my first name, you know."

She nodded, holding her arms stiff against his chest until he let her go. "Maybe. But not in the office."

"Oh, God no!" he gasped in mock horror. "Of course not."

She had to force the laugh, but she managed it.

"You need more time off, don't you? You shouldn't be here."

"No, I can do this. Don't worry."

"Jane, I'm not worried about the office. I think you've only called in sick one time since we opened. You've earned whatever time you need. Take it."

She knew he was just being kind, and she knew she needed the time, if only for her own sanity, but something inside her still held tight to denial. *You can do this,* it insisted. *You don't need a break. You don't need help.*

Her nails dug into her sweaty palms. She *could* do this without help, but that didn't mean she had to. She did have friends, and they were offering help. Quinn and Lori…and even Chase if she were being honest.

Jane took a deep breath. "I've set up e-mail notifications that should get you through the next few days."

Mr. Jennings smiled as if he were bursting with pride for her.

"But I will stop in!"

"Go on, Jane. I'm not a child."

She arched a doubtful brow.

"I can do this. I swear." He grimaced at her stare. "All right…if I can't, I'll call you."

"Okay." Her smile was real this time. "That's more like it. Promise that you'll call if you need me."

Half an hour later she'd done all she could. Quinn Jennings got lost in his work, and there was nothing to be done about that, but hopefully if his cell phone beeped incessantly enough, he'd notice it.

Jane left relatively guilt-free and headed straight for the jail to see Jessie. If he looked okay, she could stop considering fronting his bond money.

But he didn't look okay. He looked awful. "Jessie, what's wrong?" she gasped.

"My lawyer was just here. I could get six years for this, Jane."

"Jess—" she sighed, slumping a little "—you were stealing from people. What did you expect?"

"I don't know!" Tears glinted in his eyes. "I wasn't hurting anyone. I didn't threaten any of those girls and flash a gun around. I just copped a few dollars, that's all."

The fear on his face left her torn between heartache and anger. "You're not a child, Jessie. And after what Dad went through, you can't even claim ignorance. How many times did he warn you never to put yourself in this kind of situation? Even aside from the theft charges, you've set yourself up for huge trouble."

He flattened a hand against the counter. "I didn't touch those women, Jane. I swear to God, I didn't. Can't you talk to your D.A. boyfriend for me? Get him to believe me?"

Crud. She shook her head. "He's not my boyfriend. Not anymore."

He asked about home, and Jane told him about Grandma Olive and her margarita accident.

Jane tried to hide her tears behind laughter, but Jessie noticed anyway.

"I really am sorry, sis. I know I let you down."

She shook her head.

"If I get out of here, I swear I'll do the right thing. Stop hanging around with those guys. Maybe go back to school."

Jane wanted to believe that this experience would scare some ambition into him, but Jessie knew how to work a room. Regardless that he looked like a typical high-school slacker, he had eyes that puppy dogs would envy.

The one-minute warning rang in her ear and she watched Jessie flinch. The warm puppy eyes tightened at the edges, leaving him with a wary, exhausted look.

"Tell Dad I'm sorry. I should've listened to him. If they send me to prison, I know he'll never come see me." His voice broke on a sob. "So tell him I'm sorry, all right?"

Oh, God. Jane pressed her fingers to her mouth to hold back her own tears.

"Please?" Jessie begged.

She nodded because she couldn't say anything more. His cool confidence had been stripped away in here. He'd finally gotten a glimpse of the truth: he was a criminal. Not a cute slacker. Not a laid-back pothead. He was a criminal and he was in trouble.

Jessie hung up the phone and swiped at his eyes in a gesture she recognized from his toddler years.

If he got out of this without a six-year prison sentence, maybe he really could change. She'd changed. One really bad weekend had changed her course in life.

So maybe Mac was right. Jessie had been stealing and using drugs and hanging out with dealers. Maybe a few months in jail was just the kick he needed to set him on the right path.

Tears streaming from her eyes, Jane walked out of the jail. Jessie would either become a man in this place, or he'd decide to never grow up, but she couldn't make him choose the right path.

CHAPTER TWELVE

CHASE HADN'T SEEN JANE in more than a day.

It seemed strange that only a week ago he'd walked into her office, and now he felt tight with the need to call her. See her. Touch her.

And for the first time in years, his father had done something wonderful for him; he'd called Chase to let him know that Jessie MacKenzie's bail had been lowered to thirty thousand dollars. Chase had an excuse to contact Jane.

He dialed her number and held his breath. Would she be upset about the way he'd dropped her at her place the other day? He'd been torn that night. Worried over her exhaustion, distressed about her past, hurt that she was lying about her identity and pissed that she lumped him in with the "bad" guys. Sleeping with her had been the last thing on his mind.

But now her phone was about to go to voice mail, and he was scowling with regret.

"Chase?"

He was so startled by her voice that he didn't answer for a moment.

"Hello?"

"Jane! Hi. Sorry, I was just... How are you?"

"I'm okay, actually. Just… I'm good. Worried, but good."

"You sound good." She did. She sounded… *familiar.* "I heard Jessie's bail has been lowered. That's great news."

"It is! We're hopeful it means they're looking in another direction as far as that girl's murder goes. But now my mom's talking about fronting the bond money.… I don't know." Her words faded into contemplation.

"Listen," Chase said, "I've got a proposition."

"Really? What kind of proposition?"

He was almost sure he heard a note of interest in her voice, and he felt pitifully encouraged. "I'm blasting at a site today. Wanna come?"

"You're…what?"

"Blasting today. I thought, with everything going on, it would be good for you. It's a big stress reliever, watching things explode."

"Are you serious?"

"Dead serious. It'll be a blast. Get it? A blast?"

"Ouch! Yes, I think the kindergartner next door got it, too, and she didn't even hear it."

Laughing, Chase squeezed the handle of his coffee cup in nervousness. "So it's scheduled for ten this morning. You probably have to work…?"

Jane cleared her throat. "I don't, actually. Mr. Jennings gave me a few days off. But won't you get in trouble?"

"What do you mean? Because of safety? We'll watch from off-site to keep the insurance company happy."

"No, I mean with your boss."

"My boss?" He slipped his feet off the coffee table

and sat up straight. "What are you talking about? I am the boss."

"Okay." She sighed. "What about the owner, then? Surely he wouldn't want you bringing—?"

"You really do think I'm just a big piece of meat, don't you?" He actually heard her teeth snap shut, and the sound made him laugh. "You little snob. It never even occurred to you, did it?"

"I don't understand what—"

"*I* own Extreme Excavations, Jane. It's my company. I may not play the part of respectable business owner very well, but looks can be deceiving."

"You're the owner?"

The breathless shock in her voice pushed a little twinge of annoyance into Chase's nerves, but he shook it off. "Yep. I started EE from scratch about six years ago."

"I had no idea."

"Maybe that's because you were too busy using me as a birthday present to ask any questions."

"Oh…well…"

Chase decided the guilt in her voice was a nice hint at weakness and he jumped on it. "So I'll come by and pick you up in half an hour?"

Thirty minutes later Jane was climbing into his truck.

Before he'd pulled up, Chase had felt sure he had the upper hand on this date, but her appearance shocked him speechless. Not because she looked outrageous, but because she looked *normal*. Jane Morgan was wearing *jeans*. And a T-shirt. And shades. Her ponytail bounced when she hopped in and took a seat. Chase wouldn't have recognized her if he'd passed her on the street. Maybe that was the point.

"Look at you," he said, stunned.

"Look at you! Did you get a haircut?"

"Just a quick trim." He ran a palm from his neck to the crown of his head, aware that another half inch of his tattoo was exposed. Though he pretended to concentrate fully on backing out of her driveway, Chase felt her eyes on his neck. He'd thought of her when his barber had cleaned up the edges with the buzzer.

Once he hit the street, Chase snuck another glance at Jane. In her dark jeans and long-sleeved shirt, she really looked like a woman in her twenties. A cute woman in her twenties. And the tight T-shirt wasn't hurting her figure any. He saw the sweater tucked over her arm and knew she'd slip it on when they got to the site—or he hoped she would, anyway. He wasn't in the mood to show her body off to his men.

She cleared her throat. She seemed to do that a lot when she was nervous. "Your dad's been really great. Jessie's lawyer is impressed."

"He's drinking less, which is good. Good for your brother, anyway."

"Good for you, too," she said quietly.

Chase shrugged. "It happens sometimes. He'll slow down and get a job for a week or two. Once he had a girlfriend who talked him into going cold turkey for a few months. It never takes."

"I'm sorry."

He felt his jaw tightening and forced it to relax. "He's old school, doesn't believe in rehab, so I'm not sure he'll ever stop drinking. I'm not exactly at peace with it, but it's easier since I stopped helping him out. No more beer runs."

The truck bounced over a ridge of dirt as he turned into the huge building site. "I need to walk the site first, then I'll drive us farther away before the actual blast. I don't want you getting hit by debris, and it's best to coddle my insurance guy. He's paranoid."

He slid out of the truck and jogged around to open her door.

"You want me to come with?"

"Absolutely."

Thankfully, she pulled on the black sweater and zipped it up, disguising her curves. Chase breathed a sigh of relief and resisted the urge to take her hand. She wouldn't want to be led through the site like a date, regardless of his desire to mark her as his to keep all the men away from her.

It took him a good fifteen minutes to check the placement and fuses and wires. He went over the plans one last time, double-checking measurements. Everything was in order.

"Chase!" one of his technicians shouted, jogging over to him. He waved a yellow paper that Chase recognized as a permit.

"Just a second, Jane. I'll be right back."

JANE WATCHED CHASE walk away, his stride long and sure. He'd struck her as confident before, but here…here he was in his element, in control. He was the *owner.*

The men all nodded when he walked by, even as they carried on with their work. His second in command deferred to Chase, despite Chase being a good ten years younger.

Why had she never even suspected?

Yes, she was a snob, if only within the strict parameters she'd set in her own mind. But Mac was a business owner, too. She knew they didn't all wear suits and ties.

Hidden behind her dark glasses, Jane watched Chase as he worked. Maybe she hadn't considered him anything more than a laborer because that's what she'd wanted him to be. If Chase was successful and ambitious in addition to being tattooed and rough…

She watched as he folded his arms and cocked his head, looking down at the paper the other man held. Then Chase nodded and clapped his hand against the guy's shoulder before turning back toward Jane. When he glanced up and saw her, his mouth curved into a smile.

Something deep inside her chest clenched. It wasn't her heart. It couldn't be. Just her stomach. For all his muscles, Chase had the smile of a mischievous little boy.

He was impossibly cute. And this was the reason she needed him to be nothing more than a dead-end laborer.

This was bad. Really bad.

She shouldn't have come. She should've stayed home and puzzled out what Chase's revelation meant to her.

But his offer had been irresistible. She'd been pacing her condo restlessly, trying to think of some way to occupy her time before Jessie's discovery hearing at three. Then Chase had called and offered to take her to an *explosion?* She'd nearly wept with relief. But now she didn't feel anything like weeping. Now there were butterflies dancing in her stomach.

"You ready?" he asked, shocking her into a little jump with his sudden appearance.

"Oh, y-yeah," she stammered. "Absolutely."

"Come on." His hand rested low on her back for a moment before falling away. The faint imprints of his fingers tingled for a long time after as they walked across the wide lot toward his truck. But Jane forced her pulse to slow as she glanced back toward the jagged wall of rock. Perfect little holes peppered it, trailing red wires like tails. "Are you sure those little bits of dynamite will work?"

Chase winked at her. "I'm pretty sure." When he handed her up into the truck, his hands lingered at her waist and dragged down her hips. Lust shot through her like tiny explosions, racing out ahead of his fingers, and her thoughts scattered.

"Where are we going?"

"Just to those trees over there. Here." He reached into the tiny backseat and grabbed a hard hat. "You'll need this."

"Ooh, cute." She plopped it onto her head.

"It's not bad. Put it on with sexy lingerie and see how I react."

"Hmm. Maybe the same way you'd react if I wore a jester's hat with sexy lingerie?"

"Possibly." Oh, God, that smile again.

Jane put her hands flat to her thighs and pressed. "So how did you get into the job of blowing things up?"

"That's not all I do!" he protested.

"Yeah, I get it. You're the owner. But blowing things up is what you love, right? Your eyes are sparkling like disco lights."

"Ha! Okay, yes, I love it. I started working construction when I was sixteen. The first time I saw a blast…I was in awe. I couldn't believe that was actually someone's *job*. I wheedled my way onto the excavation team, and that was that."

"Well, I'm awfully glad you found a way to use your powers for good."

He winked. "The other side of that coin wouldn't be pretty. Luckily, I'm one of the good guys."

Yes, he was. He really was. And his goodness was beginning to seep into her, sneaking through her pores when she was trying to have meaningless sex with him. She'd tried so hard to feel this kind of comfort with Greg. And with Mitch. And with all the socially acceptable men she'd dated before them. But when she was with those men, she felt as if she was working. On guard. Always careful.

With Chase she felt *alive*. The way she felt alive when she boxed. But danger made some people feel alive. So did drugs. Shoplifting. Reckless sex. Those kinds of feelings didn't mean something was good for you.

"This should do it," Chase said as he backed the truck underneath a big maple tree. The new leaves fluttered around them, turning the sunlight into glitter.

Chase got out to open her door again. But he surprised her this time by lifting her up as soon as her feet touched the ground.

"Oh!"

He set her on the hood of the truck. "This'll give us

a better view." His hands rested on her thighs, both easing close to a very interesting place.

"Good," she murmured, breath coming a little faster at that harmless touch.

"Scoot over?"

She slid across the hot hood of his truck and found a comfortable spot to lean against the windshield.

"Leave your sunglasses on just in case there's any debris," he instructed as he slid his own shades into place and leaned back, his shoulder nestled comfortably against hers. She wasn't truly surprised when his big hand slid under hers and he laced their fingers together. She wasn't *surprised,* but it did shock something deep in her chest. Something warm and melty and frighteningly soft.

"So what do you love?" he asked.

Fear trembled up from that place he'd just warmed. *"What?"*

"I love blasting through rock. What do you love?"

"Oh. I guess…" She shuffled nervously through her thoughts. What did she love? She liked boxing, but she didn't think it made her eyes light up. It was just an outlet. "I…I love my job."

She saw his head turn toward her, but Jane kept staring straight ahead.

"Being a secretary? You mean like…answering phones and stuff?"

"No, I mean…I like knowing that I'm good at something. Being shown respect. Being valued. Can I tell you a secret?"

"Yes!" he said as if he'd been sitting on the edge of his seat for days.

Jane flashed him a smile. "You won't tell anyone?"

"You know I won't, Jane. You can tell me."

She nodded. "Okay. Here's the truth. I'm not just the secretary. I own part of Jennings Architecture."

Well, she'd shocked him. She couldn't see past his sunglasses, but his mouth had fallen open. There. That would teach him to hide his success behind dirty jeans and ragged T-shirts.

"It's true. Mr. Jennings couldn't pay much when he first started out, so he offered me a share in the profits. I'm the secretary and receptionist and office manager, but I'm more than that, too. Mr. Jennings consults me about the direction of the company, or risks he might take, or partnerships he enters into. He values my opinion. I never thought I'd..." Jane paused in the face of her vulnerability. "It's not explosions and dynamite, but...I really, really love it."

A piercing tone cut through the stillness around them. "What's that?"

Chase murmured, "It's the all-clear warning."

She clutched his hand tighter. "Is it about to happen?"

"Yep. Are you ready?"

"I'm ready!"

The all-clear warning sounded one last time, then warped into a clear, computerlike voice. "Five, four, three, two..." Pulling his hand up to cradle it tight to her thumping heart, she held her breath and then... Whoom! A blast of sound went through her, an invisible hand. Silence held on to its coattails—complete silence—just before the rattle of falling rock began to pop through the air. Dust and smoke billowed up as she felt the adrenaline hit her blood.

"Wow!"

"Did you like it?"

It was simplicity itself: something had blown up. End of story. But her heart was jumping hard with excitement. "That was great!"

"It's even better up close. This was a pretty small one, but I thought you might like it."

"I loved it. Thank you so much for inviting me." His knuckles brushed the bare skin at the base of her neck and she realized she was still clutching his hand. She forced her fingers to uncurl. When she let him go, his hand rose to cradle her face and turn her toward him.

His mouth touched hers. Lust spiced the adrenaline in her blood and set off a different kind of explosion. Jane ran her hand up the back of his neck. His newly cut hair prickled against her skin as his tongue rubbed hers.

Every time he touched her, she wanted him, but the adrenaline added something dangerous to her need. She wanted to crawl over him, crawl *inside* him. Her hand curled, trying to hold on to his hair.

Chase broke away. "Jane…we *really* can't do this here."

"I know that!" She laughed.

He kissed her again, tasting her, pushing into her wetness. Oh, God. This was what she wanted. Nothing more complicated than this.

"My place," she murmured as he nibbled at her bottom lip, "is only three minutes away."

"Let's go."

CHASE MADE A QUICK DETOUR to the construction trailer, pulling right up to where his supervisor stood.

He listened to the rundown, gave a few instructions and told him he'd be back at two to walk the site. Then he was free.

Before they even made it off the lot, he snuck his hand between Jane's thighs and rubbed her through her jeans. Her head fell back as she groaned.

That first time had been quick and hot, but in the shower afterward, he'd planned what he wanted next. He'd fantasized about spreading her out on his bed and *exploring* her. Tasting and sucking and biting. But she'd slipped from his grasp that night, and there hadn't been any time or space in his truck at Ryders. But today. Today he planned to make her as weak and helpless as she'd been making him.

She groaned again, her legs falling open as he stroked her through the thick denim.

"Almost there," he muttered.

"No, I'm not quite…" Jane's eyelids rose a millimeter and she smiled. "Oh, I see. My street."

"Yeah, you're not that easy."

"Not quite. But almost."

Chase grinned, tires squealing as he swung into her driveway and braked hard. She popped open her door before he'd even cut the ignition. By the time he'd raced up her three front steps, Jane had the door unlocked and wide open.

Chase had a vague impression of rich colors and dark wood doors as he glanced around the town house, but he was more focused on looking for the bedroom. "Upstairs?"

Jane didn't answer. She just started up the stairs, taking the time to drop her sweater as she walked. Her

T-shirt came off next, revealing a pale pink bra underneath. Chase got into the spirit and shrugged off his shirt as he followed.

Her bedroom was perfectly neat, not one thing out of place until Jane kicked off her shoes. He hopped on one foot and then the other, unlacing his boots so he could toe them off as Jane reached to unzip her jeans.

He liked this girl. A lot. She wasn't looking to be seduced or worn down. She wanted this as much as he did and had no stake in pretending otherwise. But when she reached to push her underwear off, Chase held up a hand. "Wait."

"Why?"

"Because we're doing this my way today, and I want you to wait."

Her brow drew tight. He met her gaze and waited. Jane didn't exactly give in, but she didn't take off her panties either. Good enough.

Chase shucked off the rest of his clothes, enjoying the way her eyes ate him up as he walked toward her. Aware of how she'd touched him that first night, Chase traced his hand down her elegant neck and over her collarbone, measuring her response by the hitch in her breath. She liked it when he dragged his thumb over the soft flesh above the line of her bra. She jumped a little when he got too close to her arm, so he veered up, away from ticklish spots.

He circled her, the way she'd circled him, and pressed his mouth to intriguing spots like the top of her shoulder and the place where it began to curve up to her neck. He licked her nape, the way she'd licked his, then dragged his fingertips all the way down her spine.

"I've never touched anything so soft, Jane. Never." He spread both hands over her full hips, then her narrow waist and the hard cage of her ribs. "Amazing," he breathed, pressing his erection to her ass.

Jane inhaled sharply, reaching back to grip his naked hips.

He thought about ripping off her underwear and sliding into her right there, but just a few minutes ago he'd been intent on taking it slowly. Jane was likely to end this affair at any moment, and he'd never even *tasted* her.

So Chase sucked at her neck and memorized her curves with his hands before he nudged her panties gently down. He took off her bra and turned her to face him.

As always, the sight of her breasts stole his breath. Amazing. Just like the rest of her.

The dark triangle of hair that covered her sex was nearly black against her pale skin. It looked…untouched. And here was the friendly mystery he'd pondered for hours.

Chase backed her up to the bed and eased her down. He knelt before her and put his hands over her knees to spread them wide. "Ah," he breathed at the beautiful glimpse of her. That triangle of hair was perfect…and there was nothing else. The rest of her was waxed bare, leaving vulnerable and naked the plump lips and pink wetness. "Ah, sweet God."

Hooking his hands beneath her knees, Chase tugged her forward until she was within reach of his mouth. And then he kissed her. Finally. He licked her and sucked her and listened to her cries as if they were music. He traced the soft flesh and flicked his tongue over her until she begged for more, and then he gave her more, plunging two fingers deep.

"Oh, God, Chase," she groaned. "Oh, God, you're so good."

Well, that was nice. It was even nicer when Jane screamed his name, her hips jerking against his hold as she came, the taste of her flooding him.

Too fast. Too fast. He cupped his whole hand over her heat as her shivers subsided.

"Oh, God," she whispered. "That was… It was good."

"It was gorgeous," he agreed, rising to his knees and tugging her farther off the edge of the mattress. Now she was only an inch from his throbbing cock, the wetness of her tempting him to slide into that heat, to feel every bit of her squeezing against him, naked and slick.

"Chase," she whispered. He looked up to see her eyes burning into him. "Fuck me."

Yes. His hands shook against her thighs. His jeans were so far away, and he wanted to fuck her just like this, the way it was supposed to be.

But he couldn't. "Damn it," he muttered and lunged to the side to snag his jeans. "Damn it." He tore open the condom and slid it on, then sank himself deep in one brutal thrust.

Jane pressed her feet flat to the floor, arching her back as she cried out. Her sex squeezed him, the muscles tightening at the invasion. If Jane ended this, Chase was going to start hanging around the Pilates classroom at the rec center. But some other Pilates girl likely wouldn't be the fix he needed. It was Jane who turned him on so much. Jane and her tight body and confusing life and incredible hunger.

He thrust into her slow and hard, watching the way she bit her lip and clenched her hands. Her back arched harder, thrusting her breasts higher. Chase watched, eyes narrowed in focus. He was the one making her muscles clench. It was his cock filling her up and pushing those cries from her throat. Growling with greedy pleasure, he quickened his pace.

"Chase," she whispered, eyes opening to show just as much fierceness as he felt.

God, she was beautiful. So gorgeous she made his heart clench with pain. And suddenly this wasn't enough, this brutal coupling. They'd already done this. He wanted more.

Gathering her body into his arms, he shifted her farther onto the bed, so that he could rise over her. Now he could kiss her. Now he could lower himself to her body and feel her skin against his. Her arms clutched him closer, and that tension inside him loosened with relief.

Now he could taste her and breathe her in and feel her and sink deep into her sex all at the same time. He was surrounded by Jane, absorbed by her, and *pleasure* wasn't a strong enough word to describe the rightness of it.

"Jane," he whispered, biting a spot just below her ear. "Jane."

Her nails bit into his back, pulling him tighter. His strokes quickened as her legs wrapped around his hips. She pressed herself into his cock, a quiet moan telling him he was hitting just the right spot. Sweat made their movements fluid and hot. Too hot. Chase felt a bright pressure building, tightening.

He shifted his body a little higher, and her moans turned to keening. "I want to feel you come," he whispered. "Come again, Jane. For me."

"Ah, God," she sobbed, her nails dragging down to his ass.

Chase gritted his teeth and kept his strokes even, despite wanting to thrust frantically into her, to come inside her, fill her up.

"Yes," he urged as her body strained toward him. *Please.* He wasn't going to last. He couldn't hold out. She was too hot, too tight, too soft and trembling. He couldn't...

"Fuck," he growled as his orgasm loomed over him. Finally Jane screamed, her body stiffened beneath him, sex pulsing tight, and Chase let go with a roar.

CHAPTER THIRTEEN

SHE DIDN'T KICK HIM OUT.

Chase wasn't so confident about his welcome that he'd dare to leave her alone and jump into the shower, but he was quietly pleased when she pulled back the sheets and motioned him to join her. The noon sun glowed through the curtains, after all. Jane had the perfect excuse to clear her throat and mention work or Jessie or one of a hundred other excuses. But she didn't.

Instead, she cuddled naked into his side, her cheek pressed to his shoulder, breath teasing over his chest.

Two nights ago he'd been angry with her, frustrated that she wouldn't share anything about her life unless she was forced to. But he'd let that go today when she'd talked about being valued and respected as if it were a priceless, rare thing. He hadn't known anyone who respected Dynasty MacKenzie, and she clearly hadn't respected herself.

Chase wanted to tell her that he understood. He'd had his own problems in high school. But considering her reaction to Jessie's stupidity…probably not a good idea. He'd just be handing her another excuse to blow him off. Better to leave the past in the past.

Certainly Jane seemed to think so. She'd changed

her name, for God's sake, as brutal a severing from her old life as she could make. She didn't want anyone to know about her past.

He could live with that.

"Tell me about your tattoo," she murmured.

Chase glanced down to the thick black ink that swirled around his arm. "It's not a very good story, I'm afraid. I wanted a tattoo, and the day I turned eighteen I went in for this one."

"It must have taken more than a day."

"It took a few weeks."

Her arms stretched across him to trace a dark edge. "It's nice. I'm glad you didn't go with a naked dancing girl."

"I couldn't decide on blonde or brunette, so I had to go with abstract tribal."

"Smart man."

"Maybe you should get a tattoo. You sure seem to like mine a lot."

"Yeah, right. Can you imagine me with a tattoo?"

Actually, he could. It would match her hidden lush body and sexy underwear and insatiable appetite. And her secret past.

But he wasn't stupid enough to say that, so he just rested his mouth against her temple and closed his eyes. God, she felt good. "So no tattoos, huh? How'd you get that scar on your knee?"

Her head shifted as she looked down, as if he was talking about someone else's knee. "Oh, that? A fight on the playground in first grade. The girl pushed me down. I had to get stitches."

"Aw. Poor Jane."

He felt her mouth smile against his shoulder as he glanced toward the clock.

"Damn," he muttered at the unforgiving numbers. "What do you say we grab a quick shower and go to lunch?"

He hadn't realized just how liquid her body had become until she stiffened against him. He could *feel* her thinking. Considering the pros and cons of going out to lunch with him.

"You're thinking too hard again, Jane."

She shook her head, her hand splaying against his stomach.

Why couldn't she just enjoy this? Just give it a chance? "It's just lunch."

"No," she whispered. "It's not just lunch."

"Okay, so it's more than lunch. What's wrong with that?"

She pushed up and leaned toward her dresser to snatch open a drawer.

Chase tried to control his anger as he watched her pull a T-shirt over her head. Just seconds ago he'd felt forgiving. Understanding. She'd missed out on a lot in her life. But, Christ, he'd lost his mom. His dad was an alcoholic. Chase had acted out. His childhood had been screwed up, too, and he wasn't afraid to try.

He growled, "I'm a person, Jane. Do you get that? A real person."

"Of course. I—"

"I spend time with you and I have sex with you and I like you."

When she stood, he closed his eyes so he wouldn't get distracted by the sight of her naked ass.

"I know. I'm sorry. I like you, too. You know I do. But…"

When he dared to open his eyes, she was safely covered by a pair of sweatpants. "But what?"

"Let's not do this."

"No, let's," he insisted. "I want to take you to lunch. I want to talk to you. I want to pretend for an hour or so that I'm more to you than just an easy lay."

"Chase—"

"Am I?"

She rounded on him with a glare. "Why are you doing this?"

"Because I'm not just an easy lay!"

"I have made clear to you from the very first day that I want—"

"Jesus Christ, Jane, we both know what you want. I'm talking about what *I* want now. Not as much of a concern to you, I understand, but you could at least pretend to listen."

Her mouth tightened. "You're asking for exactly what I told you not to ask for."

"Fine," he snapped, whipping the sheets back. He brushed past Jane to get to his jeans. "You had a bad childhood. You're damaged and uptight, and you don't want to change. A relationship with a guy like me is your worst nightmare. I got it."

"Why are you so angry?" she shouted. "You volunteered for this."

Chase paused in the act of tugging on his boots. She was right. Why *was* he so angry? Running a hand over his hair, he bit out a few curses, then shook his head. "I'm sorry." He yanked his laces tight and took a deep breath. "Sometimes it feels like it means more to you. And to me, obviously. My mistake."

From the corner of his eye he saw Jane raise a hand toward him, then slowly drop it. "Chase…"

"I'll see you later, Jane," he muttered.

She didn't try to stop him when he walked out of the room. She didn't walk him down the stairs or watch while he pulled his shirt on. She didn't open the door and wave goodbye. And he couldn't even be mad, because she'd *warned* him.

Knowing full well he was making promises he wouldn't keep, Chase told himself it was over and slammed the door behind him.

PHONE PRESSED TO HER EAR, Jane looked around the parking lot of the bail bondsman, hoping to spy her mom's long blond hair. Her stomach ached with regret over the argument with Chase that afternoon, and now she had to deal with this.

"Grandma Olive, are you sure? I've been here for five minutes. She's not here."

"She told me point-blank what she was doing."

"Does Mac know?"

"Not yet. And I'm not going to be the one to tell him."

While Olive was still sniffing her disdain, Jane saw her mom's car pulling up. "Mom's here—I've got to go."

When her mom got out of her car, her eyes widened, but she hesitated only a second before moving past Jane.

"Mom," Jane said. "You can't do this."

Her mom walked determinedly across the parking lot, mouth set in a stubborn line. An inconvenient time for her to grow a spine.

"Mac will be furious."

"Jessie is my son, too, and I'm not going to leave him to rot in that jail just because his father is angry."

She kept pace with her mother's every step. "Mom, think about this. Where is Jessie going to stay?"

"Grandma Olive has agreed to let him stay with her for a little while."

"And what if he runs? You'll lose thirty thousand dollars!"

"It's only ten thousand now. That's nothing. And he won't run. He wouldn't do that to his family."

"He brought stolen goods into your home!"

Her mother shook off the hand Jane placed on her arm and reached for the door.

"You can't put up the house as collateral, regardless. Mac has to sign off on that, too."

She whirled to face Jane. "I know that. You might think I'm too dumb for words, but I do know some things. I'm putting up my car. It's worth just enough and the title's in my name. Now, why are you trying to talk me into leaving Jessie in jail?"

"The motion of discovery was approved. Just give the lawyer time to look over the evidence. He could be cleared in a few days."

"You just want him in jail where he can't cause you any more embarrassment. You want to keep him there so he can't interfere with your fancy life!"

Jane let her mom see the full weight of her fury. "Oh, yes, having Jessie locked up has been a great relief. All that hanging around the courthouse and sneaking into the jail for visiting hours has got to be great for my reputation. Not to mention the relief of getting rid of the savings that've been weighing me down. That's been wonderful! Mom, Jessie's twenty-one and he's still a little kid. And now you're rushing in to protect him *again*."

"I am his mother!" she shouted, tears dragging through her black mascara. "It's my job to protect him!"

Jane's throat burned with the things she wanted to say. Cruel things that had built up inside her for years.

She did the best she could, Jane told herself. *She didn't know any better.* But she should have known. She should have known that you didn't drag a little girl to prison visiting hours every month of her young life. You didn't introduce her to a new "daddy" every other year, especially when those daddies were big, scary men with cold eyes and scarred hands. She should have seen that being trailer-park trash was hard enough without the added stigma of being a prison groupie piled on top of it. And that parents wouldn't let their kids go to a birthday party for the stepdaughter of a convicted murderer no matter how many invitations were sent.

But there was no point in telling her mother this. Jane was a grown woman now, and she had to let these childhood resentments go. And though Jane thought bailing Jessie out of jail was a big mistake, her mother's motivation was pure.

"All right," she made herself say. "Do what you feel you need to do. Call me if there's any trouble. I might have a fancy life, but I'm doing my best to help Jessie, too."

She stalked away, a giant fist tightening in her gut as she rushed off. Her own mother thought she was a selfish bitch. Chase did, too. Because she was. She was selfish. Determined to have *everything* she wanted. Success. Respectability. Security.

Her mother had aimed as low as one could possibly aim. She'd prided herself on winning the affections of lonely criminals locked away in barred cells. Men who hadn't seen a woman in a decade. That had been her idea of accomplishment. She'd demanded *nothing* for herself, not even a man she could touch.

They had nothing in common…so why was Jane so terrified of becoming her mom?

Jane stopped at her car, thumb hovering over the button on her key chain that would unlock the doors. Where was she going? To work? To the lawyer's office? Home?

Something was gnawing at her from the inside out. Anger and words and regrets. She found herself wishing for another explosion, something that would draw the feelings out of her, like lancing an infection.

If Chase weren't mad at her, she'd call and propose a quickie.

Crud.

Jane pulled her cell phone out and scrolled through her contacts. Nearly every single one of them was filed under the "work" heading. She found the name she was looking for and hit the call button, hoping she wasn't making a big mistake.

LORI LOVE POPPED THE CAPS off two bottles of beer and handed one to Jane. "Come on. Let's sit in the living room."

Jane clutched the beer bottle awkwardly. It was only

four-thirty. Wasn't that too early for beer in respectable society? She followed Lori into the cheery living room. "This is pretty."

Lori's eyes looked surprised when she glanced over the pale yellow walls and the white curtains billowing in the spring breeze. "Thank you!" Her gaze went to the tight grip of Jane's fingers around the neck of the bottle. "Do you need a glass?"

"Oh…" Did she? She hadn't drunk beer out of a bottle in years. "No, this is fine. Thank you."

"So… What's going on? Why'd you call?"

Jane met Lori's sympathetic eyes and couldn't think what to say. She'd come here to talk, but now… "Are you getting excited about your trip?"

"I can't wait!"

"You've really changed your life, haven't you?"

"I have."

Questions bubbled up in Jane's throat. *How did you do it? Do you feel different inside or the same? Did you turn your back on your past? Are you faking your way through every day?* But if she asked those questions, she'd have to explain, wouldn't she? She'd have to tell Lori that Jane Morgan wasn't real.

Lori's head cocked. "Jane? What's going on?"

"I…" She'd kept her secret for too long. She couldn't do it. Better to go with a smaller truth. "I'm seeing someone inappropriate."

"The big guy?"

"Yes."

"The one with tattoos on his neck?"

"Yes. His name is Chase."

Lori nodded. "Quinn told me about him. He very reluctantly admitted that Chase seemed like a nice guy before he started abusing you."

"He's not abusing me!"

Lori's grin spread across her face. "I'm sorry. I couldn't resist. Quinn's been so upset about his sweet little Jane dating a big, scary man. Do I get to meet this mystery guy?"

"*No.* It's not serious like that. In fact, it's probably over. He's... We're nothing alike."

"Well, look at Quinn and me. I was a mechanic, and now I'm a thirty-year-old college freshman dating a successful architect. We're not anything alike, we're not in the same place in our lives, but I can't imagine life without him."

Lori looked down at her hands. "You two are amazing together. You make him so happy."

"So does this Chase make you happy?"

She shook her head. "He can't. I feel nice when I'm with him. He's easy to be around. But I have plans that don't involve someone like him."

"Jane!" Lori laughed. "That sounds awful. 'Someone like him'?"

Jane's cheeks heated. They must be red, but they felt even more than that. Aglow with fiery magenta. "You don't understand. I want to get married someday and have children. I can't have kids with a man like that."

"A man like what?"

Jane felt horrible. She knew it wasn't right. Chase was a good man. He'd probably be a good father. Logically, she knew that, but in the deepest part of her heart, the idea of someone like Chase terrified her. And now that she knew he was a business owner, she couldn't pretend that it was some deep objection. Her standards were all superficial and disgusting.

Jane nodded and set her shoulders. "When I was a little girl, sometimes the other kids' dads would come to the school. To pick them up or for career day or the parents' day lunch. And those men in suits and ties... They looked like the kinds of dads I saw on TV. They were like *superheroes*. Always smiling. Always polite to the other children. They were smart and shiny and perfect. I knew if one of those men was my dad, nothing bad would ever happen to me."

"But Jane," Lori said slowly, "you know that's not true."

"I do, but...I don't want my children to ever think, 'I wish my dad was like that man. I wish *he* were my father.'"

Lori looked impossibly confused. "What was your father like, Jane?"

She shook her head. How was she supposed to answer that? Would she tell the facts? *My real father was a convicted felon in prison for twenty years for bank robbery.* Or add a little flavor to it? *I never met him, but he wrote to me from prison every week until I turned twelve, and then he disappeared.* Or should she talk about Mac, who was the only real father figure she'd ever had? *My stepdad was convicted of killing an old woman. He didn't do it, but everyone was still scared of him, and he did rob a liquor store when he was young.*

Jane didn't know what to say, so she just shook her head.

Lori shook her head, too. "My dad was a mechanic.

When he came to pick me up at school, he wore greasy coveralls. His nails were always black with grime. Always. And I never, ever wished my dad was somebody else, no matter what he looked like."

"I did," Jane whispered. She felt tears welling up and took a desperate swig of her beer.

"Then your dad wasn't a good dad for other reasons."

Oh, God. That was the understatement of the year. "I know. I know it's irrational and ridiculous. I *know* that. And I know I'm awful and ugly to think this way, but I'm just…"

Lori took her hand. "What?"

"Terrified."

"I understand about being scared. You know that. But it's something to get past, Jane. Not embrace."

"I've gotten past a lot already. I'm settled now. *Done.* I'm too tired to get past more. I just want a nice, normal husband and a nice, normal family! It doesn't seem like a lot to ask for."

"I understand," Lori said softly. "You know I do. After what I went through last year… But you've got something bigger going on, right? Do you want to talk about that?"

"No," Jane answered quickly. "I don't. I'm sorry. It's nothing to do with you. I just want to leave that all behind. I don't want to drag it along with me for the rest of my life."

"Okay, but you know it'll follow you anyway, don't you?"

"Not if I can help it," Jane muttered.

"So what are you going to do about Chase?"

What *was* she going to do about Chase? "I don't

know. He's angry with me right now, so I might not have to do anything at all. Maybe it will just fade away."

"Coward," Lori said with a smile.

Jane raised her beer in a toast, then chugged half of it down. She might be a coward, but her secret was still safe and she'd happily run away from everyone to keep it that way.

CHAPTER FOURTEEN

THE DOOR of Grandma Olive's apartment flew open and Jane found herself face-to-face with a sleepy-eyed Jessie. "Jess!" she yelped, surprised by how relieved she was to see him without the barrier of Plexiglas between them.

"Hey, sis," he said as he returned her tight hug.

"You look really good." He did. He'd been out only for thirty-six hours, but his skin had already lost its pale anxiety.

"I missed you," he said, sincerity in his eyes. Jane didn't know if he was referring to jail or the fact that she hadn't seen him for nearly six months before his arrest.

"Jessie!" Olive yelled from a back room. "Is that Dynasty?"

"Yes, Grandma!" he shouted as he waved Jane in. He glanced over his shoulder before he spoke again. "Can I stay with you?"

"Me?" Jane yelped. "Why?"

"I don't like it here. Grandma doesn't wear clothes to bed."

"Well, jeez, she doesn't make you sleep with her, does she?"

"No, she makes me sleep on the couch, which

would be fine if she didn't wander out for a snack every night at 2:00 a.m.!"

The woman herself appeared, fully clothed, thankfully. "You complaining about my birthday suit again, boy?"

"Grandma," Jessie whined.

"If you don't air out your plumbing, you get mildew. Everyone knows that."

"Oh, God," Jane muttered. "Just put on a robe, woman."

"This is my house!" Grandma Olive snapped. "If you're so concerned about his innocent eyes, take him in yourself."

Jane gritted her teeth, knowing full well what was coming.

"Oh, but you won't do that, will you? You don't want some dirty thief living in *your* house. You're too high and mighty for that. Still, I guess high and mighty is better than what you used to be."

"Jessie—" Jane ground out the words "—are you ready to go?"

They both darted for the door, while Grandma Olive shouted for them to pick up peanut butter and milk on their way home.

"Can I please come stay with you?" Jessie begged, but Jane shook her head.

"Nope. I'm not getting on Mac's bad side. He was right to let you stew, to give you some time to think about what you've done."

"I'm thinking about it now," Jess muttered.

"I'll buy you a sleep mask," she offered. Let him sleep on Grandma Olive's couch for a few weeks and realize the value of working hard enough to afford his own place. He'd had his personal space in Mac's basement. There'd been no reason for him to work hard and get out. But now, faced with the specter of prison or more of Grandma Olive's birthday suit, maybe he'd think about going straight.

Jessie reached for the stereo and fiddled with it until he found a rock station that was only slightly fuzzy with interference from the mountains. She wanted to ask what his plans were, what he wanted to do with his life, but that conversation could wait until they knew just how much prison time he faced. Right now it would be cruel to ask him to consider it.

"I didn't think Mom should've bailed you out, but I'm glad to see you anyway."

"Thanks," he said, sounding only half-sarcastic. After a few moments of silence, Jessie cleared his throat. "I'm sorry I ruined your birthday."

"It's okay."

They rode in silence the rest of the way to the lawyer's office, the Foo Fighters keeping them company.

The receptionist ushered them into the conference room, and Jane's heart slumped a little when she saw Peter Chase.

Not because of his appearance—he looked really good—but because he sat at the table alone.

Jane hadn't heard from Chase in several days now, and it felt like an eternity. "Jessie, this is Mr. Peter Chase, our investigator."

"Nice to meet you, Mr. Chase," Jessie said, impressing Jane with his lack of slacker ennui.

Chase's dad really did look good as he pushed to his

feet to shake Jessie's hand. There was healthy color in his cheeks and a robustness in his movements that had been missing before. Maybe Chase was wrong about him. Maybe he really was on the mend.

The attorney bustled in and they all sat down to go over the reports the police department had released the day before. Mr. Chase and the attorney had clearly already read them all, because they each had a list of questions.

"Listen," Mr. Chase said. "I managed to corner one of your friends, Jessie. He didn't want to talk to the cops, but when he found out I was working for you, he agreed to answer a few questions. After I offered a hundred-dollar bill, I might add. This guy said that your pal Tiny is dealing pot and a few pills. Is that true?"

Jessie shifted uncomfortably.

Mr. Chase gave him a hard look and turned to the attorney. "The name of the girl who OD'd is Rose. The informant says she's fine, though. Took a few pills with a few too many shots and her friends ran her in to have her stomach pumped."

Jane took a deep breath. "She didn't die?"

"Nope. He didn't know her last name. Jessie?" He shot Jessie a sideways look. "Last name?"

"I don't know her, man," Jessie mumbled.

"Well, it's nothing to do with this Rose girl, it seems. I just thought I'd track down that loose end."

They turned to the Michelle Brown file, but nothing surprising came up as they trudged through it. Yes, Jessie admitted, he'd stolen her purse. He'd also tried to use one of her credit cards to buy beer at the self-checkout line of the grocery store. He couldn't remember how much cash she had, but he was pretty sure it had been less than the two hundred dollars she'd claimed on the police report.

"And afterward?" Ms. Holloway asked. "When did you see her again?"

"Never!"

"You're sure? Maybe you hooked up with her later, not even realizing who she was."

"No way. I'm not such a dog that I can't remember the names of the girls I hook up with. The only Michelle I ever slept with was a girl in my high school, and it wasn't her."

They went over where he'd been the night Michelle Brown was killed, but his answer offered no comfort. "Probably getting high at Tiny's house" wasn't exactly the rock-solid alibi a jury would be looking for.

"Okay, let's move on to Kelly Anderson. She said her backpack was stolen from The Black Box on January third. Do you remember that?"

"The Black Box? No way, man."

Ms. Holloway leaned forward. "Why do you say that?"

"Because I haven't been to The Black Box in three years. It's all emo bands and folk shit now. No way."

"So maybe she was at Ryders and didn't want her mom to know."

Jessie shrugged. "I never lifted any backpack, either."

Mr. Chase flipped through the papers. "They didn't find any of Ms. Anderson's belongings in the car or in Jessie's room."

"Told ya," Jessie said.

The attorney's eyes gleamed. "So there's no connection between Jessie and Kelly Anderson at all, and nothing connecting him to Michelle Brown's murder but the fact that he stole her purse two weeks before she died."

"That's it?" Jane asked.

"That's it, which is why the judge agreed to lower bail to ten thousand."

"All right, man," Jessie said. "Great."

"Jessie," Jane snapped, "it's still serious. Six years' worth of serious, in case you've forgotten."

Jessie rolled his eyes. "Yeah, it's my ass on the line, Jane. I'm pretty clear on it."

His attorney put up a restraining hand. "Jessie, I don't want you doing anything while you're out on bail. Nothing. Stay home. Keep your nose clean. No drinking. No pot. No women. And definitely no clubs or bars."

"Jesus," he muttered, but quickly followed it up with "Fine."

"This is really good. And as long as you behave, we're in a strong position. Don't screw it up."

"I won't." He tried to give the Scouts' honor sign, but Jessie had never been in the Boy Scouts, and he raised two fingers instead of three. But no one called him on it. His expression was sincere.

He started to stand, but Ms. Holloway put a hand on his arm. "If you two will excuse us, I need to speak to my client for a moment about some procedural issues."

Jane nodded and walked out of the room, smiling at Mr. Chase when he held open the door and gave her a chivalrous little bow. She could see where Chase got his charm. And it suddenly hit her how sad it all was. That his dad was so sweet and charming and smart, because that meant Chase knew exactly what he was missing when his dad was drunk.

"I think you may be right about your brother, Miss Morgan. I don't think he killed those women."

It felt as if a giant fist squeezed her in its grip. To have someone outside the family say that about her slouching, long-haired brother... "Thank you so much, Mr. Chase."

She touched his arm as she turned toward the group of chairs in the reception area. But her body hesitated when she caught sight of someone approaching past the glass sidelight of the office door. It was Chase, looking down at his phone.

When he glanced up, his eyes locked with hers, and he smiled. He *smiled.* Chase wasn't mad anymore. Her heart jerked to a stop before sputtering back to frantic life. This was just a fling. She'd thrown that in his face so many times. So why was she so incredibly relieved that he wasn't angry with her?

She couldn't think about that now, because she was too busy smiling at him as he drew closer to the door.

"Hey, Miss Jane," he said as he walked in. Her stomach shivered at the warm slide of his voice.

"Hi, Chase."

"Dad? Are you ready to go?" Right. His dad probably didn't have a license. Chase hadn't come to see her, but he looked happy with her presence, at least. Didn't he?

"...just a few more minutes," his dad was saying. "I want to speak to Ms. Holloway before we take off." He withdrew to a seat and started flipping through the files.

Nodding, Chase turned to her, hands in his pockets, head ducked a little. "How are you?" he asked softly.

"Good. Jessie's out. He's staying with Grandma Olive."

"How's that going?"

"You don't want to know," she answered, sharing a secret smile with him. "How are you?"

"Good." He rocked back on his heels, and Jane watched, wanting to touch him. "Busy."

"I'm sorry," she whispered.

He met her gaze, his eyes immediately softening. "You just...confuse me."

"I'm sorry," she repeated. What more could she say? She confused herself.

"It's all right, Jane." His voice was so...understanding. She couldn't tell what he meant. He could be understanding because he was done with her and at peace with it. Or he could be understanding because he cared.

After finding out about his career, she'd had to admit to herself that her only objection to Chase was superficial. His tattoos and boots and beat-up truck reminded her of her past. And his drunk father and trailer-park past were just too close to her own embarrassments. She wasn't proud of her prejudice, but she wasn't afraid to accept it.

She didn't want to date Chase because of his family and his looks. But seeing him now, those worries fell away. He was smart and hardworking and nice. She missed him. Maybe she could just *try?*

"Tomorrow is Tuesday," Jane said inanely, hoping it was some sort of prompt.

"Yes, it is."

She wanted him to ask her out. She wanted to see

him, but she couldn't admit it, because she'd made clear that she wasn't serious about him. Oh, God, she'd backed herself into an untenable position. An indefensible position that she couldn't abandon. This was how the Visigoths had gone down. At least according to last month's book club selection.

Chase watched her past his lashes.

She cleared her throat as he took his hands out of his pockets to cross his arms.

"Jane," he said, eyes narrowing, "would you like to go out to dinner on Tuesday night?"

She'd been hoping he'd propose a night at home. But she knew she'd been hoping in vain. Could she do this? Go out with him on a real, meaningful date? Because there was no doubt that was what he meant. "Okay," she breathed.

"Okay?" He raised his head and looked straight at her. "All right, then. We'll go someplace nice. Maybe Miso or Antony's?"

Jane looked down at the floor and clasped her shaking hands together. Was she really going to let Chase take her out among businessmen and people who knew her? Could she make that leap?

Maybe. Maybe she could.

She took a deep breath and clenched her hands into fists. "Either would be fine."

"Really?" That one word was a laugh of disbelief. "Well, all right, then. I'll pick you up at seven."

"Seven," she agreed, her pulse galloping. She was going to do this.

As if the world had been waiting for just this arrangement, the door to the meeting room opened, and

Jessie emerged with his attorney. His face was actually serious instead of apathetic. Maybe he really was growing up.

Peter Chase stood and inclined his head toward the lawyer. "All right, Billy," he said to Chase. "I should be just a minute."

Billy? Jane glanced toward him. "Billy?" she said, her smile stretching to a grin. "That's your name?" She was starting to laugh when she registered the way his mouth tightened, his eyes going dark. "What?" she asked, thinking he must really hate the name.

But he didn't answer her, and the name formed more fully in her mind.

Billy. Bill. William. That was what the *W* on his card stood for.

Chase watched her with a gravity that scared her.

"Billy," she repeated. "Billy Chase." And it finally hit her like a flat, brutal hand. Billy Chase.

"Oh, my God," Jane murmured.

"Jane," he said, his hand reaching out as if he'd touch her.

She jerked her arm out of his reach. "Oh, my God."

"It's no big deal."

No big *deal?* Jane rushed for the door.

"Hey," she heard her brother say. "Where's she going?" But she knew the footsteps following were Chase's.

She got to the elevator, but his hand closed over her elbow when she stopped to hit the button. "I can't…" she gasped.

"Jane, don't run off."

"You knew me." She heard her own breath rushing too fast past her lips.

"Let's talk somewhere private."

"No." She yanked her arm from his grip.

"Jane, come on."

"You *knew* me. Oh, my God." Billy Chase. A vague image emerged from deep in her memory banks of a cute boy with a Coke can in his hand. Every party she'd ever seen him at, he'd been drinking a Coke. During at least one of those parties, she'd sat on his lap and sucked at his tanned neck, thrilled with the way his dick got harder with each passing second.

Jane's eyes widened with a sudden thought. "That's why you asked me out."

"What?"

"You knew who I was. That's why you asked me out—"

"That's ridiculous."

"Because you knew I'd be *easy*."

"No!" he barked. "That is not true. Just calm down and listen to me."

The door to the office opened behind Chase, and Jessie walked out. "Dude," he said when he saw Jane. "I thought you left without me."

"Let's go," she ordered past numb lips, gesturing toward the opening elevator doors. Unfortunately, Chase stepped into the elevator, too, and they rode down to the first floor in pulsing silence.

Jane pictured herself as she'd been then, her nearly white hair and the black eyeliner she'd worn like a mask. The short skirts and belly-baring tops. But her appearance had been the least of it. She'd been desperate for male attention, and that desperation hadn't manifested itself subtly. Hell, she'd sat on Chase's lap and giggled at the feel of his erection.

What else had he seen her do?

They stepped out of the elevator and were in the parking lot within five footsteps.

"Jane, wait a minute, damn it."

"I've got to get Jessie home," she muttered.

"Jessie," Chase snapped, "go wait in the car. I need to talk to your sister."

Jane set her jaw and watched her treacherous brother saunter away.

"I didn't know who you were when I met you. I thought you were *cute*. That's why I asked you out."

"When did you know?" She felt as if she'd been violated and she wanted to know the exact moment it had happened. "At Ryders?"

"No, when your grandma called you Dynasty."

She nodded, crossing her arms together and squeezing tightly. "Right. Of course."

"I was shocked. I had no idea, even when Mac said he was your stepfather. But it doesn't matter."

"Of course it matters. I don't… No one knows."

"I know. And it doesn't matter to me."

She dug her nails into her elbows. "It matters to *me!* That girl is supposed to be dead. Gone. I don't even know what… Did I sleep with you?"

"What do you mean?"

"Did I sleep with you back then?"

"No!"

"Because I might not remember. Some men…some men I don't even remember."

"Jane—" his voice dropped to a hoarse whisper "—you were just a kid."

Cold sweat prickled her brow and her stomach tightened as if it might start rolling at any moment. "You said you were raised in Grand Junction."

"I was. We moved to this area when I was sixteen."

"Oh, God," she groaned. "I've got to go. I don't want to talk about this."

He said her name one last time, but she was already rushing toward her car, hand shoved into her purse, scrambling to find the keys. Jessie, lounging against the hood, raised a curious eyebrow at her mad scramble to open the door.

"What's up with that guy?" he asked.

"Nothing. Get in."

"Christ, he really got your panties in a twist."

"Shut up, Jess." She didn't know why she felt like throwing up. All that stuff she'd done as a teenager, all the ways she'd degraded herself… It had happened, whether Chase had known about it or not. But it had been like an old movie before. Now the memories felt like true memories again. Right there. Reminding her of exactly who she was.

"Oh, God." Jane sighed, then forced herself to take a deep breath. Okay, so he knew the truth about her. Maybe it wasn't that big a deal. He had no reason to tell anyone, and she wasn't tied to him.

She'd kept it casual. She'd kept him at a distance. Her original plan had been to use him for sex and then walk away. Despite Lori's little pep talk, Jane had to stick to the original plan.

This thing with Chase was officially over.

CHAPTER FIFTEEN

IT WAS SNOWING. May 20 and it was snowing. Jane stared at the fat flakes drifting past the window. The snow was like an order for her to relax and have a perfect night at home. She'd already ordered pizza, and her pay-per-view movie was starting in two minutes.

Tonight the outside world didn't exist. Her condo was muffled by the snow, a protective blanket keeping out all the craziness of her life.

Her butt hit the couch, but as soon as her fingers touched the remote, a sharp knock sounded on the door. *Pizza.* One nice thing about being single and lonely—she could order any toppings she wanted. Spicy sausage with mushrooms, jalapeños and green olives. And leftovers galore. Maybe she wouldn't leave her apartment for days.

Jane grabbed her wallet. She opened the door with a smile, but that smile froze when she spied the man standing there. Apparently fluffy snow didn't make for a good enough shield. The outside world was standing smack on her doorstep.

"Hello," Chase said, his eyes drifting over her sweatshirt and ten-year-old leggings. Her own eyes swept down his body in turn, and the sight of him sent turbulence shivering through her nerves.

Every time she'd seen Chase he'd been wearing jeans and some version of a T-shirt. But tonight he wore black slacks and a gray blazer brightened by a deep blue shirt.

"Oh," she said. He'd dressed up. For a date they weren't going on.

"I take it you weren't expecting me?"

"No," she answered flatly just as a car squealed up to the curb. A painfully tall teenage boy jumped out and rushed toward her with a pizza box. "I was expecting him."

"Ouch."

She completed the pizza/cash exchange, then stood there, holding the hot pizza and looking up at a new version of Chase. He was even hotter than the pizza, and the sight of him was breaking her heart.

"Did you forget about our date?"

"You know there's not going to be a date."

"No, I'm pretty sure I don't. If I'd given up on the date, I wouldn't have gone shopping for big-boy clothes today."

That almost made her smile, so Jane narrowed her eyes in defense. "We're not doing this. I can't see you anymore, Chase."

"Yes, you can. Nothing's changed."

"Everything's changed."

"Just because I know about your past? I've known about it for days now."

"Yes, but now *I* know. And I just… I can't get past it. I was so desperate to leave that girl behind that I changed *everything*. My appearance, my name, my behavior. I've practically given up my family just so I won't ever have to think about who I used to be."

Chase crossed his arms, then uncrossed them, then took the pizza box from her hands before she could shift it out of his reach. "Let me bring this in for you."

"No!" She dived for the box, but he slipped past her, invading her little bubble of movie-night peace. "Damn it!" she screamed.

"Wow." Chase shot her a look of amazement. "Did you just say that, Miss Jane?"

"Shut up and get the hell out of my house!"

"Nuh-uh," he said, popping open the pizza box as he set it on the granite countertop. "What the heck have you done to this pizza?"

"It's none of your—"

"You've ruined a perfectly good pie. I mean, green olives, Jane? Come on. That's disgusting."

"Chase." She sighed. *"Please."*

He closed the box and leaned against the counter. "Something bad happened to you, didn't it?"

Icy flakes floated against her skin, so Jane reluctantly closed the door behind her, letting her weight rest against the cold wood. "No."

"It did."

She shook her head, teeth pressed together.

"You want me to believe that you were on that path as a teenager, drinking and sleeping around and partying all night, and then, out of the blue, you decided to straighten out?"

Her skin was colder now than it had been outside. "Yes."

"You're saying that's what you *want* me to believe?"

"Yes."

Chase put his hand flat on the counter and stared down at it for a long moment. Lines appeared around his mouth that she'd never seen before.

She wouldn't tell him. She'd never told anyone.

"All right, then, Jane. That's what I'll believe."

Relief swelled so strongly through her that she had to put a hand to her stomach to settle it.

Chase looked toward the television. "What are we watching?"

Shaking her head, she told herself to send him away, make him leave. He reminded her of things she didn't want to be reminded of. He was everything she didn't want.

But that relief was still rocking through her, leaving her giddy and susceptible to the sparkle of mischief in his eyes. He knew who she was, and he still wanted to talk to her, sit with her, watch a movie.

Just that made tears burn in her eyes.

And in truth, despite all her fears and hang-ups and snobbishness, she *wanted* to sit on the couch with him and watch an action movie. It would feel so normal.

Somehow he turned her from a steel-spined martinet to a wilting flower.

Jane whispered the name of the movie, and Chase's smile bloomed into a grin. "You're kidding. I haven't seen that one yet, and I can't say that very often. Do you want my green olives? And my mushrooms?"

"Yes."

"Well, all right, then." Chase shrugged out of his coat and began opening and closing cabinets until he found plates. Jane stayed where she was, back pressed to the door, and watched him.

Her weakness in the face of his smile scared her. How many times in their short relationship had she decided that it was over? And how many times had he brushed her resolutions aside as if they were made of cottonwood fluff?

"Diet Coke?" Chase groaned, half his body hidden behind the fridge door. "I think I might cry."

"Sorry."

"I'll have orange juice. What do you want?"

Jane finally snapped from her daze and went to help him in the kitchen. And every time their bodies touched, Jane grew more and more afraid of the comfort settling deep into her bones.

CHASE LAY IN THE BLUE GLOW of the muted television, his arm snug around Jane's warm body. She was asleep, they hadn't so much as shared a kiss, and yet this was one of the best dates he'd ever had.

An action movie, spicy pizza and Jane. Pure heaven.

He'd known she'd wanted to keep her past secret, but he hadn't expected the kind of stricken panic he'd seen in her eyes in the lawyer's office. Jane had looked like a woman faced with her worst nightmare. And that nightmare had been Chase.

Christ. He'd had no idea what to do, so he'd let her run. Too bad for her, she'd already agreed to this date. Now she was snuggled up against him, fingers laced in his, heart beating slowly and steadily against his wrist.

Whatever it was she'd run from, she was here now.

And she'd been lying about not being a neat freak. There wasn't a speck of dust in this place, not even on the cable box or television. Not only was it clean, but there was a vase of fresh flowers on a little table in front of the window. The occasional glint of a white snowflake pressed against the glass before melting.

Chase felt his bones molding to the couch as his eyelids grew heavier. The smell of Jane's shampoo whispered into him on every breath. Heaven.

He must have fallen asleep, because his eyes popped open when his little piece of heaven was invaded by a frantic staccato knock. Jane's head cracked against his chin.

"What is it?" she asked hoarsely.

"Someone's at the door."

She jumped up, knocking one of the empty plates off the coffee table as she spun toward the door.

"Hey, wait a second. It's late. Let me get it." She didn't wait, but he jumped up fast enough to get to the door before she'd finished unlocking it.

Chase inched the door open and cringed when he saw a uniformed police officer standing in the snow.

Jane yanked the door all the way open. "What's wrong?" she demanded.

"Ma'am, are you Jane Morgan?"

"Yes."

"We're looking for Jessie MacKenzie. Is he here?"

He felt the way her body jumped. "No. He's at his grandmother's house."

"We were told he might be here."

Her phone started ringing, but Jane ignored it,

shaking her head. "Who told you that? And why are you looking for him?"

"It's just for routine questioning, ma'am." He glanced down at his notebook. "Mrs. Olive MacKenzie said he might be here. Have you seen Jessie?"

"No."

The officer snapped his notebook closed just as Jane's answering machine picked up. "Dynasty!" Grandma Olive's voice screeched. "The pigs are on their way! It's the fuzz!"

"Oh, Jesus," Jane muttered.

"The heat is on! The cops came sniffing around here and I sent them after you. Not sure what they want, though. Call me back and let me know."

The officer looked down, but not before Chase caught a half smile flickering over his face. The man coughed, and he was all business again when he looked up. "Ma'am, we just need to ask Jessie a few questions. You haven't seen him?"

"No." She shook her head. "What are these questions about?"

"Just call me if he gets in touch." The officer handed over a card and Jane took it gingerly and shut the door.

"Oh, God, what's he done?" she muttered, moving to grab her phone from the coffee table. She dialed, but her face made it obvious there was no answer. "His phone's off."

"Do you know where he is?"

"No. Maybe he's set it to voice mail." Head down, she tapped out a text message with her thumbs.

"What do you want to do?" Chase asked.

"I don't know. Let me call Grandma Olive and my

mom, and see what they know." Five minutes later she'd talked to both women, but the lost look hadn't faded from her face. No one knew anything.

Though he was fairly sure it was a bad idea, Chase offered the only solution he had. "Do you want to try Ryders?"

She didn't hesitate for even a heartbeat. "Yes. Will you take me? Please? I'll get changed." Jane disappeared up the stairs, calling out "Thank you!" as she ran.

Chase put on his brand-new shoes and shrugged into his coat, cringing at the thought of going to Ryders looking as if he'd raided George Clooney's closet. But this was the kind of thing a man did when he was falling for a woman.

And he was falling for her, no question. A dangerous proposition, falling for Jane Morgan. *Complicated* didn't even begin to describe her. She'd seemed so simple at first: an uptight secretary with an innocent curiosity about a tattooed bad boy.

Ha. He couldn't have been more wrong. Now he was embarrassed to think he'd planned to add a little excitement to her proper life. Instead, she'd left him reeling. Jane Morgan was the female equivalent of dynamite. Innocuous and harmless...until it found a spark and exploded.

Chase was doomed.

When he heard her footsteps, he looked up, wondering which incarnation of Jane he'd find. She hadn't dressed for Ryders this time. She wore jeans again, and heeled boots and a pretty red sweater. They looked like a real couple actually, and Chase found himself smiling despite the circumstances. "Ready?"

She grabbed her coat and they dashed to his truck.

"So," he said after a few silent minutes on the road. Jane looked up from her cell phone. "How did you pick 'Jane'?"

Her gaze sharpened, and even in the faint light of the dashboard glow Chase could see her replaying their earlier conversation. Yes, he'd agreed not to ask about her teenage years. No, he hadn't promised not to ask any questions at all.

Grimacing, she faced the windshield again. "I chose the most vanilla name I could think of."

"Good job. It's pretty vanilla."

"Thank you."

"And Morgan?"

"It's my mother's maiden name."

"I like your hair now," he said. "It's pretty."

Jane reached out and poked her finger at the stereo. "Isn't there a local news channel? There's an AM station, isn't there?"

"I think so."

"I'm worried. Don't you think… Don't you think something bad might have happened?"

"Another woman?"

Jane nodded and began scanning stations. "And where the hell is Jessie? I swear, he's got the self-control of a five-year-old. He was supposed to stay *home*."

Chase eased the truck up to a higher speed, aware that Jane was frantically tapping her foot. "I'll call my dad," he volunteered. "Maybe he's got a contact at the department." He glanced at the clock, wondering if it was hopeless. Ten o'clock. Surely Dad was passed out by now.

He answered on the fifth ring, voice hoarse, but words only slightly slurred. Chase explained the situation, and his dad volunteered to call a friend with the sheriff's department.

They pulled up to Ryders and Jane jumped out before he could get around to open her side. He caught up at the front door, and noticed that snowflakes stuck to her eyelashes. "Where are your glasses?"

"I must have left them at home."

"You don't need them?"

"I do. But I can see about thirty feet before things start getting a little strange."

"So they're mostly part of your disguise."

She tossed him an irritated look and reached for the door. "Come on."

The place was packed, warm and humid inside from the press of bodies. Voices rose to a roar over the music. After so many hours spent in the quiet of Jane's home, Chase felt vaguely disoriented.

Jane shook her head. "Even if he's here, we might not find him."

"We may as well look. And no, we are not splitting up. Let's go."

They headed to the bar first to ask Arlo if he'd seen Jessie, but there were two strangers pulling drinks. Chase kept his hand on Jane's elbow as they began to edge through the crowd, searching for her brother. Chase spied Jessie's two friends at the same time he felt Jane stiffen.

She leaned up and shouted in his ear. "I'm going to talk to them!"

"I'll do it," he answered, but Jane shook her head

and raised her hand to signal him to stay. He didn't like it, but what the hell. He wasn't her father. Still, he wasn't a dog either. Chase hung back a few feet before moving in her direction.

Apparently Jane didn't think flirting would work without the skimpy clothing. She offered a nervous smile and began talking right away. But she was wrong. Jane looked adorable and sexy in her soft sweater and ponytail. Sexier than she had been in her miniskirt, even.

She gestured with her phone, talking faster, but the guys both shook their heads. The shorter one turned away to nibble on the ear of the girl cuddled up to him. She didn't look twenty-one, and Chase found himself watching her, thinking of Jane.

He still couldn't believe the change in her. Amazing.

Chase jumped a little at the feel of a hand sliding along his waist. Glancing down, he found a redhead latching onto his side. "Uh, hello."

She pressed closer, offering a smile and a startling view of her cleavage. The closer she pressed, the more the view expanded, like dough rising in an oven.

"Er…" Chase tried to shift away, to no avail.

"I've never seen *you* here before." Her smile, bright white and wide, drew his attention away from her breasts for a minute. She was kind of pretty, but her eyes were a bit too unfocused for Chase to feel flattered.

"Yeah, I'm not really into the bar scene." He squirmed again, trying to find a way to break her hold without physically picking her up and moving her.

"Well, you're super cute," she said without loosening one finger from its hold on his waist. Her long hair slid along his arm.

"Um. Thanks. But I'm here with someone."

"Yeah? Well, if she were smart she wouldn't leave a big old piece of man candy like you unguarded." She chuckled, and her cleavage jiggled enticingly. "Her loss."

He shook his head. "I don't think—"

"Excuse me," an ominously soft female voice interrupted.

Chase's head jerked up so fast the room spun. Smack in the middle of that spinning was a tight bundle of angry Jane.

Her lips flattened into a thin line as she narrowed her eyes at the woman. "Would you please remove your hands from him?"

"I don't think so, darlin'," the woman drawled, tightening her hold on Chase. He raised his free arm to show his helplessness.

Red spots appeared high on Jane's cheeks. "I don't want to be rude, but… Get. Off. Him." The words were surprisingly clear considering her teeth hadn't unclenched the whole time.

Chase was starting to feel nervous. "Jane, it's fine. Just… Lady, you'd better go on."

The woman tossed her hair over her shoulder, whacking Jane in the face with it. "I'll go on when I'm ready to go on. She ain't the kind of woman who can satisfy a man like you, baby." Her breasts slid over his arm when she wiggled against him.

Jane drew in a deep breath, her nostrils flared and he saw the flash of rage in her eyes as she went to the dark side. *"Get your tits off him, you heifer!"*

"Jane!" Chase coughed, a shocked laugh choking off his voice. But the woman finally let him go.

She seemed to weigh her options, then put a hand on her hip as if she'd decided to argue. "You can't—"

Jane took a step forward, jaw jutting out. "Do you really want all these men to see you without your weave? Because you're about to lose it."

"Oh, Jesus." Chase laughed. The redhead made her decision and flounced away.

Arms crossed, Jane watched until she was at least ten feet away before turning her glare on Chase. "You want me to leave so you can get a closer look at those?"

"No!" He held up his hands in complete surrender. "I couldn't get away from her."

"Funny, because you look awfully big and strong. Almost like a full-grown man."

Chase gave her his best puppy-dog eyes, silently begging for forgiveness.

"Oh, come on," she snapped. "They haven't seen Jessie. He's not here."

Chase studied the faces as they made their way to the door, but there was no sign of Jane's brother. They both took a deep breath when they reached the relative peace of the dark parking lot.

He let her stalk to the truck without a word, but when she reached for the handle, Chase wrapped his fingers around her wrist and turned her toward him. "What was all that about?"

"All what?"

"Potty-mouthed Jane."

Chin inching higher, she shrugged.

"You were jealous."

"I was irritated with Jessie's friends."

"No." He felt his mouth twitch into a smile. "You were jealous. Because you like me."

"I was stressed," she insisted, turning back toward the truck. "And I was in my fair share of fights during my misspent youth. I know how to handle myself."

Chase wasn't about to let her blow that off. Her little tantrum in there had been pretty damn sexy. He snuck his arm around her shoulders and turned her back, dipping down to nuzzle her neck at the same time.

"Chase!" she complained, but half a second later her head was bowing away, giving him better access to the tender skin of her neck.

"You like me," he murmured against her pulse. "Just admit it." He pressed his tongue there, sucking lightly.

"Oh…" Jane sighed. Her hands reached up to clutch his jacket. Snowflakes touched the back of his skull, like tiny bites of ice.

"I think I'm falling for you, Jane." He dragged his mouth up to hers and kissed her before she could protest. She would, he knew that, but he didn't plan on paying attention to her arguments.

She tried to shake her head, but he wouldn't move his mouth. A tense moment passed, and then she was kissing him back, rubbing her tongue hard against his. The taste of her was a drug, wrapping around his nerves, dulling the feel of the snow on his neck.

He could kiss her forever. Just kiss her and nothing else. But Jane wouldn't allow that. She'd want more, and he'd give in without any fight at all.

Ending the kiss with a faint taste of her bottom lip, Chase framed her face in his hands so she'd have to meet his gaze. "I'm falling for you," he repeated.

"No."

He let her go. "You have no say in it. Sorry." Reaching past her, he opened the truck door. "Where to?"

"Chase, we can't… There's no future for us. None!"

"You want to go to your grandma's house?"

She put her hand flat to his chest and pushed him. He took a step back so she'd feel some satisfaction. "Listen to me!"

"I'll do whatever I want, Jane. I just thought you deserved fair warning."

"Then you need to leave. Just go!"

"I'm your ride, darlin'. And right now your brother is more important than your fear of genuine emotion."

Her jaw dropped. "My *what?*"

Chase rolled his eyes. "Get in the truck, Jane. We'll talk about this after we find Jessie."

She choked on her outrage a little, still staring at him as if he'd just grown a third eye. But finally she bit out, "Fine," and climbed into the truck.

Fine was never a good thing from a woman, and it would likely be an uncomfortable ride, but Chase was glad he'd said it. A pressure was gone from his chest, as if those words had weighed a ton. But he made a sincere effort to hide his smile as they pulled onto the road and headed toward Carbondale. Jane wouldn't appreciate it at all.

His cell phone rang like an alarm, startling Jane's heart into a stampede. She was getting a stiff neck from holding her head perfectly straight, but when Chase answered his phone, she allowed herself to look in his direction.

VICTORIA DAHL225

He was falling for her.

Just that was a frightening complication, but the way her heart had responded to those words was even more disturbing. It had *strained* in her chest, as if it wanted her to jump up and down or throw her arms around him and squeal.

Her second response had been abject terror. But *not* because she was afraid of genuine emotion. It wasn't that at all.

Jane glared at him in remembered anger. Then she registered the deep lines of worry in his forehead as he listened to whoever was on the line.

"Who is it?" she whispered.

He held up a hand. "And that's all he would say?" When he pressed his fingers to his forehead, Jane began to worry. "Shit," he muttered. "All right, Dad. Thanks. I'll talk to you later."

Chase snapped his phone shut and wrapped both hands around the steering wheel. "We've got a big problem."

"What?"

"They found another girl."

Panic blasted through her body like lightning. "A girl? A murdered girl?"

"Yes."

"Oh, God. Oh, God. This is…"

"Her body was found in her house tonight. Cause of death was unnatural."

"She was strangled?"

"My dad's contact didn't know any more. He did say the time of death hasn't been determined, so my dad suspects it wasn't within the last hour or two."

"Who was it?"

Chase shook his head, the bones of his knuckles showing white through his skin. "I don't know. It was in Aspen, though, not Carbondale or Garfield County."

The panic twisted through her, squeezing her stomach too tight. "Mom should never have bailed him out."

Chase shot her a hard glance. "You think he did it?"

"I think if he was still in jail, we'd have proof he hadn't done it."

By the time they drove into Carbondale and turned onto Grandma Olive's street, Jane's body burned with tension.

She spotted Jessie as soon as the headlights flashed over the front porch. "He's here."

The truck rocked to a halt and she jumped out and ran across the grass.

"He just showed up," Olive snapped. "Won't tell me where he's been."

"Okay," Jane panted. "All right. I'll talk to him, Grandma Olive. You go on and get out of the cold."

Jessie muttered, "I wanna get out of the cold, too," but his grandmother slammed the door in his face.

Jane grabbed his arm and dug her nails into the leather of his coat. "Where were you?"

"I had to get out, all right? Grandma was watching a *Fantasy Island* marathon, and I couldn't take it any-more. She's only got one fricking TV in that house."

She shook him, hard. "Where *were* you?"

"God." He tore his wrist from her grasp. "I was with a girl, all right? Calm down."

A girl. He couldn't mean… "What girl?"

"None of your business, Jane."

"Jessie!" she screamed. *"What girl?"*

The weight of Chase's hand was a sudden comfort on her shoulder. She'd forgotten he was there.

"Jessie," he said calmly, "this is serious. Your sister needs to know where you were."

He finally seemed to get it. Her brother's eyes went wide, and she was relieved to see no sign he'd gotten high. "I was with a girl named Eve. It was only for an hour or something. She just dropped me off."

Jane swallowed hard, fearing that she might sob with relief. "She was here?"

"*Yes.* Dude, what's going on?"

For a moment there, she'd thought… She'd *feared*…

Jane couldn't speak, and she was impossibly grateful when Chase cleared his throat and stepped forward. "The police want to talk to you, Jess. There may have been another murder."

"Oh, fuck," Jessie said. Even in the moonlight she could see his face go pale.

Now that her doubt was gone, fury took its place. "Your lawyer told you to stay home! No drinking or smoking and *no girls.*"

"I'm not a fucking monk, Jane. And I didn't do anything wrong!"

"Will this Eve give you an alibi?"

He shrugged. "I think so. She doesn't have a boyfriend or anything."

"We're calling your lawyer. Right now."

To her credit, the attorney answered on the first ring, despite the late hour. Jane babbled out the whole story, feeling more calm with every no-nonsense question the woman asked.

"Stay with him," Ms. Holloway said. "Don't let him go anywhere. I'll call you back in fifteen minutes."

For the full fifteen minutes Jane paced the tiny confines of Grandma Olive's dining room. Everyone else was crowded into the living area. Jessie lounged with his feet on the arm of the couch, of course, able to relax despite the threat hanging over him like a sword. He even charmed Grandma Olive into cackling at a joke or two.

The old woman was relaxed enough to offer margaritas, but when no one took her up on the offer, she poured herself a glass, dropped into her recliner and popped out her dentures to enjoy it.

Chase seemed surprisingly unfazed.

Finally the phone rang, and Jane answered it so quickly that she cracked her cheekbone with the phone. "Hello?"

"All right, here's what I've arranged. Jessie will voluntarily meet with an Aspen detective tomorrow at ten. I'll be there. Don't worry. I've made clear that he has an alibi for the whole day, but he's happy to offer questions if they feel it will help move the investigation along."

"Okay." Good. That sounded great.

"I already spoke with Mr. Chase and he's going to get as much information as he can on his end. Tonight Jessie needs to stay sober and get to bed. *Nothing* else."

Jane nodded. "All right."

"Let me speak to him for a moment."

She happily handed the phone to her brother, and even more happily turned into Chase's arms when he offered comfort.

"It's okay," he whispered. "You're okay."

In that moment Chase's threat of falling in love felt more like peace than a complication.

CHAPTER SIXTEEN

JANE STARED at the familiar door of Greg Nunn's apartment as if it was the entryway to hell itself. The evening sun belied any dark imaginings, but it didn't make her feel better. She didn't walk up the short sidewalk or knock on the door; she simply stared at it.

How could she do this? How could she *not?*

She glanced over her shoulder to see Chase watching carefully from his truck where it was parked at the curb. He rolled down the window. "You okay?" he called.

"Yes," she lied.

Her brother hadn't been arrested, but the murder had made it to the paper, along with a note that a local man had been brought in for questioning. There'd also been one ominous line indicating that police were not yet ruling out the possibility that the murder could have been linked with the earlier death of Michelle Brown.

If her brother's name was linked to a serial killing or, God forbid, if he was framed for those deaths...

She had to do this.

Jane walked the last few feet to the door and knocked.

At first there was no answer. If Greg wasn't home, she was off the hook for a few hours, maybe for a whole day. But Jane knocked again and waited. Unfortunately, Greg answered the door a few seconds later. Her heart plummeted.

"Jane?" His eyes widened with what looked like pleasant surprise. "What are you doing here?"

"I need to talk to you."

"I'm glad! Come on in."

"No! I just… I can't come in."

Eyes narrowing, he leaned against the doorjamb and crossed his arms. He was wearing a cardigan. An honest-to-God cashmere cardigan. Jane resisted the urge to look toward Chase to see the way his muscles bulged in his worn T-shirt, but her control didn't matter. Greg's gaze rose to look over her shoulder.

"Who the hell is that?"

"Nobody," she said automatically, but the word sent a shock of painful guilt through her heart. Crud. Drawing a deep breath, Jane squared her shoulders and made herself stop wringing her hands. "I need to, um…I need to talk to you about Jessie MacKenzie."

"Who?" he snapped.

"Jessie MacKenzie. The police suspect that he's been involved somehow in those murders. I figured you might know something."

"What the hell?" His groomed eyebrows drew together. "What does any of this have to do with you?"

Jane would've swallowed in nervousness, but her throat was too dry to manage it. If there was anything worse than the prospect of asking a bitter ex-boyfriend for help, it had to be this. Asking him for help while explaining that your life was a lie, and a messy one at that.

"I know that Jessie couldn't have done it. The police act as if they don't believe me, so I'm coming to you for help. You said that you genuinely cared about me...."

His mouth twisted with impatience. "I said I *had* feelings for you. Past tense. Regardless, what possible interest could you have in Jessie MacKenzie?"

For a moment she considered blaming Chase. *The guy in the car is Chase. I work with him. Jessie is a friend of his and he needs help.* It would be an easier connection to admit, but the lie wouldn't last through one inquiring phone call to police. And it wouldn't be the truth. The last thing Jessie needed was lies piled on top of his situation.

Jane wanted to look down, but she met Greg's gaze straight on and spoke over the mad pounding of her heart. "Jessie's my brother."

That knocked the impatience off his face. "Excuse me?"

"He's my brother."

"Jessie *MacKenzie?*"

"Yes. So I wanted to know if—"

"Jessie MacKenzie is your *brother?*" Now his lips were drawn so tightly down that white showed at the edges. "You're kidding me, right?"

"No," she bit out.

"You weren't friends with Michelle Brown. You were calling for your brother."

"Yes," she admitted, her pulse pounding faster.

His gaze swept up and down her body. "This has got to be a fucking joke, right? Your dad's an ex-con? A murderer?"

"My stepfather," she muttered. "And that murder

conviction was overturned. He was never charged again. He didn't do it."

"*That's* what you want to talk about?" he growled. "You lied to me. You've been lying to me for months."

"I'm sorry, Greg. I never… I don't really like to talk about my family—"

"No wonder!"

"I didn't lie about them. I just—"

"You let me think you were from a decent family! And you're nothing but garbage."

Jane's chest burned with anger, but she couldn't let it out. She needed his help.

"And you proved it by trying to coerce information out of me for a murderer."

"He didn't do it."

"I really… I can't believe I almost took a piece of trash home to meet my parents."

Shock sang through her body at his words. She should have expected them, but she hadn't. No one had called her trash in a decade. No one except her, anyway.

The shock broke quickly into old pain. Jane stuffed it down where it belonged. "I wanted to speak with you about Jessie's case. I know what the police suspect him of. And I just want you to take a closer look at the evidence. For me."

"For *you?*" Greg had never struck her as anything other than a decent person. Aggressive and short-tempered yes, but decent. But now…now he looked ugly and cruel, cheeks flushed and eyes bright with rage. "You broke it off with *me,* Jane. Now you're standing in my doorway with your nose still in the air and asking me for help?" The bitter sneer in his voice was not a good sign. If he wanted her to grovel, she would grovel.

"I'm sorry I broke up with you, Greg. It wasn't working." Her brain offered up an excuse. "We're from two different worlds."

He cocked his head. "Now, that's something you might be right about. *My* brother's not a killer."

"Neither is mine! I swear to you, Greg, he didn't do it. I *know* that. That latest girl, she was killed the day before she was found, wasn't she?"

"Where did you hear that?"

"It doesn't matter. What does matter is that Jesse was with me that day. He couldn't have killed her."

Greg sniffed. "You want me to go to my boss and tell him I've cleared a murder suspect on the word of his sister? Maybe I'll also mention that I used to sleep with you."

"Regardless, I—"

"'Hey, boss,'" he mimicked, "'my ex-girlfriend is a skank from a family of criminals.' That'd be a great note in my file when promotion time comes around."

"All right," she snapped. "I'm sorry I hurt your feelings, Greg, but this is more serious than your damaged pride. We're talking about somebody's life."

"We're talking about a few lives, Jane. Two women are dead, maybe three, and from what I hear there's plenty of evidence that your brother did it. So get the hell out of here. Now."

"He didn't do it, and I'm providing you with evidence that he didn't! On Monday evening he was with *me*. We met with his attorney and then stopped at the grocery store before having dinner with his grand-mother. You can check with his attorney. You can check the security cameras at the store. He was with *me*."

"And how late did dinner run? I've got a feeling Grandma doesn't eat at nine o'clock."

Jane clenched her teeth together. She didn't know the exact time of death. Mr. Chase's contact had revealed only that she'd died about twenty-four hours before she was found.

When her fingers went numb, she realized that she'd twisted them tightly together. "Can you at least look into it? Please? Look at the evidence with a new eye. Just assume, for a minute, that it wasn't him."

"We treat every case with the same objectivity. Nobody is out to get your brother. If he didn't do it, he won't be charged."

"Oh, please. Don't give me that."

"Jane," he snapped, then paused to take a deep breath. "I'm sure his lawyer will be contacted with anything important. I couldn't show you favoritism even if I cared to. And I don't."

Hoping to see some glimmer of reason in his eyes, Jane stared at him for a long moment. *Please help me,* she pleaded silently. But Greg's scowl was back.

"Who's that guy, Jane?" He jerked his chin in the direction of the truck. "Are you working your way back to your roots?"

Jane set her shoulders and calmly turned to leave.

She should have waited to break it off with him. Why had she been in such a hurry? If she'd held on for one more week…

But the thought made her shudder, and her instincts

had just been confirmed. He'd liked her well enough when she was sleeping with him, but now she was trash. Just trash.

She slipped into the truck.

"Jane? You okay?"

"Yes."

Chase pulled away from the curb, but she could feel his attention on her. "That didn't seem to go well."

"He was posturing. Maybe when he gets into the office he'll take another look at the files."

"Mmm."

She'd claimed to be okay, but was she? Jane closed her eyes and took an internal inventory. She'd just revealed part of her past to Greg. And she felt…okay. It was the part of her past she would have been forced to reveal if their relationship had continued.

Yes, he might spread it around, let other people know where she came from, but her family was hardly the worst of it.

She was okay.

"So," Chase said, "is that the kind of guy you usually date?"

"Yes."

"Doctors, lawyers, that sort of thing?"

"Yes."

"Mmm," he said again. Jane wondered what that noncommittal hum could mean.

She hadn't wanted to bring Chase along, but he'd decided that every solitary woman in Aspen was in danger. He also seemed to have decided that Jane was *his* solitary woman and he wasn't going to let anything happen to her. In all honesty, she probably could have convinced him to leave her alone. He had no control over her. She could've kicked him out.

But the truth was that she had the perfect excuse to have a few more unwise days with him, so she'd asked him to drive her to Greg's house.

"So what about guys like me?" he asked, startling her out of her thoughts.

"What do you mean?"

"You said you'd never done this before. I assume you meant you don't usually keep a guy like me on the side?"

"No!"

Chase nodded, his hand hanging casually over the steering wheel, as if he hadn't just said something outrageous. "Well, that guy doesn't look like he'd be able to handle someone like you."

"What?" Jane heard her voice echo through the cab of his truck and realized she was shouting. "What do you mean, 'someone like me'?"

When Chase turned to her, his face was flushed with anger. "I'm not calling you trash like your *classy* boyfriend did, if that's what you mean."

All the blood seemed to drain from her head. She felt clammy and cool and confused. "You heard that?"

"Yes. And I came damn close to getting out and putting my fist in his face, but I figured that wouldn't help your brother."

"No," she murmured, shame drifting over her like wisps of fog. She'd let Greg call her garbage and trash. She'd stood there and let him say those words, and Chase had heard them. For some reason that was worse than knowing what Greg thought of her.

Chase cursed under his breath and wrapped both

hands tightly around the steering wheel. "When I said he didn't seem like he could handle a woman like you, I meant that he seemed like a jackass. And a wimp. And a pussy."

Her throat got even drier.

"I meant that he wasn't good enough for you."

Oh, God. Why did Chase have to be the one to say the right things? Why did he have to be the man who made her feel tight with need? "I called it off with Greg because I wasn't in love with him. And in the end, I guess I didn't really like him."

"I'm glad to hear that. I would have doubted your judgment otherwise, Jane."

"I suppose. But he wasn't that bad before. Maybe he'll come through. Maybe he'll give Jessie a fair shake."

Chase shrugged. "We'll see," he said, but his voice still held the censure of disappointment.

Jane stared out the window and willed herself not to cry.

CHAPTER SEVENTEEN

"WHY IS THERE A HEAVY bag in your spare bedroom?"

Jane looked up from the book she was reading to try to take her mind off her worry. The book wasn't working. Neither was the movie playing on television. "I box for exercise."

"Really? Boxing? That's kind of hot."

"You say that about a lot of things."

"Seriously, you sweating and half-naked while you beat the shit out of that big red bag? That's hot."

"Why would I be half-naked?"

"Er… Because you like me?"

Jane rolled her eyes and punched him in the arm.

"Ouch. Do that a couple more times and I'll give you what you want."

"Shut up!" Jane laughed, throwing a few light punches at his shoulder.

"Oh, yeah," he said. "Do it, baby."

"I thought I was supposed to be half-naked," she teased.

"Shit, you're right. Come 'ere." Chase unzipped the hoodie she was wearing while Jane pretended to slap his hands away. He was just sliding his hands under her shirt when his cell phone rang. His hands didn't stop sliding.

"Chase!" she protested as his palms covered her breasts. "Answer the phone."

"Later." His hot mouth sucked at her throat.

"It might be important."

"*This* is important."

Yes, it was. It really was. Especially when his teeth scraped down to her shoulder. The phone stopped ringing, and Jane sank back into the couch, sighing when Chase followed her down. His body pressed into her....

And his phone rang again.

"*Shit,*" he barked, pushing up to sit on the edge of the couch and grab his phone. "Don't move." He flipped open the phone. "This is Chase." His back straightened, and Jane heard an urgent male voice speaking rapidly on the other end of the line.

"Okay," he said. "Okay, we'll be right there."

Jane jumped off the couch and began pulling on her shoes. "What is it?" she begged when he closed the phone.

"My dad has something to show us."

"What is it?"

He shook his head. "Something to do with a police report. He said he'd tell us when we got there."

Jane grabbed her purse and coat and they were out the door. The fifteen-minute ride seemed to take an hour, but Jane comforted herself with assurances that he must have found something good.

Jane raced up to the door and knocked, but couldn't make herself wait for him to answer. Horrified with her own rudeness, she pulled the door open herself. "Mr. Chase?"

"Hello, Jane! Would you like a beer?"

"No, thank you. What did you find?"

"Hey, Billy!" he said when Chase pushed past Jane. "Can I get you a brewski?"

"No, Dad." Jane could hear the edge of impatience in Chase's voice. Or perhaps she was projecting her own vibrating impatience onto him.

"Mr. Chase," she pleaded, "did you find something?"

"Oh, I sure did. I already called Ms. Holloway to tell her. You two want to sit down?"

Jane launched herself toward a chair and sat down so quickly it skidded across the linoleum. She counted to ten while Chase approached and took the chair next to hers. She made it all the way to twenty while his father puttered around, straightening out files and re-arranging papers.

Finally he sat down and opened one of the files. "As soon as I heard about the last murder victim, I went down there to see if she'd filed a complaint about a stolen purse in the past couple of months."

Jane swallowed. Maybe it wasn't good news after all.

"I found the report. It's all a matter of public record. Her purse was stolen from a place called Steel. Jessie mentioned it in one of his interviews."

"Oh, no," Jane whispered.

"But—and here's the important part—she said her purse was stolen on May thirteenth."

Jane frowned. "The thirteenth?"

"Jessie was arrested on the seventh. He was in custody on the thirteenth."

"It couldn't have been him."

Mr. Chase shook his head. "It couldn't have been him."

Overwhelmed, Jane grabbed Chase's hand and squeezed it. "This is it, right? This is why they didn't arrest him again. They don't have anything."

Chase's dad smiled. "They don't have anything. Jessie admits he stole Michelle Brown's purse, but there's no evidence he was involved in the theft of Kelly Anderson's backpack, and he couldn't possibly have committed this last theft."

Jane nodded, blinking back tears. "So all we have to worry about are the legitimate charges of theft."

"Probably. But let's not get ahead of ourselves. Cops don't like to give up on a hunch. Right now Jessie is their only lead, as far as we know, and they won't want to let him go. I want to give them something else to think about."

"Like what? I don't understand."

"We're going to go through these files and find something they've missed. Even if it's just an idea. Every single page. You sure you don't want that beer now?"

Jane shook her head, and they got to work.

An hour later they'd made a list of possible connections between the women. Most of them were tenuous, and the police had probably connected most of the dots, but it was better than nothing.

Churches, schools, doctors, friends. If those details had been collected, they hadn't been included with the evidence provided to Jessie's lawyer. But despite all their hypothesizing, it was clear that the women were linked by the thefts.

"All the reports were taken by different officers, but that's not to say another officer couldn't have taken an interest in each woman as she came in."

Jane couldn't quite believe what Chase's dad was saying. He'd been a policeman himself. "You really think an officer could be involved?"

"I don't think so, but that doesn't mean it should be dismissed out of hand. Now then, her purse has been stolen, she's filed the report—now what does she do?"

"Cancels her credit cards," Jane suggested.

Mr. Chase wrote that down. "And maybe her cell phone account?"

Chase flipped open a file. "The first two had the same brand of phone."

His father raised an eyebrow. "Maybe it's someone working at the local cell phone store." His hand flew over the notebook. "I noticed all the women reported that their keys were in their purses. They must have had their locks changed, too."

Jane added, "And they would've needed a new driver's license first thing."

She felt Chase's elbow touch her. "Don't go down to the DMV anytime soon. There could be some psychopath there taking license pictures."

By the time they left, Jane was nearly giddy with hope. Mr. Chase would give all these ideas to Ms. Holloway, and Ms. Holloway would make clear to the police that they'd better start following up on these other leads before the press got the idea that they weren't doing their jobs.

Pretty soon Jessie would be cleared, and Jane's life would get back to normal. Only, she was beginning to suspect she no longer knew what normal looked like.

ON WEDNESDAY AFTERNOON, Jane was sitting at her desk in Jennings Architecture, looking around with a sense of wonder. She'd been back at work for three days. The mess of indecipherable notes that Mr. Jennings had piled on her desk had been weeded down to two remaining scribbles.

These were the kinds of mysteries she enjoyed. What had Mr. Jennings meant when he'd written "8 south boy here"? He had no recollection of such a thing, so it was up to Jane to puzzle it out. The second note was less cryptic—"Thursday 9:00"—but equally mysterious. Still, that puzzle would likely solve itself on Thursday at nine o'clock, so Jane was less intrigued.

But her sense of amazement had nothing to do with her personal little *Da Vinci Code* and more to do with the utter calm around her. Jessie's lawyer had played her cards with great success. It had helped that the lead detective on the case was losing faith in the Jessie-as-serial-killer scenario. A preliminary report from the medical examiner placed the girl's death at a time when Jessie's alibi was strongest.

The detective hadn't appreciated the lawyer's suggestions of how to conduct the investigation, but Mr. Chase had dropped the same thoughts into the ear of his contact at the sheriff's office. Hopefully someone would pick up on a hotter trail than Jessie MacKenzie. But regardless of whether or not they found the real killer, the D.A. in charge of Jessie's case had made overtures of a deal. They were no longer awaiting additional charges. The case was moving forward.

"Thank God," Jane murmured just as Outlook notified her that Mr. Jennings's phone call with a reclaimed-wood dealer was coming up in five minutes. She hit the intercom button. "Mr. Jennings?"

Silence.

She tried again. "Mr. Jennings?"

Experience had taught her that she might startle her boss from his work with that second inquiry, but once he ignored that, it was hopeless. Jane got up and walked to his office. His door was partially open, and she could see him hunched over his drafting table, glaring at a quiver of straight lines that meant nothing to her.

"Mr. Jennings." She tapped him on the shoulder.

"Hmm?" he grumbled, not looking up from the sharp edge he'd started to draw.

"You have a call coming up in three minutes with Hatlock Wood. Shall I go ahead and place the call?"

He finally looked at her, eyes cloudy with distance. "What?"

"Hatlock Wood, Mr. Jennings. Are you ready for the call?"

"Oh." He cast a mournful glance at the sketches before rolling his shoulders. "Sure."

"Still no idea about the 'south boy' note?"

"The what?"

"I thought so. I'll have Hatlock on the line momentarily, sir. Can I get you a cup of coffee?"

He said yes, and she was so thankful to be busy again that she grinned while rushing around to get coffee and place the call. She had her own meetings this afternoon. One with their accountant and another with a school representative interested in placing an architectural intern with Mr. Jennings. Adding a young kid to the office would upset Jane's perfect balancing act, but Mr. Jennings seemed enthusiastic. She needed to be sure they got a quality candidate and a school willing to work carefully with the office. Then there was Lori's bon voyage party to nudge along…

A landscape architect came through the front door to drop off a series of sketches he'd done for one of Mr. Jennings's clients, and Jane noted that his eyes looked right through her. Despite the way she'd been living for the past two weeks, her disguise hadn't been compromised. This man didn't see her as anything other than an office fixture. The scarlet letter on her head was still invisible. He hadn't heard any rumors, didn't notice any difference in her body. She was still invisible Jane. And that was the biggest relief of all.

She'd had a wake-up call, at least. Her family was still her family, no matter how sharply she'd tried to separate herself. She wasn't foolish or naive. She didn't plan to throw a party to introduce all her colleagues to her leather-clad kin, but she realized she needed to find a better balance. A less fragmented way of living her life while still working toward the white picket fence.

No problem.

A glitch appeared in her bubble of calmness when a client called in a panic. The woman had finally gotten a look at the stone the builder had installed around the outdoor fireplace, and she was convinced that it wasn't the stone Mr. Jennings had described. Jane made a note and set it in front of Mr. Jennings, who was deeply absorbed in a conversation about old beech wood.

When she walked back into the reception area, Greg Nunn had appeared like an inexplicable ghost. He stood in front of her desk, hands in his pockets, smiling with all the confidence in the world. Alarm rang through her. Surely he hadn't come to deliver good news.

"I've got good news, Jane," he said.

Well. She glanced toward Mr. Jennings's office to make sure he was still on the phone. "What's going on, Greg?"

"You asked me to take another look at the case."

"Yes."

"I decided to do it. For your sake."

"Oh, well… Thanks."

He walked farther into the office, stopping to lean against the wall only two feet from her. "I'm sure you'll be very pleased to hear I've recommended that we turn our focus elsewhere."

"Oh. Really?" Jane made herself smile despite the fact that she'd already heard this, and she didn't believe for a second that the suggestion had come from Greg Nunn. "That's great."

"So how are you going to thank me?"

She watched the shameless smirk twist his lips and could hardly believe she'd ever liked this guy. Chase had been right. Greg was a jackass.

"Why don't we go out for drinks tonight and toast your good luck?"

She shook her head. "No."

"You should wear that red lingerie I like so much."

"Greg, we're not dating anymore, so I have no idea what you're talking about."

He winked. "I'm talking about you making sure the heat stays off your brother."

Jane stepped back in an effort to avoid shoving him away. "Get out of here, Greg."

Greg stepped closer. "You don't get to brush me off, Jane. You don't get to look outraged. Your whole life is a goddamn lie." He was close to shouting now and Jane looked frantically over her shoulder.

"Get out of here," she whispered furiously.

"What, you don't want your precious Mr. Jennings to know about your past?"

His face was pure ugliness now. She should have expected it. On the rare occasions he'd lost a case, his fury would show itself like that. Fury. Disbelief. Petulance at having been bested in public.

He could be petty, and she didn't want his pettiness anywhere near Jessie.

Jane took a deep breath. "I'm sorry, Greg. Thank you for helping. I mean it. But I can't meet you for drinks."

"*Can't* is a strong word, and one you'd better reconsider. I'll let you think about it for a few days...*Dynasty.*"

It didn't quite register for a moment. She'd heard that name too many times over the past week.

Dynasty.

No. Oh, no. He knew. That little rat *knew.* He'd snooped around her past, and oh, my God...

"Yes," she rasped. "I changed my name. It wasn't dignified. I hated it. So I'd appreciate it if you'd—"

"Have you ever looked up old classmates online?" he purred.

"What?" Again there was a sweet, welcome moment of blankness over his implication. And then the blast of it hit her.

"The social networking sites make it so easy. Type in the name of a high school. Type in a year. Pages and pages of names pop up. And boy, do people love old gossip."

The air inside her lungs was rushing to get out. Fighting. Struggling. No matter how hard she gasped, she couldn't seem to move enough air.

He was going to tell. He would tell his friends, her friends. He would tell Quinn Jennings. *Your precious Mr. Jennings,* he'd threatened.

Greg would tell Mr. Jennings that Jane Morgan was a lie. He'd reveal that she was really Dynasty Alexis MacKenzie. That she'd taken a new name with the sole purpose of covering up her past. That her father and her stepfather were both convicted felons. That her brother was a thief. He'd probably even bring up Jane's two citations for underage drinking. And he'd definitely tell him what kind of woman she really was.

Quinn Jennings would feel betrayed. He'd feel lied to. He wouldn't trust her. She'd no longer be Jane, the perfectionist office manager and partner. She'd be that girl from a family of criminals who was probably embezzling money from the business. That girl who drank and slept around. And what if the police report from Denver turned up?

Lori wouldn't want Jane in the office, wouldn't want her so close to Mr. Jennings every day.

Jane finally managed to draw a deep breath into her lungs. Some oxygen leaked into her tumbling brain and calmed her down a little.

Okay, maybe she was overreacting.

She took another deep breath.

Probably she was overreacting. Even if Greg found

out the very worst things she'd done...would Quinn Jennings hate her? Or was it just fear telling her that?

"You don't get to end it with me, Jane. I'll pick you up tomorrow after work," Greg said. His mouth smirked, but his eyes were cool and grim. "Wear something I'll like."

Her mouth was still parted in shock when he turned and opened the door. She couldn't think. Couldn't move.

"Oh," Greg said, pausing for a moment, "that guy you've been hanging out with? William Chase? I don't ever want to see you with him again. I don't want to see you with anyone until *I* say it's over."

He tried to slam the door when he walked out, but the pressurized hinge kept the landing soft. What an utterly civilized, polite evisceration.

Lowering herself into her seat, Jane closed her eyes.

What was she going to do? She'd hidden her past for so long that she couldn't imagine people knowing about it. Now she realized just how much trust she had in Chase. She didn't like him knowing—not at all—but she'd never truly feared he would expose her to the world.

But Greg? She'd made him feel stupid. First by breaking up with him, then by revealing that she'd lied about who she was. She'd hurt him and used him and he was angry.

It seemed as if the whole world were conspiring to reveal her for who she was. Even her own body was pushing her back toward the past.

She stared at the door. The clock on the far side of the office ticked loudly, the second hand counting down to disaster. What the hell was she going to do?

Just as the question threatened to overwhelm her, an

Outlook window popped up on her computer with a little ding. The meeting with the accountant. It was time for her to head over.

She gaped at the computer. Going to this meeting seemed an impossible task in her current mind-set. And yet, as she stared at the familiar shape of the Outlook alert, her frantic pulse slowed. This *was* something she could do. She could meet with the accountant for Jennings Architecture. She could do her job. Calm down. Think.

Jane had a big decision to make. Would she continue to run from her past? Or would she turn around and face it?

She had no idea. So in that moment she made an easier decision. She gathered her papers, picked up her purse and headed to see the accountant. Her past would still be there when she returned.

CHAPTER EIGHTEEN

THE PLEA DEAL WAS ARRANGED. In two days Jessie would plead guilty to ten misdemeanor charges of theft. He'd do nine months in County. He wasn't going to prison.

And in her family this meant they were having a party.

"Seriously," Jane muttered to her mother. "This is ridiculous." Her shoulders burned with tension. The deal wouldn't be final for two days, and Greg was acting like a wounded bear. He was going to show up at her office the next evening, demanding a date and rabbit sex, and she was going to turn him down. What would that mean for Jessie?

Jane rounded on her mother. "He's going to jail, Mom. It's not something to celebrate."

"You know how close he came to something far worse. We are celebrating, Jane, and I don't want to hear another word about it."

Jane glanced over to where her stepdad was carefully coaxing the briquettes to a perfect glow in his grill. He didn't look happy, but there was a less rigid line to his shoulders. He was relieved. He'd even allowed Jessie to set foot on the property, but only for this special occasion. After he'd served his time, Jessie would have to find his own place to live. Mac would never let him live in his house again.

But for tonight, the men of her family had called a truce. And Jane felt like a traitor in their midst. Did she really have the right to put her nonexistent virtue above Jessie's future? She'd spent years having sex with men she barely knew. Why was it so hard to consider sex with Greg?

Her gut burned. She wanted to get out of here. At least it wasn't crowded. Who did one invite to an "our son is going to jail instead of prison!" party, after all? Grandma Olive was there, of course. And Arlo. And that girl named Eve who was apparently a girlfriend of Jessie's. But his best friends weren't there, because Mac wouldn't allow it.

This was her whole family. How could she let them down? She could either sleep with Greg one last time—just enough time to finalize the plea deal—or…

She looked down at the bright green shoots of spring grass poking through the brown mat of dead leaves. Maybe Greg wasn't as smart as he thought he was. Maybe she could turn this around.

For the first time all day her heart beat hard with an emotion that wasn't fear. She couldn't stop Greg from ruining her reputation, but she could stop him from ruining her family.

Raising her chin, she looked up to see Mac taking a long swig from his bottle. When she walked closer, the glow of the fire pressed against her skin. "Are you all right?"

"Yeah. I'm gonna break down and buy a new grill

one of these days." He'd been saying the same thing for eight years.

"You're not mad at Mom?"

He shrugged. "She meant well."

"Regardless, you can still be mad at her."

He shot her a measuring look. "Yeah, I know that. I'm plenty mad. But she does her best. She's a good woman."

This was uncomfortably close to a conversation they'd had years before, and Jane's neck tightened with remembered tension. *She's a good woman. She might not have been the perfect mother, but she did her best.*

Her best.

Across the yard Jane's mom pulled Jessie into her arms and held him tightly. When Jane had been little, her mom had held her like that, too. Then Jane had discovered anger and bitterness and rage, and a good portion of that had been directed at her mom. And after the bitterness and rage had gone, there'd been guilt.

Somehow Jane had never been able to bridge the gap she'd created. "I know she's a good woman," she murmured. "It's just hard for me."

"I know."

She'd never understood how Mac could comfort her with so few words. He was a simple man, yet he'd always understood her most complicated feelings.

"You want a beer?" he asked, divining her deepest need once again.

"Heck, yes," she said with a sigh.

He reached into the cooler, twisted off the top and pressed the icy wet bottle into her hand. Mac to the rescue once again.

"Thank you," she breathed.

Before she'd gulped a quarter of the bottle, she heard the sound of a door slamming above the Eagles music blaring from the kitchen window. When the two new party guests walked around the side of the house, Jane was darn glad she had a beer.

"What is *he* doing here?" she gasped.

Her mom shouted a hello from the far side of the yard. "Oh, the Chases are here. I'm so glad you could make it. Thank you so much for everything you did for Jessie."

Chase made the rounds, shaking hands, introducing everyone to his dad.

He looked right at home as he strolled past the skeletons of dead bikes lined up along the shop wall. Totally comfortable as he shook hands with Mac.

When his father stopped to grab a beer and stand over the grill with Mac, Chase continued the last few feet toward Jane. "Hello, Miss Jane."

"Did my mom invite you?"

"Yep."

"I'm sorry. This party is kind of…inappropriate."

Chase opened his mouth as if he'd say something, then glanced toward Jessie and seemed to change his mind. "Your mom is relieved, and she should be. Your brother has the chance to turn his life around."

Jane shook her head. "I don't know. He's a convicted thief now. I worry that… My stepfather was wrongly convicted. The state never acknowledged it, but the evidence is clear. He didn't do it. But Jessie did. He's a criminal. A thief. I've never known any thieves who went on to good futures, have you?"

"I…" Chase's head cocked as he frowned down at her. "I'm sure…"

Jane waved her hand. "Don't worry about it. It could've been so much worse. Thank you for bringing your father in to help us."

He took a deep breath. "Dad was happy to do it, and it was good for him."

They both watched as his dad twisted open a second beer. He'd made quick work of the first. Jane winced. "Maybe he could work for Ms. Holloway as an investigator."

"Maybe," he said, then shook his head. "He doesn't have a driver's license, and he can't do that kind of work without one. Anyway, it would get boring after a while, and then... You know what? I've come to realize that I can't fix him, so I try not to think about it."

"How did you manage that? Getting over his drinking?"

"I don't know if I'm over it. I guess I... A few years ago I was in a long-term relationship. She needed to move to Utah and I let her go, because I was afraid to leave my dad. I'd taken care of him from the time I was nine, and I couldn't leave."

Jane just nodded. She had no idea what to say. It felt strange to imagine Chase in love with some unknown woman. Holding hands and watching movies and taking her out for explosion dates. It felt more than strange. It felt awful.

"Frankly, I was kind of a mess last year. I was so worried about my dad that I couldn't sleep. I felt guilty when I didn't see him, but when I did he'd ask me to bring beer. Then my stomach would hurt at the thought that I was helping him kill himself. I went to a few Al-Anon meetings, and things have gotten clearer. Now I see him, but I won't bring beer. I don't feel great about it, but I feel better."

"But how do you…? Aren't you mad at him? How do you get over the anger?"

"I haven't gotten over it. Sometimes it sneaks up on me and I just want to shake him, yell and scream. I used to have a real dad, you know?"

Jane took a sip from her beer so she wouldn't cry.

"But now this is the dad I have, and I can either accept it or kill myself fighting it."

She nodded again.

"You must've had a lot of anger toward your mom."

"Oh, yeah."

"So how did you get past it?"

Jane looked at him as if he was crazy. Couldn't he see the truth about her? "I didn't. I never have. Every single day I think about what my life would've been like if I hadn't been raised within spitting distance of razor wire. What it would've been like to be normal, not the girl who got dressed up once a month to visit scary strangers in scary places. To have had a real father instead of a pen pal. I think about what kind of choices I would've made and…"

She swallowed hard. "I was mad at her for so long, but it's past time to let it go. And I just keep thinking once I have everything I want, it'll be easier to reconnect with her."

"Will it?"

"Probably not. I keep pushing her further away."

He tucked a strand of hair behind her ear, and the touch swept over her like sunshine. "Is that what you want? To push her away?" he asked.

258 LEAD ME ON

"I don't know." She honestly had no idea anymore. Run away or get closer? She'd didn't know.

"You were right," Chase said. "You are a mess." That startled a laugh out of her, and Jane was grateful for that. He did that often, she realized. Made her laugh when she was close to crying.

"Say there, boy!" a voice wobbled from across the lawn. They both turned to see Olive looking right at Chase.

He raised his hand in greeting. "Hey, Grandma Olive!"

"Get me a beer and come over here."

"Oh, shit," he breathed. "Wish me luck."

Grinning, Jane watched Chase jog over to get a beer before he headed for Olive.

"Where's *my* beer?" the old woman yelled before he'd made it halfway across the big yard.

"It's right here," he answered, holding up the bottle.

"Then where's your beer?"

Jane followed casually behind him, eavesdropping, and heard him say "I don't drink."

Grandma Olive's eyes snapped to narrow slits. "What kind of man doesn't drink beer?"

Chase shrugged.

"You a mean drunk? Can't hold your liquor?"

"No, ma'am. I just don't drink."

"Pansy?" she snapped.

"Um, no."

"Hmph." She snatched the beer from his hand and eyed him up and down. "Well, I suppose, considering the size of those hands, a woman can forgive a few flaws."

Jane jumped in before Olive could explain her

theory about the relationship between the size of a man's hands and his "private pieces." "There's nothing wrong with not drinking, Grandma Olive."

"Thins the blood," she replied, as if thin blood were the epitome of good health.

"No wonder you almost bled out from that cut the other day," Jane muttered.

"Never been sick a day in my life."

Jane rolled her eyes. "You were in the hospital with pneumonia last year."

"Hmph," Olive grunted in disgust. "That was asbestos poisoning from that dust I inhaled when they remodeled the supermarket."

Well, there was nothing to say to that, but at least they weren't discussing Chase's privates.

"Say, did you see that new movie about that big robot?" Grandma Olive asked, and she and Chase fell into a ten-minute conversation about science-fiction movies, which ended with Olive hanging on his arm and laughing so hard she had to hold her dentures in.

Jane's heart beat hard as she watched the scene play out. Mac put his arm around her shoulder. "If Grandma Olive likes him, maybe you should keep him around."

"I was thinking just the opposite."

"Good point."

She leaned her head into his arm as the shade of the trees darkened into dusk.

"He's a nice guy," Mac said. "I like him."

"Me, too. But I'm not sure he's what I'm looking for."

"I thought you might say that." His arm squeezed her closer.

Jane sighed. Mac was good at that—offering silent comfort and no judgment.

"Sometimes, baby, you've got to stop thinking and go with your gut."

She kept her eyes closed and her cheek pressed to his chest. It was good advice. Except that her gut had always been the thing telling her to run far and fast to escape her beginnings.

Now she had no idea what to do.

CHAPTER NINETEEN

JANE WATCHED the office clock count toward five-thirty. She still couldn't figure out if she was imagining the ticking of the second hand or if it had always made noise and she'd never noticed it before. There was a perfectly good digital clock on the computer. Maybe she should throw the ancient, ticking menace in the Dumpster out back.

Still, throwing it out wouldn't stop time. The day was over. Her executioner would be walking through the office door sometime in the next half hour.

Jane could help Jessie, but she couldn't save herself. She was resigned to that. There was no way to put that dirty little genie back into the bottle. All she could do was try to soften the blow and mitigate the impact.

Strange, but she felt fairly calm in the face of her worst fears coming true. Her pulse didn't even quicken when she rose to knock on her boss's open door.

"Mr. Jennings?" she said. "I need to speak with you."

"Hey," he murmured as he clicked around on something in his drafting program. Jane sat on one of the chairs in front of his desk and waited patiently. A few moments later he looked up, frowning.

"Jane, what's wrong?"

She took a deep breath, clutched her hands together and leaped. "The reason I've been out of the office is that my brother was arrested for larceny. He's going to plead no-contest tomorrow and start serving his nine-month sentence. Also, my stepfather is an ex-con. So is my real father. And before I turned eighteen, my name was Destiny Alexis MacKenzie. I changed it on my eighteenth birthday."

Mr. Jennings didn't move. He watched her as if he were waiting for more.

"That's who I am," she said softly.

His brow furrowed. "Okay."

"I wanted to tell you the truth. I acted out as a teenager. I wanted to leave that behind, so I changed my name."

"To Jane Morgan?"

"Yes."

"Okay." He shook his head, frowning harder. "So…that's the truth about the past, but Jane Morgan is the truth now."

Her heart twisted. "Yes."

"I don't understand. Were you afraid to tell me this?"

"Yes."

"Why?"

Why? Because despite her earlier calm, she felt as if she was going to throw up and cry and run away, all at the same time. "Because nobody knows."

He smiled at that, a wide grin that stretched across his face. "Well, I'm glad you trust me, then. I won't tell anyone. You're not going to ask me to hire your brother when he gets out, are you?"

"Oh, God, no!"

"Do you need tomorrow off to go to his hearing?"

"Just an hour or so."

He nodded. "All right, then."

And that was it. She'd done it. She'd told Mr. Jennings the truth. It hadn't been terrible at all really, but it was just the beginning. Three people in Aspen knew the truth about her now. More would find out. Things were going to change, and the harbinger of that change was walking into the office with a disarming smile when she closed Mr. Jennings's door behind her.

"Hi, Jane," Greg said so cheerfully that she was struck with a moment of vertigo. He was trying to blackmail her into sex, so why did he look ready for a real date?

Jane stared at Greg, forcing her face to stay impassive. "One moment," she said as she sat down and picked up the phone to take care of the last bullet point on her to-do list. A phone call to her least favorite surveying manager. The man was rude and foulmouthed, but for once she didn't want the conversation to end. She waited until the contractor hung up and the line began to beep before she set the receiver down.

"Are you ready?" Greg asked. His eyes swept down her plain black jacket, and the sight tightened his mouth a little, but he didn't say anything. Had he expected her to wear something low cut?

Arrogant dog.

"Are you really going to do this?" she murmured.

His smile betrayed no hint of guilt. "I'm just trying to reconnect with my girlfriend. What's wrong with that?"

Jane got up and stepped around to the front of her desk so there was no chance of Mr. Jennings overhearing them through his door. "Just a few days ago you made clear I wasn't good enough to be your girlfriend. I'm trash, remember?"

"Oh, I remember," he said happily.

Great.

Greg's eyes slid toward Mr. Jennings's office. "Are we going out or not?"

He couldn't threaten her with Quinn Jennings now, but Jane grabbed her purse and headed for the door regardless. She needed to get this over with before she chickened out, but her blood was singing with alarm.

This was dangerous. It was real. She was furious and afraid and hurt. But her face was blank as glass as she walked to his car. She could feel the cool stiffness.

He opened the door for her before circling around to the driver's side. "I've missed you," he said, still looking pleased with himself as he leaned in to peck her on the lips.

She felt nothing at the kiss, not even disgust. Maybe she could salvage something. Maybe this didn't have to get ugly. "Greg, I am so sorry. Honestly."

"It's all right," he said easily. "I forgive you."

"That's not what I mean. I mean I'm sorry that I had to end it, but I'm not in love with you. Please don't do this."

His jaw tightened.

Heat washed over her face. "Whatever I've done, it doesn't give you the right to threaten my brother."

He shrugged. "You were in my bed two weeks ago. It's no big deal."

"It *is* a big deal. It's blackmail."

His smile was gone as if it had never existed, and a flush of guilt crept up his cheeks. "You made me wait for months, and that guy… Were you sleeping with him when you were with me?"

"*Who?* Chase? No, of course not."

"So you made me wait, but not someone like him, huh? Not some fucking low-class criminal loser? I'm not as good as *him?*"

"It's not… Chase isn't a criminal."

Greg snorted. "He's just as bad as the rest of your family, which is probably what you like. Lucky for him he got caught before he was eighteen."

"Wha—?" She cut off the word and snapped her mouth shut, hoping he hadn't noticed her shock. What did he mean?

"Ready?" Greg asked, flipping the car keys around in his hand.

"No," she whispered.

"Just drop it, Jane," he snapped. "I don't know what kind of game you were playing with me, but you certainly haven't been restraining yourself since we broke up. Now that I know what you are, I want another taste. So let's stop pretending it would offend your morals."

"It would!"

"You were my girlfriend, Jane. It's no big deal. Let's just have a good time."

"Or what?"

He started the car, ignoring her. "I should've known what you were the first time I saw that body. It's in your fucking blood."

Jane clutched the edges of her purse harder. "I'm saying no," she insisted.

"No, you're not."

"Or *what?*"

"Let's go out and have a few drinks. It's nothing you haven't done before. Your brother's hearing isn't until tomorrow. Things could still go wrong."

"I see. Just one night, then? That's all you want?"

"No. You'll go out with me until I'm ready for it to be over. And in return, I'll keep your secret safe."

Jane took a deep breath, trying to calm the storm of rage and hurt tumbling in her chest. "It's too late. I already told Mr. Jennings the truth."

Greg's eyebrows flew up. "Really? You told him about your past?"

"Yes."

"Wow. Well, let's be clear that you won't be banging him while you're with me, all right?"

"He wouldn't—"

"But that wasn't what I meant. I meant that none of your old classmates know your new name, Ms. Morgan, and I'm sure you'd like to keep it that way."

The world lagged, as if this were a slow-motion scene in a movie she was watching. This was exactly what she'd feared her whole life. People pointing, sneering, calling her trash. Seeing through her facade of Jane Morgan to the sick, worthless girl inside. Men looking at her and seeing someone who deserved to be used.

That was what Greg was thinking. She could see it in his eyes. *You're going to sleep with me because that's what you're good for.* She'd seen that look often enough to recognize it. *You'll do it because you have no pride.*

What a complete bastard. "This is blackmail and it's illegal."

"Blackmail?" His face paled a little, but he smiled

and shook his head. "Hardly. Come on, Jane. You're single, I'm single. What's the harm of meeting up for a few drinks?"

"You threatened me."

"With the *truth?* You *are* Dynasty MacKenzie. You're the one who's been lying to everyone. You've been dishonest and sneaky." Greg watched her for a long moment. "You lied to me throughout our whole relationship." Pain flashed in his eyes. "I can't just let it go and pretend it never happened."

"I'm sorry," Jane said, reaching for the door handle. She was halfway out of the car before he had time to react.

"What do you think you're doing?"

She slammed the door just as Greg opened his. "Get in the car, Jane."

"Nope."

"I'll tell everyone."

"Do it."

"I'll stop your brother's plea deal."

Hand on the door to her office, Jane froze. She turned back toward Greg and measured the distance between them. Ten feet. That was safe enough. "No, you won't. You won't do anything like that. You're going to be too busy fighting for your job."

He sneered. "What the hell does that mean?"

"It means there's a nifty little cell-phone program that works like a mini recorder." She tugged the phone from her purse and held it up. "You're on tape. And you're never going to bother me again."

All the color in his face blanked to a sick white. "What? You can't... You didn't really—"

She opened the door. "Us white-trash sluts are sneaky. It's our nature. Goodbye, Greg."

"If you send that to my boss, I'll—" The door closed and she locked it from the inside, just in case. His face was like a mood ring now, skin flushing from white to magenta as she watched. She flipped her phone closed as Greg was tugging his from his suit pocket. When her phone began to ring, she turned it off.

She could no longer hide from Dynasty. But she was Jane Morgan now, and she was determined to prove it.

CHAPTER TWENTY

CHASE RANG THE DOORBELL, then stepped off the small front step to wait for Jane to answer. It was eight o'clock. Her porch light was on, so hopefully she was home.

Though he'd spent the previous week with her, he'd seen her only at the barbecue since then, and he felt strangely nervous about dropping by.

The barbecue had been nice, though. For some reason, spending the evening with her *without* going home with her afterward had felt…good. Evidence that there was more between them than sex. Of course, Jane hadn't meant to spend time with him at her family party, but that was too bad. She'd done it, and he'd enjoyed every second of it, even with Grandma Olive calling him a pansy.

He'd had paperwork to catch up on, so Chase hadn't minded giving Jane some space, but now he was ready to move forward.

Jane finally opened the door, and Chase's body tingled with happiness at the sight of her wearing workout shorts and a T-shirt with her cute black glasses. "Hey, I'm just in time for boxing."

Jane cocked her head. "I wasn't expecting you."

Ouch. "I have something important to tell you."

She glanced past him before nodding. "Okay. Come in."

Chase looked over his shoulder as he stepped inside. "Is everything all right?"

"Everything's fine. I'm glad you're here, actually. I wanted to talk to you, too."

That was more like it. "About what?"

She hesitated, lips parting for a moment before she shook her head. Her ponytail bounced, distracting him into thinking about how soft her hair felt when he made love to her.

"You go first," she said, waving him toward the couch.

"All right." He dropped onto the couch and she sat down next to him. "My father heard something yesterday, but I didn't want to say anything until he'd confirmed it. The police have another suspect."

"Who is it?"

"I don't know his name. They're keeping it quiet because they haven't brought him in yet."

Jane looked down at her hands. "All right. It's great to hear, though. I'll let Jessie know."

"Yeah, hopefully they won't be looking in your brother's direction again. But don't say anything that might tip off the suspect."

"I'll wait a few days."

Chase took her hand and rubbed his thumb over her knuckles. "Are you okay? You look tired."

She shrugged.

"What did you want to talk about?"

"I…" Frowning, she looked down to their hands. "I need to…"

Jane was worried about their relationship again. It

was easy to see. But he'd meant what he'd said about falling for her, and he wasn't going to let her go easily. He'd made that mistake with his ex-girlfriend. This time he wasn't letting go without a fight.

Chase leaned close, and when Jane looked up, he kissed her. He knew how to work her. He knew when her neuroses were about to overwhelm her real feelings. And he knew full well that he was her weakness, and he was pretty damn thrilled about that.

Though she didn't pull back, her lips were cool against his for a moment. And then they weren't. Then they were soft and hot and opening for him.

She kissed him back and let him keep it slow, which was unusual for her. They tasted each other for a long minute, and then he pulled away. "What's wrong, Jane?"

Her fingers dug into his hand, she took a deep breath…but then she shook her head, denying she was upset. "Do you want to watch a movie?"

"A movie?" It was nine o'clock and he had to prep a site at 6:00 a.m.… "A movie sounds perfect."

Jane got him a Coke—a real Coke, as if she'd gone shopping for him—and poured herself a glass of red wine. Then she turned on a romantic comedy, snuggled close to him, and Chase was back in heaven.

At first he thought they'd re-create Saturday night when they'd watched a movie in platonic relaxation. But he'd already seen this movie, and he hadn't touched her in so long, and her lips looked rosy and red from sipping the wine.

Soon enough, he found himself stroking her knee, then the inside of her thigh. It felt like years since he'd touched her there, and he was rock hard and aching within minutes. Jane sipped her wine and laughed at the movie while Chase closed his eyes and thought of the way he'd licked her last time. The way she'd screamed in pleasure.

Shit. He forced his eyes open and tried to watch the show, but there were other scenes playing behind his eyes.

Holding his breath, Chase slid his hand higher, and Jane's thighs eased apart.

Thank God. He gave up any pretense of looking at the TV and turned to her. She kissed him and tugged him close. He laid her on the couch or she pulled him down, but somehow he ended up over her, kissing her, pressing his whole body into hers.

God, he'd missed the taste and feel and sound of her. Her sweet mouth and soft hair and greedy sighs. Jane's hands ran up his chest, stealing the breath from his lungs. She shoved off his shirt and he knew then that she was as hungry as he was.

He touched her everywhere, running his hands over her skin, dragging off her shorts, pushing up her shirt. "Jane," he murmured over and over again. "Jane."

In no time Chase was slipping on a condom and sliding deep inside her.

"Ah, God, Jane," he whispered as she wrapped her arms around him. Every inch of her body touched his as he took her, plunging slow and hard.

Her nails dug into his back, her sighs turned to moans. His whole world was Jane beneath him, surrounding him.

He shifted higher on her body and Jane cried out, her nails dragging down to his ass. He felt her rising into him, her sex tightening around him. She shuddered beneath him, her scream a mixture of pleasure and tears. Just as her cries faded, Chase was pulled deep into the vortex of release, the world giving up all its light for one spinning moment.

Before he'd finished spinning, Jane went stiff beneath him. "We have to talk," she said, pushing at his chest.

Oh, Jesus. Seriously? He couldn't even feel his legs.

"Chase!"

Okay. All right. Chase took a deep breath and pushed up on his arms. He grabbed his jeans and headed for the bathroom. By the time he got out, Jane was up, wearing her shirt and underwear and pacing like a madwoman.

She swiped a tear off her cheek and his heart fell, but there was no getting around the truth.

"Jane, I think I'm falling in love with you."

"What? Why did you say that?"

"Because I love you."

"No!" she yelled.

Chase knew it was a really bad idea to smile, but he felt his lips twitch in the wrong direction.

"This is not funny!"

"Jeez. Do you do this every time a man tells you he loves you?"

Her mouth snapped shut so quickly that he heard her teeth crack together.

"I'm sorry. I can't do this. I need to break it off. Completely."

"Uh-huh."

Jane stopped in her tracks and spun to face him. "What does that mean?"

"It means I don't believe you."

"Why?" she huffed.

"I'm not sure. Maybe because we just made love?"

"No. We had *sex,* Chase."

Intellectually, Chase knew that should have hurt, but it was so obviously a lie that his heart didn't even twitch. She'd meant to break it off when he'd shown up, just as she'd meant to break it off several other times in their short relationship. But she couldn't do it. Not when she wanted him.

She liked him, and she needed his body, and Chase knew that eventually those two things would mesh together and create something much more intense. Just as it had for him.

"It's over," Jane insisted.

"Why? What happened?"

"Nothing happened. It's just over. It was supposed to be over after the first night!"

"When you came to the door today, you were upset. What happened?"

She shook her head. Crossed her arms, then uncrossed them. Her chin rose. "I told Mr. Jennings."

"Um…" A flush of embarrassment crept up his face, as if Quinn Jennings was her dad and had just walked in on them. "You told him we were sleeping together?"

"No! I told him about my family, about my name."

"Oh, I get it. But that's a good thing!" He started to reach for her. "I'm proud of you, babe."

Jane threw up her hands to hold him off. "It is not a good thing! Dynasty MacKenzie isn't a secret anymore. You know about her, and so does Mr. Jennings, and now…now Greg knows, too, and he'll tell people. I have to *live* with her now."

"Maybe she's not so bad, Jane."

Fists tightening as if she might practice her boxing on him, Jane advanced. Chase actually took a step back. "You have no idea how bad she was."

"Well, I knew—"

"You knew me when I was, what? Thirteen or fourteen? I spent two more years perfecting my bad-girl image. I was completely out of control. I was... I can't be anything like her. I can't date a man with tattoos or visit my brother in jail or...I *can't*. Or people will think I haven't changed."

"But Jane... Who cares what people think?"

"*I* care! You don't understand."

"So tell me."

Her eyes were fever bright, sparkling with pain.

"Tell me what happened."

"No!" She looked so panicked that Chase no longer cared if she was going to hit him. He grabbed her and folded his arms around her. Her breath blasted against his bare chest as if she'd just run a race. Her knuckles dug into his stomach.

"Jane, you need to talk to someone."

"I don't need you to play therapist. I know what happened." Her breathing slowed, so when she pushed away, he let her go. "My dad, my real dad, wrote to me every week when he was in prison. *Every* week. I had all the fantasies you'd expect about what a great time we'd have when he got out. What a great father he'd be. He *encouraged* those fantasies. Then he was paroled when I was twelve, and I never heard from him again. Ever. He'd moved on. He didn't need a pen pal anymore because he had a life."

Chase's throat tightened with sympathetic pain for her. "Jesus, that's really awful. You must've been—"

"It couldn't have happened at a worse time, of course. Puberty. I started craving male attention, and I had the body to get it. Men wanted me and I loved it. There you go. Therapy session over!"

His chest burned so hot that he had a momentary fear he was having a heart attack. "You were just a kid."

"Sure, when I was twelve, I was a kid. But at some point I was old enough to know better. At some point I couldn't blame my mom or my dad or my past anymore. It was just me drinking and getting high and having sex with men twice my age—"

Oh, God.

"And living with that is hard enough without everybody knowing about it!"

She was pacing again, hands wound together, mouth pressed into a tight line. He remembered how sexual she'd been. A thirteen-year-old seductress on a mission to lose herself...and apparently she'd succeeded.

"What happened when you were sixteen?"

"Ha! I thought I knew what I was doing. I thought I could handle myself."

It seemed ridiculous, but he was afraid. Afraid for that girl she'd been. Whatever had happened, it had been a long time ago, but the terror of it sent his heart racing. "What happened, Jane?"

Her laugh sounded like a sob. "I thought I was so cool."

"Jane."

"These guys asked if I wanted to go to a real party down in Denver, and I was so damn ready to get out of this town and have some real fun. I hopped into their car at midnight and left town without thinking once about my family or my safety or who these guys were."

Chase rubbed his hand over his skull, hoping it would relieve some pressure. "Jesus." She stood still now, but Chase suddenly found himself pacing, prowling across the length of the room.

"We went to their house in downtown Denver. They had pills and beer and I was so high, I was happy to do anything, you know? I *did* do anything. I had sex with three guys. In the same room, at the same time. That's who I was, Chase." Her voice had been quiet, but it rose now, tears shining on her pale cheeks. "That's who I was! And I deserved everything anyone ever said about me. I deserved it when girls called me a skank and whore, and when boys grabbed me and asked when they could get their next blow job."

"Jane."

He wrapped his hand around her arm and tried to hug her, but she shoved him away. "That's who I was and I can't bear to have anyone think that about me again!"

"They won't," he whispered, tugging her back before she could escape. "They won't think that." He folded her into his arms and squeezed too tightly.

"I just want a boring life that no one looks beyond," she said, her voice muffled by his chest. "That average woman who fades into the background. I don't want anyone to know what's inside. Ever. And *you* know what's inside. I can't be around you."

He pressed a kiss to her hair. "You'd rather be with someone who doesn't *know* you?"

"Yes!"

"What kind of life is that, Jane?"

"It's… It will be peaceful. And *good*."

"No, it won't." God, her whole body was shaking like a live wire. "It will be a sham."

Chase led her to the couch. He lay down and pulled her on top of him. Holding her, stroking her hair, he waited for her shaking to stop. Eventually her body started to melt into his. The rough sound of her breath began to smooth at the edges.

"Did they hurt you?"

She gave a watery laugh. "Not really. I took care of that myself. But the next day they kept saying they'd take me home. Then all of a sudden it was getting dark again, and they said, 'Hey, don't worry. We've got a few friends coming over who want to party with you. We'll take you home tomorrow.' I panicked, and I snuck out. But I was in Denver. I didn't know anybody, didn't know what to do, so I just wandered around for a few hours until I finally got picked up by a cop."

"Thank God."

"I was so tired and freaked out, I told him what had really happened. I honestly believed he was going to help me, you know?"

Chase felt his relief vanish at her disgusted huff of laughter. "What do you mean?"

"He wasn't exactly sympathetic. He took me back to the station and called Mac to tell him I was going to be charged with solicitation if I wasn't picked up by morning."

"Solicitation?" Chase barked.

He felt Jane nod against his chest. "He told Mac…"

Her breath hitched. "He called Mac in front of me and stared right in my face while he talked. He said, 'I found your daughter walking the street. She admits she had sex with three men last night in exchange for drugs. Come get her or I'll charge her with prostitution.' I wanted to die. I didn't... I never wanted Mac to know that."

Eyes wide with shock, Chase stroked her back.

"He came. And I was so ashamed. He didn't say a thing at first. He just started driving. When the sun started coming up, he pulled over, flipped the visor down and said, 'Look at yourself.'"

"Classic dad move," Chase whispered, hoping to make her laugh.

She did. Just a soft huff of laughter, but her spine relaxed a bit.

"It worked. I looked at myself, and I was a mess, and I knew he didn't doubt what the cop had told him. I looked hard and sad and used. I told him it had all been a mistake. That I hadn't meant to end up with those guys. And then Mac started talking. He never talks. But that day he talked, slow and quiet. He talked about how much he wanted to do right by me, how much he loved me."

She paused to swallow hard. "He said he knew that my dad had hurt me and how mad I was at my mom. He said, 'You throw your mom's decisions in her face, but she tried. She tried. And all you're trying to do is ruin yourself so you can prove she did a bad job.'"

"Ouch."

Her hand rubbed his upper arm, back and forth in little strokes. "He didn't ask any questions. He didn't berate me. But he stopped at the hospital in Vail and told them I needed to talk to a doctor in private. He took care of me, Chase. And sometime during that drive I realized I did have a real father. I'd done nothing to make him proud and everything to push him away. I'd been *awful* and he *still* loved me."

"Is that what changed you?"

"That was part of it. I wanted to make him proud, to repay him for loving me. And I wanted to be better than my mother, instead of worse. Most of all, that night…once the pills wore off, I was so horrified and ashamed of what I'd done. And so scared of what might've happened. And I knew that cop hadn't offered help because he thought I'd deserved what I'd gotten. It was like I needed to feel *that* awful, that low, for any emotion to soak through the rage and alcohol and defiance."

Chase brushed his lips over her forehead, breathing in the scent of her hair. The burning in his chest started to fade, but some of it just migrated to his eyes. "I can't believe you actually pulled yourself together after that. At sixteen? That's amazing."

Now her fingers were tracing his tattoo, running slowly up and down the black lines. Her weight pressed him down. Goose bumps raced across his skin.

"It didn't matter. That's my point, Chase. It didn't matter that I'd changed. All anyone saw was who I had been. My good behavior was suspect. People at school and in town said I'd had a baby or that I had AIDS. They said I'd been a prostitute and I was on probation. The boys I'd once hung out with were cruel, but the girls were worse. Sometimes it does matter what people think of you."

"Sometimes," he acknowledged, "but not anymore. You're not sixteen. You're not in high school. You have a good life now and you should be proud of yourself."

"Well, I'm not. Not when I think of that. I need the security of pretense and appearance. I'm sorry, but that's the truth."

"It's not the truth. I love who you are now, Jane, but part of that love is because of who you used to be. The changes you made…I don't know anyone who could have done that out of sheer will. Don't you want someone who knows who you really are? Who *loves* who you really are?"

"No. I want someone who doesn't even know that world exists."

Chase rolled his eyes. God, she was thickheaded, lying on top of him, caressing his tattoo and claiming to want someone like Ned Flanders. "Okay, what about the rest of your wants? You're going to marry some up-standing white-bread kind of guy, and then… What? Keep someone like me on the side?"

"No!" She put her hand on his chest and pushed up to glare at him. "Why would I do that?"

Chase curved his hand around the back of her neck, spreading his fingers over the heat of her. "Because I turn you on. Because those high-class guys don't do a thing for you." He pulled her down until her lips were only an inch from his. "Good girl or not, you're passionate as hell, Jane."

He tried to kiss her, but she twisted away. "Stop it!"

"You want to live your whole life like that? Hiding from yourself?"

"Yes! I don't need this. *I don't.*"

He held her still when she tried to push farther away from him. "Yes, you do." Her heart hammered, her pulse vibrating through his ribs. "You were starving for it. For *me*."

When he pulled her down, she resisted again, but when his mouth touched hers, her lips opened. The kiss was hungry and hard. She devoured him, her hands clutching his head. Now instead of struggling to get away, she seemed to be fighting to sink into him.

Her kiss was violent, her fingers digging into his skull, but Chase didn't care. He was hard within seconds, thrilled to be used.

Aside from framing her face with his hands, he didn't touch her, but Jane touched him. She dragged her hands down his neck, his shoulders, arms. Her mouth followed, biting and sucking at his skin.

He closed his eyes when she reached for the button of his jeans, then sucked in a deep breath when her hand wrapped around his dick.

Her hand slid down all the way to the base of his erection, then back up, slowly. She watched her own movement, bottom lip caught between her teeth as she worked him.

Chase shuddered, watching her jack him off. Her cheeks flushed, her nipples hardened beneath the thin shirt, her fingers squeezed tighter.

"Ah, God," he gasped.

Her eyes flew to his, flashing triumph. She let go of him so she could whip off her shirt and wiggle out of her panties. Then she leaned down and came up with one of the condom packages he'd dropped in his hurry to have her earlier.

By the time she rose over him, Chase was panting, but he still didn't touch her. Instead he clenched his hands to fists as her hot sex touched him, as it slid down, taking him in, squeezing him.

Jane threw her head back and sighed, the lines of her face relaxing. He knew how to make her look that way. He knew how to make her laugh and scream and smile and cry. He knew her. Whether she liked it or not, he knew her.

She began to ride him, and Chase let her take what she needed. Not that it was hardship. She was beautiful, lost in her own pleasure. *Sex* with her was beautiful, and it made his heart twist every time.

Despite his vow to let her have her way with him, Chase soon found his hands holding her thighs as he surged up to meet her. He watched the place where their bodies joined, watched his dick sliding in and out, and it was nearly too much. He'd just come a few minutes before, but his body was already tightening to an ache.

Sliding his hand higher, Chase pressed his thumb to her clit.

"Yes," she whispered as he rubbed her. "Chase. *Please.* Yes."

His fingers brushed the slick heat that coated his shaft, and Chase shivered.

"Yes," she breathed, repeating it over and over like a prayer. He felt her tighten around him, but she shook her head, holding back, one hand digging into the back of the couch. "No," she moaned, but it was too late. Her hips jerked and she screamed.

He managed to hold on long enough to watch her

as she came, but the sight sent him quickly over the edge, plunging into his own world of painful pleasure.

Jane collapsed onto him, and he gladly wrapped his arms around her sweat-dampened body. "Jane," he whispered. "I love you."

She didn't object this time, though her breath hitched a little.

"I love you," he repeated, "but that's the last time I'll let you use me."

The muscles of her back stiffened. "What?"

"If you want me, Jane, you have to take all of me, even the parts that complicate your life. Even the parts that make you self-conscious."

Chase's legs worked a bit unreliably, but he had no choice but to get up and make good on his words. This time when he came out of the bathroom, Jane wasn't pacing and glaring. She sat on the couch, head in her hands.

He watched her for a long moment, but when she didn't look up, he grabbed his shirt and shoved his feet into his boots. "We'll talk later, all right?"

Jane didn't respond, so Chase kissed the crown of her head and walked out without saying goodbye.

CHAPTER TWENTY-ONE

HER EYES FELT GRITTY and swollen before she even opened them. Not a good sign. And she felt as if she'd been asleep for only an hour.

Jane cracked one eyelid open and looked at the clock.

No wonder she was exhausted. It was only 1:00 a.m.

She was letting her head sink back to the pillow when she caught a glow of blue light at the edge of her vision. The numbers on her clock were red and she didn't leave any lights on at night, so what could it be? Jane frowned into her pillow for a sleepy moment, then shifted to her side to look.

For a moment it was just the blue light. Then she saw the shape of her cell phone and the lower half of a man's face illuminated by the glow.

Someone was in her room! She gulped down a gasp as she watched a hand rise into the light to push a button. She couldn't see anything else, not even the arm that must be holding the phone.

It was a man, but who? Her heart forced blood to race too fast to her brain, mixing her thoughts into a jumble. Should she jump up and run or stay quiet? Her lungs screamed for air, but she tried to keep her breathing slow.

Was it the killer? Was he disabling her phone so he could take his time without worrying about the police?

She couldn't just lie there. There was another bedroom on the other side of her wall, but she couldn't remember now if the owner had rented it out for the year or just for ski season. Regardless, Jane had to take a chance. The man stood between her and the door. Running was not the best option.

Opening her mouth, she drew in a deep breath and watched the man's face shift toward her.

"Help!" she screamed as loudly as she could. "Help!"

"Oh, shit," the man barked, lunging toward her. The voice was familiar, but Jane screamed again.

A hand slapped over her mouth, cutting off her cry.

"Shut up," the man growled. "I'm not going to hurt you."

Greg? Jane snapped at his hand, trying to bite him, but she didn't catch any skin between her teeth.

"Calm down."

She shook her head and grabbed for his arms, but Greg let his weight fall on top of her, trapping her hands.

"Anh!" she screamed against his hold.

"Shut up. Don't scream and I won't hurt you. Are you going to scream?"

Jane shook her head, hoping he'd be dumb enough to let her go, but his hold stayed tight.

"I'm not going to let you ruin my career over something that didn't even happen, all right? Just take the recording off your phone, and I'll leave."

She nodded and closed her eyes, waiting for his hand to ease off, but his fingers dug harder into her cheek.

"Don't try anything, Jane. That killer is still on the loose, you know."

Tensing, she frowned at him.

"You don't want to be written off as his last victim, do you?"

Oh, my God, was he really threatening to kill her? No way did he have that in him. Then again, she hadn't really expected blackmail or breaking and entering either.

"You know who he is?" Greg asked. "A locksmith. And I used that spare key you hid on the side of the building. There's no sign of forced entry. Everything will point to him."

Jane nodded, serious this time. She felt his hand slide off. For a few heartbeats she considered screaming, but his story about the locksmith sounded well thought out. Maybe he really would hurt her. When he brought the phone closer to her, she decided on a better plan. She'd already screamed three times anyway. Either neighbors had heard her or they weren't going to.

"Delete the message," Greg demanded, holding out the phone.

"This is ridiculous," she said. "Do you think I won't tell the police about the blackmail? Not to mention that you've broken in to my apartment and threatened me?"

"It would be your word against mine. And I've got to tell you, your word just isn't worth as much."

Jane grabbed the phone, but Greg snagged her wrist before she could push any buttons.

"If your finger comes anywhere near the nine or the one, you'll regret it."

"Fine. But I have to call in to the system. It's not saved on my phone."

"I'm watching," he warned.

Jane pulled up her recent calls and quickly moved down to the one she wanted. It was a risk, but…

The line opened and began to ring. Jane held her breath, and so did Greg. There was no sound but the electric tone ringing through the ether. Finally it clicked into silence.

"Hello?" a deep, hoarse voice said.

"Chase!" she yelled just as Greg barked, "God-*damn* it," and knocked the phone from her hands. "It's Greg!"

He slammed his fist into the phone, turning the screen dark. "You bitch," he growled.

"You're an idiot," she snapped. When he twisted toward her, hand raised as if he might strike, Jane punched him. Hard. But not as hard as she could, not from this angle.

The feel of his jaw shifting under her knuckles freed some tightly controlled animal inside her. Jane pushed up to her knees as Greg sat back on the bed, both hands cradling his jaw.

"Hey," he whined. "You hit me!"

Putting years of practice into every movement, Jane drew back her arm and envisioned putting her fist right through the dark oval of his face. When her knuckles hit his nose, bone crunched.

Greg screamed. Her phone began to ring.

"You stupid, arrogant shit," she muttered, reaching out for the light next to her bed. When it snapped on, she saw Greg dressed in a black sweat suit and black knit cap, but the hands cupped to his nose were bright red and getting redder by the second.

He stood and backed away from the bed. "You broke my nose!"

A few seconds ago she'd been scrambling for a plan to get away from him, but now Jane jumped out of bed and followed. His eyes widened. Before he could turn and run, Jane jabbed him in the gut. When his hands fell, she aimed an uppercut for his jaw.

Greg fell backward, crying out in a high-pitched little scream that made her smirk.

"Don't you *ever* threaten me again."

Flat on the floor, Greg began to curl into a little ball to protect his body, but Jane was done with him. She grabbed her phone, which had finally gone silent, dialed 911 and strolled past Greg without even a twitch of nervousness.

By the time the 911 operator answered, Jane had slammed the door on Greg's whimpering and was headed downstairs. She filled the police in on what had happened, but her explanation came out in bits and pieces due to the constant beep of the other line.

"I need to answer this other call," Jane said.

"Ma'am, please stay on the line until the police arrive."

"But my friend—"

"Ma'am, the intruder is a continued threat. The arriving officers need to—"

"I told you he's incapacitated."

"Ma'am—"

The phone beeped again, and Jane hung up on the operator, worried that Chase thought she was being murdered by the serial killer. Before she could click to the other line, the hot squeal of tires on the street outside interrupted. Funny, she hadn't heard any sirens.

Jane opened the locked front door and was nearly trampled by Chase.

"Jane!" he yelled as his hands latched onto her shoulders. He was wearing gray sweats and nothing else. His hair, which she would've thought too short to get mussed, was lying in a funny direction on one side of his head.

"I'm fine." In fact, she felt fine, despite the throbbing in her right hand.

"What happened?"

"Greg… He broke in."

"He *what?*"

"He threatened me earlier today, and I recorded it, and—"

"What?" Panic widened his eyes. "What the hell are you talking about?"

"He said if I didn't sleep with him, he'd interfere with Jessie's plea, and spread the word about my past. But I recorded the conversation and told him I was going to get him fired."

"Oh, Christ," he muttered.

"So he broke in tonight and tried to make me erase it."

His gaze rolled toward the open door. "Is he gone?"

"No, he's upstairs, but—"

He broke for the stairs so quickly that Jane felt the breeze on her pajamas. "I already took care of it," she called out as she chased after him.

She heard the door slam open before she was halfway there. Greg's startled yelp of fear mixed with Chase's low "What the hell?"

"I said I took care of it." She stopped at Chase's shoulder, and he looked down at her in complete disbelief.

"You did *that?*"

They both turned to look at Greg, who had one hand to his still-bleeding nose and one held out to ward her off. Both eyes were already turning black. "L-Look," he stammered. "I was just leaving. This doesn't need to… Oh, God, I think my jaw's broken."

Jane shook out her aching hand. "That might explain why my hand hurts so much."

Greg cringed. "We don't need to involve—"

A siren wailed, cutting him off, mouth still open.

Chase looked down at her again, carefully taking her hand in his. "Wow, Miss Jane. That is totally hot. Wish I could've seen it."

Rolling her eyes, she slid her hand out of his just as Greg darted forward. If he'd thought he was going to make a run for it, he was sadly mistaken. Chase shoved him back so hard that Greg went sprawling on his ass. New blood spurted from his nose when he landed.

"Stay down, dickwad," Chase muttered.

"I need to let the police in," Jane said, but then she heard a rush of footsteps in the entry. "We're up here!" she shouted down.

Two officers came up, guns drawn. As soon as they spotted Chase, they aimed straight at him and yelled for him to get his hands up.

Jane put her hands up, too. "It's not him. The guy's in the bedroom." The guns stayed trained on Chase. "This is my friend! The intruder is in my bedroom."

Chase backed up until his back hit the wall, because

the police seemed hesitant to edge past him. When they got a look at Greg, one of them swung the pistol back toward Chase.

"Seriously," Jane said. "The man on the floor is the intruder."

They finally swooped down on Greg, who immediately began babbling about the D.A.'s office and who he knew at the police department.

Chase reached out for Jane's arm and tugged her toward him. "Why didn't you tell me what was going on?"

"You know why."

"Damn it, you can say I'm not your boyfriend, but you called *me* when you needed help."

The emotional part of her brain finally started working again. Jane felt her eyes burn with the start of tears.

It was true. It hadn't occurred to her to call anyone but Chase, and she hadn't been thinking about how close his place was to hers. She'd been thinking that if she needed help, Chase would help her. "You're a good guy," she said lamely.

"Jane…" he said as if he was about to lose his patience, but then the exasperation fell from his face like a mask and he snatched her into his arms to pull her close. "God, you scared the hell out of me. I thought… Are you sure you're okay?"

"My hand's starting to throb a little, but…" She didn't say anything more. The skin of his chest was so hot against her cheek, and he smelled warm and sleepy. She snuck her arms around his waist and just held on. Greg's voice seemed very far away as he demanded to be taken to the hospital.

Jane closed her eyes and listened to Chase's heartbeat vibrate through her. They stood like that for a long time before the police began asking questions. Nearly an hour later the police were gone and she had to face him alone.

"You want me to sleep on the couch?" he asked, but Jane shook her head.

"You have to go. Greg is going to make sure everyone in town knows about my past now. And there have been flashing lights outside my place for an hour. My neighbors are already talking. I can't have you sneaking out of here in the morning, adding fuel to the fire."

"I wasn't planning on sneaking out."

She shook her head and crossed her arms. "Thank you for coming. Thank you for caring. But I can't be with you, Chase. My reputation is going to be in shreds."

"And why do I detract from it? Because of my tattoos? Half the *girls* in this town have them, for Christ's sake."

She crossed her arms tighter. "Do you have a record?"

That shocked him. He pulled his chin in. "What?"

"Greg said you had a record. Is that true?"

He stared at her and said nothing.

"Oh, my God," she huffed. "I never asked because I figured you couldn't get permits with a criminal record. This is unbelievable."

"I was seventeen. It was my first offense. My record was expunged after two years."

"That doesn't mean it didn't happen! What did you do?"

Chase shook his head and shifted from foot to foot. "I stole a truck from my boss—"

"Oh, perfect!" She laughed, throwing her hands in the air. "A thief! No wonder you fit in so well with my family."

"I wanted to go to Grand Junction for the weekend, and I didn't think he'd miss it. He reported it stolen and I was picked up on my way home. My boss accepted my apology and the charge was lowered to criminal mischief. I did community service and paid reparations to the company. It was no big deal."

"No big deal? Then why didn't you tell me about it?"

Chase's jaw dropped. "You're kidding, right? After all the stuff you kept from me? Christ, you aren't the only one who struggled through shit as a teenager. I was pissed off, too. And I figured I'd poured all my money into rent and groceries since my very first job, so I decided I deserved a little joyride. Get over it and stop being self-righteous."

"I'm not being self-righteous, I'm saying I want to be with a man who's never seen the inside of a jail cell! Is that too much to ask?"

Chase shook his head and sighed. "I'm sorry I didn't tell you about it. I didn't *want* to tell you about it."

"So you kept it from me on purpose."

"Yes. Do I look like a fucking idiot? I knew you'd use it as an excuse, and that's exactly what you're doing now. It's an excuse, Jane. We're good together, and you said yourself that I was a good guy."

"It doesn't—"

"And you were right about one thing. Nothing's changed. The way you feel about me hasn't changed, and I still love you. But that doesn't mean I have to take this kind of shit. I'm going to go, and you can call me when you're ready to talk like a grown-up, all right?"

"No!"

"Put some ice on that hand, Sugar Ray."

"Chase…"

He gave her a perfunctory wave and walked out. After a moment of stunned silence, Jane locked the door and checked all the windows. The police had already found the key in Greg's pocket, thank God. Jane wasn't planning on calling a locksmith.

Still, she felt nervous as she walked around. Her eyes drifted toward the sofa where Chase had offered to sleep.

She'd made the right decision. They needed a clean break. There was nothing she could do about the past, but she could damn well do her best not to get it mixed up with her future.

CHAPTER TWENTY-TWO

HALFWAY THROUGH THE WEEK, Jane couldn't stop thinking about Chase. She'd thought of him a lot during their fling, but now it was pathological.

She wanted to call him. Wanted to call and say, "My mom is at my house!" But then she'd have to explain that her mom had never been to Jane's condo before, and that would sound awful, considering she lived twenty minutes away.

Jane poured two glasses of lemonade and went to sit next to her mom on the couch.

"So Jessie looks good?"

Her mom nodded. "He does. Really good, actually. And if he keeps up the good behavior, his lawyer says he'll probably be out in six months. That's not so bad."

"No, it's not."

"Are you gonna go see him? He can receive visitors until eight on Thursdays. You've still got an hour."

She looked into her mom's hazel eyes, noticing how deep the lines were getting beyond the mascara. "I don't think so, Mom. I sent him a letter a few days ago, though."

"He told me he got it. And thanks for paying for the attorney. She was real good. I'll try to pay you back someday."

"Please don't. I wanted to do it."

"Thank you. But I'll still try." Her mom sipped her drink and looked nervously around. "It's real pretty in here, Jane. Like something on TV."

"Thank you."

Her mom's neon-pink nails plucked at her skirt and Jane felt her gut lurch. Her own mother was nervous in her house. She had no idea what to say to Jane, and Jane didn't know what to say, either. This was ridiculous. And shameful.

"Oh!" her mom said. "I knew there was something I wanted to tell you. Do you remember Mrs. Jackson? She used to live next door? She stopped by to see me."

Jane nodded, hiding her anxiety about what was coming next.

"She said she'd heard how well you were doing for yourself now and she was just tickled pink."

Jane ducked her head. The stories were starting already.

Though Greg had been charged with breaking and entering, it hadn't made it to the papers. Probably the D.A.'s office was trying to keep everything quiet. They'd fired Greg immediately, and Jane had been relieved to hear he'd left town to go stay with his parents.

Still, his departure didn't really change things. He'd made sure to spread the word about her before he'd left. Mitch the dentist had already called to ask if everything was okay. Lori had come by the office just today, having heard some of the story from Quinn. Lori had brushed off Jane's concerns and taken her out for lunch without batting an eye.

But it hadn't been enjoyable. Jane had spent the

lunch wondering whether she knew the other diners and what they might think of her.

There was no hiding anymore.

Her mom smiled and patted her hand, seemingly oblivious to Jane's worries. "You remember Patricia, her daughter? She was younger than you. Only twenty-one years old and she married an Egyptian man and moved all the way over there. Can you imagine that? Married to a man from such a different culture? And so far away." She gave a disapproving hum.

Amazing that marrying an Egyptian man at twenty-one would shock Jane's mom. She'd married her first convict at nineteen, after all. That was only three years older than Jane had been when she'd gone off to party with three strangers.

Though her mom kept talking about Mrs. Jackson's recent visit to her daughter in Egypt, Jane's thoughts were on the past.

Her mom had made some really bad choices, but she'd had no one around to pull her out of them.

It should've been easy to forgive her, considering some of the bad choices Jane had made in her own life. But somehow it wasn't. Maybe because if Jane was going to forgive her mother for making bad choices, she'd have to forgive herself, too. That made her feel nauseated.

Maybe she could take baby steps.

"Mom, I was thinking I could bring some pizza by this weekend. Maybe we could all watch a movie or something?"

For a moment her mother looked as if Jane had proposed they paint their faces blue and rob a bank. But then she smiled, a grin so wide it showed off her back teeth. "That would be great, baby. Maybe we could invite Grandma Olive."

Jane's smile twitched into a sick grimace for just a moment before she managed to straighten it out. "Oh, sure. Whatever you want."

"She's a little lonely now that Jessie's gone."

"Of course." Lonely like a beta fish after it had eaten all its young. "Whatever you want, Mom."

"Oh, this is going to be so much fun! That new *Fast & Furious* movie is out on DVD. Have you seen it yet?"

"Um…no."

"Okay, I'll order the pizza, and you pick up the movie, all right? I'm so excited!"

Everything she said just made Jane feel worse, but thankfully her mom was gathering up her purse and phone.

"I've got to get home and make dinner for your dad. You think about going to visit Jessie, all right? We'll see you this weekend. Oh, Jane, I can't wait."

Jane stood, waiting awkwardly. When her mom passed her, Jane reached out and gave her a quick hug. "I love you, Mom."

"Oh, honey. That's so sweet! I love you, too!"

"I'll see you this weekend. Is Saturday okay?"

"You know us. We're just an old married couple. We only ride on Sundays now."

As soon as the door closed, Jane's eyes flew to the phone. She was shaking with nervous energy. She needed to talk to someone. Was Chase home?

It didn't matter. She'd broken things off. He meant nothing to her.

But she wanted to tell somebody that she'd reached

out to her mom. She could call Lori, but Lori wouldn't understand what a big step it was.

Heaving a sigh, Jane walked over to her coffee table and stared down at the phone. It seemed so innocuous, the screen staring blankly at nothing.

It was over. He wasn't the kind of man she wanted to date. It had been a clean break.

Eyes narrowed, she glared at the phone.

He'd said he didn't want to be used anymore, but that had been days ago. Surely he was horny by now. Maybe she could lure him over for sex and a quick conversation. Only because she was stressed out.

Comfort food. Chase was comfort food, and she was dying for a little comfort right now.

Jane snatched up the phone and flipped it open. She'd promised herself she wouldn't call him, but there was a way around that.

Pulling up his number, she typed out a text message.

Want to come over?

She counted to ten. Then counted again. Then she set her phone down and walked away from it to make it beep. It worked. Jane raced back and picked it up.

Dinner? A walk? It's a beautiful evening.

She scowled at the screen.

No, just here.

This time she didn't put it down—she only glared and waited, tapping her foot. Finally her answer arrived.

Thank you, but no. Have a good nite.

"Oh, you bastard," she huffed, tossing the phone onto the couch. "What kind of man refuses sex?"

She had no other outlet now. Nothing but boxing. And nowadays even boxing made her think of Chase. But at least she could imagine punching his face while thoughts of him tortured her.

The thought made her feel guilty. The guilt made her think of her mom. Then of Jessie. She was drowning in guilt and a helpless need to do *something*.

She'd taken a first step with her mom. Things were over with Chase. But what about Jessie? She glanced at the clock.

Her reputation was in a shambles, so she'd vowed not to set foot in the jail again. If anyone saw her, another juicy tidbit would be added to the delicious story of her true identity. Mitch would remember that he'd seen her at the jail, too. Everyone would wonder what she'd done. Perhaps they'd wonder if she was following in her mother's footsteps.

She couldn't do it.

But she'd vowed to be a better sister, a better person. Her relationship with Chase was effectively over, but she couldn't cut off her brother. Not if she wanted to help him.

Jane grabbed her keys and hurried out before her cowardice could gather itself up and stop her.

Half an hour later, when she saw Jessie's face, the

strange tension that had been tightening inside her eased a bit. He did look good.

"Hey, sis," he said into the cracked and dented phone, "I didn't expect to see you."

"I wanted to see how it was going."

He shrugged. "Not too bad. You know…it's jail."

"Yeah."

"Thanks for the letter."

"Of course," she said, no longer sure what she wanted to talk about. "Do you need anything?"

"Mom brought me cigarettes. Maybe some books would be nice. I used to read that sci-fi stuff, remember?"

Yes, she did remember all of a sudden. When he'd been thirteen and he'd asked to spend the night at her place, and she'd said no as she always did. Jessie had thrown one of those books at the wall before slamming the door to his room.

Jane nodded. "I'll ask around and see what's popular now."

"Great."

Silence fell between them. A stupid silence, considering they had only a few minutes. But Jane didn't know what to say. *I'm sorry I never let you spend the night at my place?*

"Hey!" Jessie said suddenly, a smile blooming over his face. "I heard they arrested someone for those murders!"

"Finally," Jane said.

"Dude, that's great. What a relief."

"I suppose."

"What's not great about it?"

Jane watched him, looking into his eyes. The same big

blue eyes he'd had as a sweet little boy. She didn't want to hurt him, but she didn't want to treat him like a kid, either. Not if she expected him to start acting like a man.

She straightened her shoulders. "He changed the locks on the homes of all three women after their purses were stolen."

Jessie nodded.

"He kept copies of the new keys."

"That's devious, man."

He didn't get it, so Jane took a deep breath and said it as clearly as she could. "Jessie, if you hadn't stolen Michelle Brown's purse, she might still be alive."

His face fell, crumpling into shock. "I didn't mean for that to happen."

"I know, and the truth is, with or without you, there was a killer out there looking for his next victim. But your actions had real consequences. First of all, a person's life can be ruined if they lose their rent money or the payment for their child's day care. And even worse things, things you couldn't imagine, like what happened to Michelle. I know you didn't mean it, but… You didn't mean it, but it still happened, Jessie."

His gaze fell to the counter and he rubbed a hand over his eyes. She felt as if she'd just stuck a knife into his back, but it wasn't about her. He needed to spend his time in jail thinking, and she wanted him to start at the right place. She wanted him to regret his old life, so he'd start a new one. Sometimes regret was a powerful force.

"I love you," Jane said just as the warning chime sounded.

Jessie looked up, his eyes bright with tears. "I'm

sorry about Michelle. And I'm sorry I let you and dad down. Mom, too. I really am."

A tear slipped down her cheek when she nodded. "I'll come see you again next week, okay?"

Her love life was one thing. She could give that up if she had to. But her family…she didn't want to lose them again.

CHAPTER TWENTY-THREE

"HEY, NICE FLOWERS!" Mr. Jennings said when he came out to grab the three-hole punch.

Jane tossed a glare toward the gorgeous bunch of multicolored tulips that had arrived at eleven. "Thanks."

"Are they from Chase?"

"Mmm," she hummed noncommittally. Yes, they were from Chase. They'd come complete with an adorable message. "You make my heart go boom. Love, Chase."

Mr. Jennings disappeared back into his office, only to reappear seconds later. "Maybe I should send Lori some flowers. Do you think she'd like that?"

"Oh, of course! Do you want me to order them?"

"No, no. A man should order his own flowers, right?"

"Sure."

His office door closed, but opened again only twenty seconds later. "Jane, who should I order flowers from?"

"I'll bring you a number," she said, trying to hide her smile. A few minutes later she had the number of a place in Tumble Creek, and a backup number of her favorite florist here in Aspen.

"Mr. Jennings," she said as she handed it over, "there's a florist in Tumble Creek, but it's called Randolph Gifts and Fly Fishing. I wasn't sure if—"

"Oh, Mr. Randolph! Right. He's perfect—thank you."

"He sells flowers and…worms?"

"Well, it's a small town. You're coming to the party, right? You did the work, after all."

Lori was leaving for the big tour of Europe in a week. Mr. Jennings would be joining her for two weeks, but before she left he was throwing a going-away party at her house in Tumble Creek. "Absolutely. I wouldn't miss it."

"You should bring Chase."

"No! Chase and I aren't… We only went out on one date. Maybe two. Anyway, it's over. He's not my type. Obviously!"

"Are you sure? He's a good guy."

"Mr. Jennings, last week you were convinced he was roughing me up!"

He shrugged. "Eh, I was freaked out. It's too bad it didn't work out. I hope it won't be awkward for you when he comes in."

"No, I'm sure I'll be fine." She hurried out to escape his eyes. The man never noticed anything around him, and suddenly he was Mr. Inquisitive. "Unbelievable," she muttered as she sat down.

This bad habit of talking to herself was going to have to stop. The whole point of pushing Chase away had been to make herself *more* normal. But she couldn't help her nervous energy. She'd gotten hooked on sex with Chase, and she needed a fix. God, how could he be so stubborn?

And she wanted to tell him that she'd seen Jessie, that he seemed to be growing up. Wanted to tell him she was trying to reconcile with her mother.

Sadly, it turned out that the man she'd been using for meaningless sex had become her best friend. A man she'd known for less than a month was her closest confidant. How pitiful was that?

Jane sighed. For once, her work felt tedious, but she forced herself to dive back into the next quarter's budget and wrestle it to the ground. When the door whooshed open, she was just reaching into the closest filing cabinet to grab last year's receipts. She glanced over her shoulder, and Chase was standing there.

Chase. He smiled and her heart tumbled over and over and landed somewhere near her feet.

"Hi, Miss Jane."

"Chase," she whispered, taking him in on a wide-eyed glance. He'd cut his hair. Actually, he'd buzzed it so low it was practically shaved. He looked as if he belonged in a Mad Max movie. He looked…incredibly hot.

Jane cleared her throat. "Mr. Chase."

His eyes slid to the vase of tulips. "You got the flowers?"

"Yes, thank you."

"I hope you like tulips."

Finally pulling herself together, she straightened in her chair and forced herself to be stern Jane. "You shouldn't be here."

"Why?"

"What do you mean, *why?* You need to go! This is completely inappropriate!"

"Jane, this isn't—"

Mr. Jennings's door opened. "Hey, Chase."

Jane stifled a groan. *Great.* A scene at her office. "Chase, you need to—"

Mr. Jennings stepped past her. "Are you ready to go?"

"Yep," Chase answered.

Jane froze. "Wait a minute. What's going on here?"

He winked. "We're going to lunch, Jane. Want to come with?"

"No!" she yelled, but Mr. Jennings's words made perfect sense now. *I hope it won't be awkward…* Crud. "Mr. Jennings, you didn't put this on your schedule. I'm…"

Chase's smile widened.

"Oh, just go," she muttered.

"Bye, Miss Jane," Chase said with another wink that made her face flash hot. But when he turned to follow Mr. Jennings out the door, more than just her face burned.

She knew why he'd cut his hair so short. That sneaky, slimy *dog*. With his head buzzed she could see all of his tattoo. The way the black ink curved lovingly up his strong neck and cupped the base of his skull. The way the tendrils narrowed like flames before they faded away.

Oh, God, she wanted to lick him so badly. She wanted to follow that ink with her tongue all the way from his arm to his skull. His hair would be rough and prickly under her mouth…. Jane shivered.

"Oh, crud," she groaned, but that wasn't the least bit satisfying. She glanced around as if someone might have snuck back into the office, and then Jane put her shoulders back and said, "Shit." Then "Fucking bastard."

The cursing helped her feel a little better. Not much, but a little.

She couldn't date Chase, no matter how much she

missed him. After all these years of striving to transform herself, she couldn't just throw up her hands and admit defeat. Not for a *man*. She'd be telling herself and everyone else that it didn't matter how fast and far she ran, she was still Dynasty Alexis.

Dynasty, who liked big men with criminal records. Who had emotionless sex with men in their cars. Who got turned on by steel-toed boots and tattoos and dirty T-shirts. Chase brought all that out in her, so it couldn't matter that he was also kind and considerate and generous. It *couldn't*.

Sniffing, pretending it was allergies and not emotion, Jane wiped her nose and glanced at the clock. The men had been gone for only ten minutes. She'd give it another thirty before taking her own lunch. She couldn't see Chase again.

The sight of that tattoo would break her.

CHAPTER TWENTY-FOUR

"Mom?" Jane opened the screen door and stuck her head inside her parents' house. "Dad?"

"We're here, sweetie!" Her mom rushed out, black heels clomping on the wood floor. She'd dressed down, though. She was showing no cleavage, and Jane was pretty sure her mother had picked out the plain blue sweater in Jane's honor.

"The pizza should be here in a few minutes." She gave Jane a quick hug, as if afraid her daughter would pull away if she squeezed too tight. "We're in the den looking through old pictures. I'm thinking of trying scrapbooking."

Jane followed her mom past the kitchen to the sunken living room, remembering how excited they'd both been about this house when Mac had announced he was buying it. A den. A *fireplace*. It had seemed like a fantasy.

Jane had thought everything was going her way when she was nine. She'd even dreamed that her real dad would move to Colorado when he got out, and she'd get to have everyone she loved in her life. Her mom, her stepdad, her new little brother and her real dad, too.

When I get paroled, the first thing I'm going to do is take you to Disneyland, baby girl.

She vividly remembered sending off for a Disney brochure. She'd kept it under her pillow for months.

Calling Chase a bastard had been unfair. She knew what a real bastard was like.

Lost in thought, following her mom, Jane didn't register at first that it wasn't Mac going through photos with her mother. It was Grandma Olive. Oh, Jesus.

"Look who's graced us with her presence," Olive said.

"Grandma Olive." She sighed.

"Where's that big man of yours?"

"Chase is just a friend."

"Pfft. Even I'd be tempted by a man like that, and you never said no to anything in your life."

"Grandma," Jane's mom snapped. "Stop it."

The old lady sniffed. "It's just the truth."

Jane had been hearing it for years, so she gritted her teeth and dropped into a recliner.

Her mom turned concerned eyes on her. "Are you doing okay? That ex-boyfriend hasn't bothered you again?"

"No, I'm fine. He's gone to stay with his parents in Fort Collins. I'm sure the D.A. will drop the charges, and once that happens, I don't think he'll be back."

"Good," her mom said, handing over a thick photo album. "Here, sweetie. Most of your pictures are in this one."

Happy to avoid any further conversation about Greg or Chase, Jane cracked open the album. The first few pages were mostly pictures of Jessie as a baby, and she smiled as soon as she saw them. He'd been painfully adorable. It was easy to see how he'd wrapped their mother around his finger.

The pictures progressed, and Jane was there, grinning and stick-thin. In the summer pictures her hair was lightened by the strong mountain sun. The winter photos showed her wearing a collection of brightly colored knit caps, all of them topped with pom-poms. She'd forgotten those caps. Her mom had developed a passion for knitting, and Jane had been the number one benefactor.

"Mom, do you still knit?"

"Oh, my God, I haven't knit anything in years!"

"You should try it again. You always looked so happy sitting in front of the TV with your yarn."

"Oh, now I'm busy using Twitter. I can't figure out *Lost* without my Twitter friends. And I don't have any reason to knit. Neither of you kids seem anywhere close to giving me grandbabies."

Olive piped up. "That Jessie might end up with a kid sometime soon. 'Course, it'd be a bastard. But probably cute as hell."

They both ignored her. Jane flipped through a few more pages, noticing the way her appearance began to change. She'd started getting curvy in the fourth grade but still had that bright glow of childhood. A few pages later a different Dynasty began to appear. This one had short hair and too much makeup. Her eyes still flashed, but the smiles were hard and flirtatious. Soon the smiles stopped altogether, replaced with pouting lips and narrowed eyes and hair bleached nearly white. The girl got taller and the clothes got shorter.

Jane snapped the book closed. She always felt as though regret were stitched into her skin, but looking at those photos, she could feel the string pulled tighter and tighter, as if the seams of her body might tear themselves apart at any moment.

She took a deep breath, telling herself it was all long past, but when the doorbell rang, Jane jumped as if she'd heard a shot fired.

"It's the pizza!" her mom called, jumping up. "Mac! Pizza's here."

Jane pulled the DVD out of her purse and stuck it in the machine. Mac brought in the paper plates and pizza, and Jane sat next to him on the couch.

A movie, beer and pizza. Everyone settled in happily to watch the show. But all Jane could think about were the pictures. She'd been so…young. One minute she'd been a little girl, and the next minute she'd been throwing herself at boys…and men.

She'd known that already, but the pictures had shown her something else, something she hadn't known.

At one point she'd been happy. Oh, not as a teenager, but before that…before that, she'd been happy.

In her mind she'd remembered those awful years of moving from town to town, prison to prison. She'd remembered the hard-eyed new "daddies" and the guards with guns. The thin walls of rented trailers and the roaches in the sink. But for a while there, after Mac had been freed and they'd become a real family…she'd been *happy.*

She'd had a family and a house and a real yard to play in. She'd had her own bedroom and a dad who actually lived at home with them. Schoolwork had come easily to her. She'd done well.

In those few short years, everything had been perfect. How could she not have remembered?

Sipping her beer, Jane leaned her head against Mac's shoulder, hoping he wouldn't notice if a few tears soaked into his T-shirt. Her head was wobbly, and she needed her dad to lean against for a few minutes.

Prison tattoos and all, he was the best man she'd ever known. The best man. So what the hell had she been running from for so long?

CHASE WOKE LATE on Sunday morning, bleary-eyed from a rough night. His dad had called him at ten, obviously drunk, to offer some new ideas about how to get Jessie clear of murder charges. Chase had reminded him that Jessie had already been cleared, then listened to his dad reminisce about his mother for a little while before hanging up.

That call had kept him awake until two in the morning. Now it was 9:00 a.m. and his eyes felt gritty and swollen. He felt as if he had a hangover, though he could judge only by the way his employees looked after partying too hard. They always looked like shit, and he definitely felt like it.

Groaning, he let his head fall back to his pillow, wondering why the sun was so insistent on crawling across the top of his bed.

Then he heard it. The faint beep of his phone. He sat up and glared suspiciously at his empty bedside table. Why wasn't his phone there? Jesus, maybe he really had gotten drunk last night. Maybe he'd thrown caution to the wind and downed those two bottles of beer in his fridge, then passed out in an embarrassingly low-level stupor.

He finally identified his jeans as the source of the

beeping and snatched them off the floor to dig his phone out of a pocket. When he saw the missed call on the screen, his exhaustion disappeared like a bad dream.

Jane.

Sunday morning seemed an odd time for a booty call. Maybe she was calling for something else?

He hit a button and held his breath while the phone rang.

"Chase?" she said, and the sound of her saying his name made him smile. Ridiculous.

"Hey, Jane."

"You sound tired. Are you okay?"

Chase stretched and collapsed back onto the mattress. "I'm still in bed."

"Oh. I…see."

Was she picturing him naked? He was sure as hell thinking of her nude body stretched out next to him. Damn.

"Late night?" she asked.

"Yeah."

"Did you go out?" Her voice sank a little.

Chase smiled. "No, I stayed home and moped around, missing you and wondering when you'd call."

"Look, you don't have to be a smart-ass. You can go out all you want. You don't answer to me, obviously."

"I wasn't being a smart-ass, Jane."

He heard her breathing for a moment before she said, "Oh."

Stretching again, he rubbed a hand over his stomach. "So, did you call to find out if I was cheating on you?"

"You can't cheat on someone who's not your girl-friend."

"Mmm-hmm. So you won't mind if I hook up with the new check-out girl at the grocery store? She's cute and she's been checking me out. Ha! Get it?"

Jane didn't laugh.

"She always shakes her head over my pile of frozen dinners and asks why I don't have a woman cooking for me."

"Shut up, Chase. I just wanted to talk to you, all right?"

"All right. Meet me at The Stube for breakfast?"

A pause. She was probably imagining who else would be at the most popular breakfast place in town. "I already had breakfast," she mumbled.

"Okay, then. Brunch. Or coffee. Or a piece of toast."

"Chase… I can't… You practically shaved your head, for God's sake! And I know *that's* why you did it. You did it as a *challenge*. To see if I'd still go out with you!"

Chase ran a hand over what was left of his hair. "I thought it was time for a change. I also thought my tattoo might attract the interest of other complicated girls. I seem to have been deserted by mine."

"You're thirty-four years old, for crying out loud. And you look like you're the lead singer in a punk band."

"Yeah, I'm clear on my age. I'm also clear on the fact that I'm a grown man who runs his own company and wipes his own nose, and I can do whatever the hell I feel like doing. You should try it sometime, Jane. It's called living your life."

"Screw you," she muttered halfheartedly.

"Sorry, but that gravy train is off the tracks."

The line clicked dead in the middle of her vicious growl. Jane had hung up on him. Chase chose to take it as a victory, even if his heart gave a startled yelp of pain.

He was trying not to take it personally, but, truthfully, sometimes it hurt like hell. She'd never beat around the bush. Jane's message was simple: you're not good enough for me. Even when he told himself it had nothing to do with him... Shit, it still stung, and he had to wonder how long he'd give her.

A week? A month?

He thought of the way her sweet body had cuddled against him in her bed.

Probably a month. Something about her proud and prickly nature pushed all his buttons. The good, pleasurable buttons, not the bad ones. Jane Morgan was like dynamite. On the surface she looked safe and stable and easily managed. But beneath the surface calm she was contained danger that left him shaking. He loved it.

Still clutching the phone, Chase let his arm fall across his eyes to shut out the ruthless sunlight, so he was startled as hell when the phone rang right next to his ear.

"Hello?"

"Can you meet me in half an hour?"

Chase grinned at the sound of her grumpy capitulation. "At The Stube?"

"Yes." The word was bitter and hard, but he'd take it.

"I'll see you there, darlin'."

She hung up again, but this time Chase didn't even flinch. A month. Ha! In her dreams.

CHAPTER TWENTY-FIVE

JANE CLUTCHED her too-hot coffee cup and watched Chase exchange a few words with the older lady at the hostess stand. Good Lord, he was a beautiful thing. When he moved toward Jane's table, the hostess turned to look at his tattoo with wide eyes, but then Jane was too distracted by his smile to notice the rest of the world.

"Good morning, beautiful," he said, leaning down to give her a quick kiss before she could stop him. When he moved toward his chair, Jane glanced around to see if anyone had noticed. Nobody was looking their way. Nobody but Chase, whose warm blue eyes cooled at her panicked look.

"Sorry," he mumbled, not sounding sorry at all. "Were you going to pretend I was just a friend?"

She shook her head, even though that had been exactly what she'd planned to do. "No."

Chase scowled and picked up his menu without saying another word. The waitress stopped by less than thirty seconds later, but he was ready. Jane shook her head when the girl asked if she'd decided to eat, but Chase ordered an enormous amount of food, plus coffee and orange juice.

"How's your dad?" she asked when she couldn't stand the silence anymore.

"He's good."

"That's great! Maybe he really is on the road to recovery. If he—"

"Actually, I lied. He's not good. He called me up drunk last night, which probably gives you another reason not to get involved with me. Grandparents' Day at the kids' school would be a real bitch. Which grandparent would be the least embarrassing? Hard call."

Jane looked down at her coffee, distressed by the hurt in his voice. He'd looked so happy until she'd gotten worried about that little kiss. Crud.

"I'm sorry," she said.

Chase met her eyes over the edge of his coffee cup. Those eyes saw through her. They saw through her and he didn't like what he was seeing. "Why'd you call, Jane? I thought maybe you were coming around. I guess I was wrong."

"I…" She was afraid to say it. Afraid to say that she couldn't stop thinking about him and she missed him and maybe she'd been wrong the whole time. "I…I called my mom last week!" she blurted out. "I invited her over for a drink and then yesterday I went to her house for pizza and a movie."

Frowning, he set the cup down. "Why are you saying that like you've never done it before?"

"Because I've never done it before."

"Wow."

"I don't want you to think my problems have anything to do with you."

"I know it's not about me, but that doesn't make it easier to be treated like trash."

"Oh. I've tried to tell you how I—"

"I get that, Jane. Why would I be here if I didn't get it?"

"I'm sorry. I'm trying to change. I'm reaching out to my mom, but…" They fell into silence. Chase added another sugar to his coffee. He played with the empty paper packet.

When he cleared his throat, Jane jumped.

"Look," he said. "I'm sorry I kept that arrest from you. You were right. I did it deliberately. I knew you wouldn't like it, so I kept quiet. But I swear to you, it was a onetime screwup. My boss didn't even fire me."

She nodded. Of course she understood. She wasn't that big a hypocrite. "You don't have to apologize. I've been keeping so many secrets for years.…"

While she was still trying to put her thoughts into words, the waitress rushed over, setting four plates in front of Chase. The lumberjack special with blueberry pancakes, plus a side of wheat toast and half a grapefruit.

Chase poured syrup on the pancakes. "So what was it like, hanging out with your mom?"

Relief tightened her throat. She didn't want to argue. She just wanted to *talk* to him. "It was nice. It would've been nicer if Grandma Olive hadn't been there."

He smiled, and Jane's skin flashed hot. For a moment she just watched him eat, aware of a creeping feeling of jealousy for the blueberry pancakes. He seemed to be enjoying them immensely. She wanted Chase to be enjoying *her* like that.

Chase pushed the plate toward her. "You can have the rest."

"No, thanks. I'm not hungry."

"Why are you drooling over my pancakes, then?"

Crud. Jane took the pancakes just to avoid saying "I'm starving for *you.*" Still, she watched him while he ate. The muscles of his jaw shifted, drawing her eye to his temple and beyond to the last little tendrils of his tattoo.

Funny, this whole situation had started because she'd lost it over Greg's chewing. Now she was getting turned on by Chase eating breakfast.

Unbelievable.

Chase cleared his throat. "So why did you call?"

Because I miss you so much I can't stand it. She swallowed those revealing words. "I wanted to talk."

He set down his fork. "About what?"

About anything. But he was watching her too closely and she couldn't get any words out. "Go ahead and eat. I don't want your food to get cold."

He picked up his fork and started on the eggs.

Jane began with something easy, telling him about Lori's upcoming trip to Europe and how Quinn would be joining her in Spain because he'd lived there for a year in college. Then she updated him on how Jessie was doing. "He wrote to the family of Michelle Brown."

His eyebrows rose. "He did?"

"He wanted to apologize for the part he played in their loss. His lawyer said it would leave him vulnerable to a lawsuit, but Jessie said he didn't have anything to lose anyway, so he wrote to the family to say he was sorry."

"That's good."

And then there was nothing easy to talk about. She wanted to reach out and touch him, but she'd drawn a line between them, so how could she cross it now?

"I've been thinking about my mom," Jane said.

He started to set down his fork again, but when she frowned, he sighed and picked it up.

"My mom had photos out when I went over. Family pictures. And I noticed something in those pictures."

"What?"

"I think there were a few years that I just forgot. I forgot them because there was nothing dramatic going on and everything was okay. And I was looking at those photos and I thought…maybe I've been mad at the wrong person all these years. My mom made mistakes, but she was *there,* and…and I think I was actually happy."

"But you talked about those prisons, all those moves from town to town."

"That was bad. But after Mac was released and Jessie was born… We were a family. And everything was really good until my dad was paroled. My dad…"

She glanced up to find him staring at her, but his eyes dropped to the plate so that she could continue. "I learned to write when I was four, just so I could send him letters. From the moment I sent that first letter, he wrote to me every week. Told me how proud he was and how much he loved me and all the wonderful stuff we'd do together someday. But as soon as he got out of prison, he disappeared. He had better things to do. He didn't need to entertain himself with a kid. I was mad at him, but I think deep inside I blamed my mom."

"Because she chose him?"

"Yes. It was her fault he was my dad, but mostly I blamed her because she was *there*. It was easy to hate her. But if I've been mad at the wrong person my whole life… That's kind of awful, isn't it? That's really, really bad." She heard his fork hit the plate, but she couldn't see much past the tears pooling in her eyes.

"No, I'm fine," she said, but as soon as his fingers slid over hers, two fat tears dropped down her cheeks.

"Jane, you need to talk to your mom."

She tried to sniff hard enough to make the tears disappear. "I can't. I don't know what to say."

"Tell her what you told me."

"I don't want to admit that I'm a bad person. How can I just say that? 'Mom, I'm an awful person. Sorry about that.'"

"Oh, come on." His chuckle sounded a bit panicked, perhaps because the tears were escaping her control. "You're not a bad person, Jane. Jesus." His fingers tightened. "Don't cry."

"Of course I'm a bad person. I like you so much. But I tell myself I can't like you, because I need to have a man who comes from a stable family. A man without a record. Someone who's refined and settled and educated. Because I'm *not*, and I need that pretense. On my own I'm just a low-class girl with a sordid past who lucked into a good job."

"Jane, look at me."

She grabbed a napkin and wiped her eyes, then let her gaze rise as far as his mouth. Chase hunched down until she was looking at his eyes.

"Listen to yourself."

"What?"

"You're looking for a man who can *fix* you?"

"No! I don't expect a man to fix me! I'm not an idiot. I just want a man I can hide behind."

Chase's eyebrows flew high. His mouth twitched up, and Jane felt her mouth twitch, too.

"Jane, I'm no Dr. Phil, but I'm pretty sure you're certifiably fucked-up."

"Shut up!"

"It's true. Man, if I wasn't already in love with you, I'd be out of here."

For the first time, his talk of love didn't make her feel nauseated. In fact, she felt rather warm inside. Scared to death, but warm.

"Do you love me?" he asked softly.

Okay, now the scared-to-death part had arrived. Oh, God. Since he'd walked out of her condo that night, Jane had been telling herself she missed his body. She'd stared at the phone, hands sweating with the need to call him, sure that she wanted only to climb on top of him and use him as stress relief again.

But the brutal truth was unavoidable. More than anything, she'd wanted to talk to him, to hold his hand, to watch a movie with his arms curved around her. And, yes, she wanted to have sex with him, because he used her body just the way she liked and then whispered of love afterward.

"It doesn't matter," she whispered.

"Sure, it's totally inconsequential, but humor me."

She loved him. She did. Even the things holding her back made her heart speed with sheer joy. His calloused hands and dusty shirts. His muddy boots and inked skin. And his frickin' hair was turning her on like crazy. "You should hate me for the way I've treated you."

He shrugged. "I'm pretty tough."

"I'm scared. I don't think I can do this."

"You changed your whole life when you were sixteen years old. You really think you can't change your dating habits at thirty?"

"Twenty-nine," she muttered.

He winked. "I know."

Her hands shook against the cup. "If I love you, I'll have to be me for the rest of my life. Really me."

"Don't you think it's about time?"

"Oh, God," she breathed. Be herself? Her *real* self? "Maybe. Maybe I'd like to try."

Chase smiled, not looking nearly as surprised as she'd expected.

"Can you give me a couple more days? You were right. I need to work a few things out first."

"Sure. I can get by that long."

She picked up her purse, a red-hot mix of hope and terror swirling through her chest.

"But…" Chase stopped her with a hand around her wrist as she stood. "I'm gonna let my hair grow out next week, so you'd better make up your mind."

Her eyes flew to his tattooed skull. Jane licked her lips.

"You're going to miss your chance, darlin'."

He knew. He knew she wanted to nibble her way all the way up, wanted to lick him, wanted to look down and see that tattooed head between her thighs… God, he was so arrogant.

He pulled her hand toward his mouth and slowly lowered his lips to her wrist.

"Chase," she whispered.

His smile was pressed to her skin. "You didn't look around that time, Jane. What if people are watching?"

She shook her head, too consumed with the shivers spreading up her arms from the feel of his breath on her pulse.

"You want to touch it?"

Jane pulled her hand away, afraid that she'd start to pet him and things would get out of control. "I'll be in touch. Soon."

"Okay."

She didn't want to go, but if she stayed, she'd be hypnotized by his blue eyes and wide smiles. She took a step. Then another.

"Jane?" he called when she was only one table away.

She turned back.

"I've got a degree in geology, so you can use me for my educational achievements anytime."

"What?"

"Do you think they hand out dynamite to any firebug with fuse and a prayer?"

"I…"

"Want me to have it tattooed on my other arm? 'College educated with love and Jane Morgan approved'?"

She gaped at him in utter shock.

"Ha! You're such a snob. They let guys with tattoos into college, too. I'll call you later to find out how you're doing, Miss Jane." And with a wink, he turned his attention back to his food.

Jane stood there in the middle of the restaurant, watching him eat bacon. When she finally recovered enough to think, she glanced around. Sure enough, the people at the nearby tables were staring at her, most of them with knowing smiles. She looked back to Chase sitting there, muscles bulging in his T-shirt, black tattoos glowing dark against his skin, looking like a damned punk-rock criminal.

Then she caught the smiling eye of a woman at the next table, and Jane's fear seemed like a pitiful thing. Something easily ignored. She found herself suddenly smiling back.

That man—that big, gorgeous, scary-looking man—would be Jane's if she had the courage to claim him. He could *belong* to her. And it had nothing to do with his degree. None of these people knew about that, but Jane felt proud all the same.

As she walked out, the tiny little kernel of bravery she'd hidden beneath layers of fear began to burn and grow. If she wanted a chance to lick that man's tattoo again, she was going to have to find a way to resuscitate her courage completely. She was going to have to set aside decades of guilt and shame and anxiety and learn to live.

It seemed an insurmountable task, but Billy Chase's skull might be the only motivation in the world strong enough to help her overcome her terror. Maybe there was hope for her after all.

TWENTY-FOUR HOURS AFTER her first visit to her mom's house, Jane was back on her parents' couch. She'd come to face her demons, but the battle was less than dramatic. Her mom was out getting groceries and Mac was working, so Jane sat alone on the couch, clutching the photo album so hard that her knuckles began to ache. The sound of revving power tools echoed through the open window from the direction of Mac's shop. A motorcycle roared past the house before it slowed and turned into the shop drive.

All familiar sounds.

For a while after she'd stopped sleeping around, Jane hadn't been able to go to the shop to see Mac. Too many times his customer would be some biker she'd hooked up with at one of the bars. Too many times she'd had to hurry out and hope Mac hadn't noticed the knowing gleam in the man's eyes.

When she thought about it now, she couldn't quite believe she'd escaped that life so safely. She'd gotten a second chance, and she'd clutched at it with desperation.

Jane looked back to the picture she'd been staring at for the past fifteen minutes. Most of the photos were posed family shots, but this one had been taken when she wasn't paying attention. Instead of staring boldly at the camera with a smirk or a pout, she was sitting on the hood of Mac's old truck, looking into the distance. Her knees were tucked up to her chest, her arms wrapped around her legs. Without the camouflage of a defiant glare, she looked very young. And sad. And lost. She looked like a girl grown men should have gone to jail for touching.

She traced a finger around the edge of the photo. Chase was right. She'd been a kid. And if she saw this young girl hanging around Ryders today, Jane would feel sorry for her. She'd think this was a girl who needed help, not a girl who could never be forgiven.

If I forgive my mother, I'll have to forgive myself.

The motorcycle started again, a roar that would've carried through the window even if it hadn't been open.

Jane could hang out in Mac's shop with him now if she wanted to. No one would recognize her even if they knew about Dynasty's new name. But it was a catch-22. If she wanted to remain separated from her past, she couldn't hang out with her stepfather. She couldn't be Mac's daughter. She couldn't be Jessie's sister. She couldn't be herself or she had to be Dynasty, too.

The hinges of the front door squealed. "Jane?" her mom called.

"I'm in here!"

"Mac said you were waiting for me." She walked in with two shopping bags clutched in each hand.

"Let me help," Jane offered, jumping up to grab a bag.

"Thanks, sweetie."

She helped her mom put the groceries away, surprised that she remembered the exact spot for each item.

"Jessie called me," her mom said. "Did you hear they're charging that locksmith already? Jessie's so relieved they caught the guy. He was worried about you living alone. We all were."

"I'm fine, Mom."

"Are you sure? You've been acting a little odd. Is everything okay?"

Jane stared into the cupboard, hand frozen on a box of cereal. The same kind of cereal Mac had eaten twenty years before. "I'm sorry, Mom."

"Sorry for what, baby?"

She couldn't move, couldn't face her own mother. "I'm sorry for the kind of person I've been."

"What?"

"And I'm sorry I've been so awful to you."

"Honey, you haven't been awful to me."

Jane couldn't just stand there with her hand on a box of cereal for five minutes. She finally closed the cupboard and turned to meet her mom's troubled eyes. "I've been mad at you since I was twelve, and I've stayed away so I wouldn't have to think about it, but you don't deserve that. I'm sorry."

"Well, you've been busy with your own life, baby. It's okay."

"No, Mom. Don't make excuses for me. I live twenty minutes away. I haven't been *that* busy."

Her mom looked down before giving a small nod.

"I'm trying to make some changes, but first I wanted you to know that I thought I was mad at you, but mostly I was mad at myself. It was easier to resent you than it was to admit the truth. That I hated myself."

"Oh, Jane," her mom said, reaching out to pull her into her arms. "Don't say that. You're so smart and pretty and strong."

"It's okay." Her throat burned, but her eyes were dry. It felt good to admit it. "I hated myself, but I think I'm going to give up on that, too. I was just a kid. Teenagers do dumb things. It's part of the job description."

"What do you mean? What happened?"

Jane shook her head. If her mom wanted to pretend she hadn't known anything, then Jane would let her have that. "Just growing pains, Mom. It doesn't matter now." She tightened her arms. "I love you."

"I love you, too. But you know that. We always had each other, didn't we?"

That much was true. It wasn't as if her mom had been

out on the town with a new boyfriend every week. She'd worked and spent time with Jane and that had been it.

Her mom stepped back, taking hold of Jane's hand to pull her toward the kitchen table. "You are so much smarter than I ever was. So much more determined. Do you know why I married your father?"

Jane held her breath for a moment, trying to calm her galloping heart. "No."

"My stepdaddy… You never met him, but he wasn't a nice person. He beat my mom when he was drunk. Screwed around on her when he wasn't. And sometimes…sometimes he paid too much attention to me, if you know what I mean."

She squeezed her mom's fingers in answer.

"I didn't trust men. I liked them, but they made me nervous. I never knew what to expect from them. Like your dad…I knew him before he was sent away. He was reckless and arrogant, but charming as hell. We went out once, but he had lots of girlfriends. I knew he'd never settle for me. I was too…small, I guess.

"But when he was arrested, I wrote to him. I figured he could use a friendly word. And he wrote back, Jane. He wrote me so many letters. He said he loved me. Asked me to marry him. I guess he figured I was small enough that I'd marry a man who was about to be sent to prison for twenty years. And I was. I was scared of men, but I so wanted someone to love, and this wild and handsome man had chosen *me*."

"So you married him," Jane said past a tight throat, fighting against the sad need she could hear in her mom's words. Jane knew how it felt to feel worthless and still want to be loved.

"I married him. And I got you out of the deal, and I was so happy. But your dad started getting mad that I wasn't writing as often, and I made too many excuses not to come visit. I got tired of the arguments. The woman next door was married to an inmate, too, and she had a brother in a Texas prison, so I started writing to him. I don't know what I was looking for, but I kept on looking."

Jane nodded.

"And then I met Mac and you know what happened after that."

"Why'd you stay with Mac? After he got out, I mean. I kept expecting that one day he'd go to work and we'd just pack up and leave." Her mom frowned, and Jane saw wrinkles she'd never noticed before.

"Did you want to?"

"At first, yeah. There'd never been a man around. I was scared of him."

Her mom laughed, but it turned into a tiny sob and she pressed her fingers to her mouth. A few tears leaked from her eyes even when she managed a smile. "I was, too. I was so shocked at first, I didn't know what to do. I told myself, the moment he lays his fist on me, we're out of here. When that didn't happen, I told myself I'd leave if he said one mean word to you. But he didn't. He was just like his letters—thoughtful and fair. And sometime later I realized I felt safe with him, even though he wasn't behind bars anymore."

She shook her head, sniffing back the last of her tears, and she managed a watery laugh. "I don't know what would've happened to us without Mac. But I…I'm sorry for everything that happened before him, baby doll. I thought I was keeping you safe, living without a man in the house. I thought that was best for you, but…I guess I just didn't understand."

"You did your best," Jane whispered, finally believing it.

"I did, but my best was nothing compared to yours. I'm so proud of you."

They hugged and cried a little more before Jane walked over to the shop to watch Mac work. It had been one of her favorite hobbies before she'd turned into a sullen youth, and it was the perfect place to find the strength she needed before her next stop.

CHASE FINISHED WASHING the last of his dad's dishes, then took a very long time to dry his hands. When he turned around, he'd be faced with the sight of his father shaking on the couch.

Chase felt stupid now for imagining they would have a nice Sunday dinner together. But this afternoon when his dad had asked him to come over, for the first time it hadn't sounded like a request for alcohol. In fact, it hadn't been. His dad had been trying to quit cold turkey, but by the time six o'clock had rolled around, the tremors had started. Now he sat with an open beer, the contents dribbling out when a bad tremor hit.

"I'm sorry," he said, eyes falling away from Chase's gaze.

"You can't do this on your own, Dad."

"I'm not giving it up to a higher power!" he snapped. "It's not a disease. It's a defect."

"All right. Fine. Call it whatever you want." Chase opened a drawer and pulled out a stack of brochures. "There are other programs besides AA. You don't have

to do it that way if you don't want to." He put the brochures on the coffee table, but his dad just eyed them
as if they were contaminated with nuclear waste.

"Will you think about it?"

"Yeah, yeah."

"You helped to catch a killer, Dad. You could still
do something with your life. It doesn't have to be like
this forever."

When Chase's phone beeped, he pulled it from his
pocket with a hard stab of relief. That relief swelled to
happiness when he saw there was a text from Jane.

Where are you?

Chase nearly fumbled the phone as he slid open the
keyboard. At my dad's.

Can I come over?

Chase snuck a glance at his father leaning down to
grab one of the unopened cans of beer at his feet. The
shaking was subsiding, but his pants were covered
with damp splotches of beer.

Meet me outside?

Now he was the one hiding his family. Great.

Her car pulled up five minutes later and Chase
rushed outside, a smile tugging at his mouth before she
even got out of the car. "That was fast."

"I was at my mom's."

"Oh?"

She shrugged and stopped ten feet away from him.

This was it, he thought, tension winding through his muscles.

She glanced toward the west, where the sun was beginning to sink behind ragged peaks of snow-covered mountains. She tilted her head toward his truck. "Want to sit with me?"

"Sure." He thought she'd meant in the cab, but Jane boosted herself onto the hood and settled against the windshield. Chase raised an eyebrow.

"I like it up here. And the sun's setting."

"Okay." He scooted up next to her, still teetering on the brink of uncertainty. Serious talks could end in many different ways.

Jane took a deep breath. "I love you," she said simply.

Chase waited. He steeled his heart against her words. She'd said it, but she was fully capable of following that up with a *but...*

She turned to him and took his hand, a nervous smile playing over her mouth. "I love you."

"And?"

Her gaze fluttered over his face, and she gave a breathless little laugh. "I love you and I want to be your special gal. If you're up for that."

He was squeezing her hand too tight, but when he tried to relax his fingers, he realized it was her squeezing him. "In public?"

"Yes."

Unwilling to be happy just yet, despite the shout that wanted to rise in his throat, Chase narrowed his eyes at her. "Why?"

"Because I love you. And you know me. And I'm

ready. I thought I'd left that girl I hated far behind, but really…really I've been sinking deeper into her this whole time. I've been a child, hiding from everything that scared me. I'm ready to grow up. I want to not be scared anymore."

He nodded. "Good. I'm glad. But I don't want you to use me anymore. I don't want to be your therapy, Jane."

Her free hand rose to touch his face, the palm pressing into his skin. Despite his brave words, there was no force in the world that could have stopped him from closing his eyes so he could concentrate on the feel of her hand.

"I won't deny I need to work through a few things, but I promise I'll never use you again. I'm sorry for that. I love you so much already, and I've been fighting it so hard. I…I want to know how good it feels not to fight you, Chase. I'm sorry for how cruel I've been to you. For using you. Can you forgive me?"

"There's nothing to forgive," he whispered, turning to kiss her palm. "If you hadn't used me, I wouldn't love you right now."

She pulled him down for a kiss. A soft kiss that didn't hold any of that familiar, desperate need.

When she leaned back, her smile made her look ten years younger. Younger than she'd ever looked back then. "I lied to you about something, though," she warned.

"What?"

"I actually am a neat freak."

"That was kind of obvious. Just don't sneak any fresh flowers into my place and we'll be fine."

They smiled at each other like idiots for a few long seconds, then her eyes shifted to a spot over his shoulder. "How's your dad?"

Chase shook his head and pulled her against his side so they could watch the sun as it darkened to pink. "He's looking at brochures for treatment centers again. I think that locksmith being arrested…it kind of shocked him out of a daze. He helped to stop this guy. But don't get your hopes up for Grandparents' Day. We've been here half a dozen times before."

"Okay."

Her head settled against his shoulder. Her fingers loosened their death grip and relaxed in his hand. The sun slid lower.

Chase cleared his throat. "I mean, you can use me *sometimes*. I don't want to be maniacal about that." She laughed and snuggled closer, and Chase finally felt the last of his doubt fall away. "I'll start growing my hair out so you don't have to take a guy with a shaved head out to dinner."

Her head popped up. She met his eyes and raised a hand to slide it over the side of his head. Shivers tingled down his neck and Jane's eyes dilated. "No. Leave it. For me? For a little while?"

He felt more than a hint of wickedness in his smile. "I don't know. It's a lot of work. I have to buzz it every other day."

"Really?" She sighed. "Can I watch?"

Oh, yeah. His grin was full-on predator now. "You want to watch?"

She licked her lips. "Yes, please."

"You have any ideas for making it worth my while?"

She leaned close, then closer. Her mouth touched his ear and Chase closed his eyes at the small pleasure.

He'd met potty-mouthed Jane only once, but he had

no trouble recognizing her reappearance when she whispered in his ear. No trouble at all. His face heated. So did other parts of his body.

Her teeth closed over his earlobe, and Chase drew a sharp breath. "How do you feel about paying in advance?"

"I'll do whatever it takes," she whispered.

Chase meant to slide her gently off the hood of the truck, but it veered toward a push. Jane landed with a grin.

"Meet you at my place?" he asked, jumping to the ground.

"My place is a few seconds closer." Jane tore out of there so fast that dust rose from her tires, forming an orange cloud in the last rays of the sun.

Jumping into his own truck, he swung it around, braking when he was lined up well enough to see through his dad's storm door. His dad still had a beer in his hand, but he was hunched over a brochure, reading. Chase honked and waited for a wave, then tore out of there just as quickly as Jane had.

His future was waiting for him, and this time he wasn't going to let it go, not even for his father.

CHAPTER TWENTY-SIX

THE FRIDAY-NIGHT DRIVE to Tumble Creek was beautiful and quiet. They rolled the windows down and turned the music off and just enjoyed the green scent of spring. Chase's hand cradled hers. She leaned over to press an occasional kiss to his shoulder.

But when they pulled up to Lori's place, Jane sat straight up with a gasp.

"What's wrong?" Chase asked.

"Nothing! I just can't believe how pretty it looks."

Lori's house was attached to an empty auto mechanic's shop, and beyond that was a private dump filled with rusting parts. But in the dark, all that was visible was the big white tent that filled the lot. It was lit from within with thousands of tiny lights. Music drifted through the air.

Jane had helped Mr. Jennings set up the rental and the catering, but she hadn't quite expected such a complete transformation.

"You sure you want to introduce me to all your friends?"

She shot a look at him, remembering the way she'd clutched his tattooed head an hour earlier. "I'm sure. Plus, I only know about four people here, so it's no big deal."

"Well, thanks."

Laughing, she got out of the truck. She wasn't the least bit nervous, despite this being their first public appearance together as a couple. Oh, he'd talked big about taking her out on the town this week, but in the end they'd stayed behind closed doors, making up for the nights they'd spent apart. And last night Chase had been busy helping his father narrow down the brochures to the three he was most open to. His dad had never taken that step before, and Chase had hope in his eyes when he talked about it.

Jane took his hand and they walked toward the music. She spotted Mr. Jennings right away and pulled Chase in that direction.

"Jane, you look great! Hey, Chase." He slapped Chase on the back. "Congratulations on getting back in Jane's good graces."

"Thanks."

"You're a lucky man. And by 'lucky' I mean don't even *think* about screwing her over. Got it?"

Chase smiled, but tipped his head in agreement.

"Have you met Lori?" He turned and tugged Lori out of a conversation with a grouchy-looking old man who had a pencil poised over a little notebook. He looked like a reporter from the sixties.

Mr. Jennings snuck his arm around his girlfriend. "Lori Love, this is Chase."

"Oh, *Chase,*" Lori said, eyes flying wide at the sight of him. Chase shook her hand while her gaze fluttered up and down. "Nice to meet you."

"Nice to meet you, Lori. Congratulations on the big trip."

"It's not that big of a deal." Her elbow struck Quinn Jennings's arm. "I still can't believe you did this."

"You can thank Jane. If I'd done this myself we would've ended up with a camping tent and a couple two-liters of soda. Thank you, Jane."

Jane felt her face heat with embarrassed pleasure. "You're welcome...Quinn."

Both Quinn and Lori made oohing sounds, while Jane laughed and wished she had a drink.

"Listen to that!" Quinn said. "She called me Quinn! Does she still call you Mr. Chase?"

"Only in private," Chase answered, drawing more oohing sounds from the couple.

"Oh, jeez." Jane laughed. "Get me a drink already. I'm not used to having a fun boyfriend. I need a liquid buffer."

As soon as he wandered out of earshot, Lori grabbed Jane's arm in a death grip. "Oh. My. God. Are you kidding me?"

"What?" Jane asked, grinning so hard her cheeks hurt.

"I thought Quinn was exaggerating! But now I'm thinking he left a few things out!"

"The shaved head is new."

"The *shaved head* is new? I can't believe that just came out of Jane Morgan's mouth. About her *boyfriend*."

Jane pressed her hand to her stomach, laughing too hard to answer.

"And that was no lie about him being big. Wow." Lori stepped close to pull Jane into a hug. "I'm so happy for you. He's really cute."

"Thank you. Your advice...it helped."

"Good."

When Chase came back with a glass of wine, Lori

slipped away to mingle with her other guests. "Don't
forget to take your box of books!" she called.

"What books?" Chase asked Jane.

"Lori and I are starting our own book club when she
gets back."

"Oh, yeah? Can I be in it?"

Thinking of the kind of books they'd be reading,
Jane shook her head. "No way. Girls only. Plus, you
don't read."

"But—" he started, cut off by a blur of movement.
A blond woman darted past them and ran straight to
Lori to give her a hug. She picked Lori up and spun
her around, squealing with excitement the whole time.

"Who's that?" Chase asked.

"That's Molly. She's Quinn's sister. She's in the
book club, too."

"Are you kidding?" His eyes stayed locked on the
gorgeous woman in skintight leather pants and impossibly high heels. Molly was still squealing. "That girl
is related to *Quinn?*"

"Yep."

As they watched, a man in jeans and a police
uniform shirt stopped next to Molly and put his hand
over her mouth to stifle the noise.

"And that guy?" Chase asked. "Is he her parole
officer?"

"That's her boyfriend, Ben Lawson. He's the
chief of police here in Tumble Creek. Come on. I'll
introduce you."

While she made the introductions, Jane waited for
a twinge of self-consciousness. That old feeling of
being exposed. But it didn't surface. She just felt…

lucky. Even when Chief Lawson's eyes focused sharply on Chase's tattoos before he held out a hand. And especially when Molly hid behind her hand and mouthed *Oh-my-God-sexy!* to Jane.

Chase belonged to her now. She'd pulled it off.

She was floating on triumph and barely paying attention to the conversation around her when Chase slid his hand around her waist. "Want to dance?" The sounds of an old Clint Black love song drifted through the tent.

"I sure do."

Chase led her to the wooden platform that served as a dance floor and curled his arms around her. "I love you," he whispered into her hair. "You look so beautiful."

She felt beautiful and happy as his heartbeat thumped against her ear. They swayed in time to the music. A tiny breeze brushed over her back.

"I probably shouldn't tell you this," Chase whispered, "but I'm going to marry you someday."

Her eyes popped open. "What?"

"Don't freak out. I'm not asking you now. I'm just giving you a heads-up. I know you'll need time to adjust."

"We've only been dating for a few weeks!"

"Yeah, I know. But somebody's got to make an honest woman of you. You'll never manage it on your own."

"Chase, I…" She didn't know what to say. She didn't even know what to feel. Her mind was sending out electric sparks of terror, but her heart was melting into a warm, gooey mess inside her. Eyes still wide, Jane cautiously laid her cheek back on his chest.

"We'll buy a house and I'll build a white picket fence first thing."

Jane shook her head, but couldn't stop a small smile.

"And we'll have two kids," he continued. "A boy named Junior and a girl named Sparkles."

"Shut up," she huffed.

"And two rottweilers named Critter and Nutz."

"Shut up!" Jane gave up and laughed so hard that tears wet her cheeks.

He pulled her tight against him again and kissed her head. "Don't worry, Jane," he murmured. "We'll wait until you're ready. But I will ask you."

Jane closed her eyes. All the tension had faded from her body. "All right," she whispered as the last notes of the song danced away. She waited for the urge to run away, the panicked need to free herself from this commitment. It didn't come. Instead, a sweet hope opened up inside her.

She leaned back in his arms so she could meet his gaze. "Promise?"

His smile faded and his blue eyes darkened with emotion. "I do."

Jane stood on her tiptoes and kissed him, and her one single worry about the people watching was a brief moment of pity for the women who couldn't have Billy Chase.

A very brief moment. This big, tattooed man was all hers, and she was going to keep him.